*Embers of the Dead*

*Embers of the Dead*

ROY LEWIS

First published in Great Britain in 2005 by
Allison & Busby Limited
Bon March  Centre
241-251 Ferndale Road
London SW9 8BJ

*http://www.allisonandbusby.com*

A catalogue record for this book is available from
the British Library.

10 9 8 7 6 5 4 3 2 1

ISBN 0 7490 8344 1

Printed and bound in Wales by
Creative Print and Design, Ebbw Vale

Inspector Raoul Garcia stared out of the window and cursed under his breath.

He was a Mediterranean man, in blood and outlook; the scenery in the Pyr n es was spectacular at this time of the year, with the high peaks clothed in snow that glittered and shone in the morning sun. When the sun deigned to shine. But on a late afternoon like this it was a different matter. The snow had begun to fall some two hours earlier, a slight sprinkling at first, whirling and dancing in the darkening air, gradually cloaking the valley, but falling now thick and fast, large silent flakes clinging to the windows of the hotel room the group had obtained to set up the equipment, and making it impossible to get a view of the house below them on the hillside.

He had been warned, of course, the Minister, but he was a stubborn, dismissive man ruled by sentiment and the regular stirring of his loins. It was common knowledge among the intelligence services that he kept several mistresses: it was, after all, a common enough practice in France where the failure to have at least one mistress tended to be regarded as a serious deficit in a politician. But the Minister took the attitude to the extreme: few of his female assistants seemed to have escaped his clutches if intelligence reports over the years were to be believed, and in addition to the stream of power-dazed young women who were taken to his bed there was also the one woman who seemed to have maintained a regular grip on his affections.

Garcia had seen photographs of her: straight blonde hair, an elegant figure, startling blue eyes and a classical profile. She would be at least forty years old now, Garcia mused reflectively, but the Minister was still clearly obsessed after a twenty year affair, and his wealthy but rather more dowdy wife seemed to have accepted the situation with an indifferent shrug: theirs had probably been a marriage of convenience right from the beginning – money married to politics.

Garcia broke off from his musing to glare out of the window at the swirling snow again.

"How is it now?"

The man seated beside him, with a camera and telescopic equipment trained on the building below them, shook his head, leaned back in his chair and locked his hands behind his neck. His knuckles cracked; he sighed and glanced at Garcia. "Impossible, sir. The snow blanks out the scene."

Garcia swore under his breath again. He glanced at his watch. The Minister would be due in perhaps twenty minutes. Why the hell he had chosen the small town of Argel s-Gazost for his assignation? Why on earth he had decided to marry a few days of skiing at Cauterets with a meeting with his mistress were matters for speculation. Garcia assumed the Minister needed to demonstrate his physical condition by attacking the slopes of the Midi-Pyr n es, to impress himself as much as his voters, as he launched himself at the Cirque du Lys. Perhaps it was at Argel s-Gazost the Minister had first met his mistress twenty years ago, and this was a romantic rekindling of a special occasion, a first meeting of minds and bodies two decades earlier. Whatever the reason, the *Groupe Speciale Contre Terrorisme* now had its work cut out.

The electronic chatter had been going on for weeks. Ever since the Minister had made his controversial speech at the Hague surveillance units had been picking up information on the air waves that suggested a spectacular event was on the way. The information had poured into the co-ordination offices of Interpol: all the signs suggested that an attempt was to be made upon the life of the Minister, and Garcia had been assigned to assist in the GSCT operation. His was a supportive role, of course: he was no muscle man, no AK47-wielding front line stormtrooper. There were enough of those waiting elsewhere, here in the hotel and elsewhere in the quiet houses beyond the square. But he was aware the men in charge expected some kind of lead from him. He glanced across the room to where the Pole, Krwzlinski, sat quietly. Their eyes met: in the Polish officer's glance he read a cold determination.

They had been together now for two weeks. They were different in character: Garcia's warm nature was distinct from Krwzlinski's dour stolidity, but they had come to respect each other, as they followed the Minister's political dance through Europe. Each event, each location presented its own problems for the GSCT. Surveillance to be carried out; discreet security arrangements to be made. Most of it could be done in collaboration with the *S ret* , Interpol, and with local agencies. Most of the Minister's movements were scheduled by political considerations. But this one was different; it was personal, secretive in part, and it demanded special arrangements. And they were under no illusions: the Minister's movements and intentions were well-known to the men who sought his death.

And it was now coming to a head. Garcia read the message in Krwzlinski's eyes. It was time to make the move.

"We can't wait until the Minister returns," Garcia said softly, in agreement.

"In the snow, with our surveillance compromised, it would be foolish," the Polish officer confirmed. The German beside him nodded, and the man from the *S ret* rose to his feet. Garcia clucked his tongue: international terrorism demanded international, European-wide co-operation. He watched as Krwzlinski flicked open his mobile phone. He spoke briefly, and then led the way out of the room. Raoul Garcia followed.

They shrugged into their heavy overcoats just inside the hallway of the small private hotel the GSCT had commandeered. In the narrow street outside the snow now swirled thickly: Garcia shivered, missing the sunny shores of his home. He and the rest of the group knew they had to take their men before they left their posts in the house below: if the targets emerged before the Minister arrived it would be impossible to find them. The group had no knowledge of the location of the strike.

In the main square of Argel s-Gazost men of the GSCT would be emerging, Garcia knew, ready to regroup and storm the house of the assassins. He glanced at his watch: the Minister would have already left Cauterets some fifteen minutes ago. His mistress awaited him in the private house in the *haute ville* that he had rented discreetly for their meeting. There had at one point been a suspicion that the mistress was possibly involved in the planning of the assassination, but that had now been discounted. This meeting was merely an affair of the heart: the danger was that it could end in a room awash with the politician's blood.

The peaks of Pibeste and Midi de Bigorre were now lost to view, the air was darkening, the snow swirled in a dense, drifting mass across the streets as they moved slowly down the hill. The house was square-built, the garden at the rear already covered with a white carpet, tall palm trees thrusting their heads incongruously through the blanketing snow. The anti-terrorism group was already surrounding the premises: they waited for the signal as the Polish officer moved into position. Garcia peered at his watch again, brushing his arm to free it of the snow that clung to his jacket. In a matter of minutes, the Minister would be arriving. A decision would have to be made.

It was made for them in the next second. A crack of light glittered through the snow-laden air, its shaft gleaming across the rear garden. There was a brief hesitation and then someone shouted. The light disappeared as a door slammed; Krwzlinski screamed something into his phone and all hell seemed to break out. From the front of the house there was an explosion, a shattering of glass; at the rear, as Garcia watched, masked men in dark protective clothing stormed the doors at the rear, smashed the windows with explosive devices, creating the kind of noise and havoc that would disorientate the men inside so that they would be panicked, unaware of which direction the danger came from.

This was no hostage situation such as some Garcia had known, and participated in. The storming of a house when there were hostages to be killed demanded this kind of turmoil, to save the prisoners while their captives were disorientated. But though the method was similar this assault was different: its purpose was to kill, because the men inside the house were committed to death. All the signs over the electronic networks had pointed to it: the code words, the chatter over the ether, the reasons for the political killing, the commitment of the men chosen to undertake the action. Garcia moved forward with care as the doors burst open and the GSCT men stormed into the building.

The crackling of automatic gunfire echoed through the deadening snowfall. There were two more explosions, and hysterical shouting, men under pressure, adrenalin surging through veins, sharpened instincts as they faced death and dispensed it themselves. Krwzlinski was waving, plunging forward; almost without thinking, Garcia followed him into the house. The open, shattered back door led into a kitchen that had been destroyed by the first explosion; smoke still swirled in the air, and there was the smell of gas in the air. The lights of the house had gone out, and the flashing of torchlight played against the dark walls as Garcia followed the Polish officer into the hallway. Two bodies lay under their feet, arms splayed, both officers from the first storming assault. The rooms to the left and right of the hallway had been blown open, doors smashed; there were still sounds of fighting above their heads, gunfire, the stamping of feet, the fall of heavy bodies, the screaming of defiant, terrified men.

Then, suddenly, everything was silent. The gunfire ended. There were a few long moments when nothing seemed to be moving in the house, nothing stirring, no one making a sound. But slowly it returned, the sound of men moving, dragging, turning; feet pounding on the floors above, shouted enquiries, the breaking of glass. A mopping-up operation. Krwzlinski turned his head, looked at Garcia. He nodded. "It's over."

Garcia shrugged. He wondered whether the Minister had now been told. There would be no rendezvous with the mistress tonight. Within the next half hour the Minister's car would be sweeping past Argel s-Gazost, heading for an area outside Lourdes. There would be a quick transfer to a helicopter – if the snow allowed. And then the bewildered Minister would be on his way to Paris, and a discreet dressing-down. He would bluster, of course: why hadn't he been informed of the danger?

He would think little or nothing of the men who lay dead, or bleeding here in this darkened hallway.

Krwzlinski was heading for the stairs. Garcia followed him. GSCT officers stood to one side, silent as they passed. There was the stink of cordite mingled with odours of mingled fear and relief in Garcia's nostrils as he followed the Polish officer to the back room of the house. Flashlights lit their way: men were breathing hard from exertion and adrenalin-pumped excitement.

"In here, sir," one of the men said.

Krwzlinski entered the room, Garcia just behind him. The room was a shambles. Electronic equipment that had stood near the window had been smashed to pieces; a shattered table had been thrown against the wall, riddled by gunfire. Garcia coughed as a bitter taste touched his tongue, and a rawness entered his throat. The remains of what had once been a man lay huddled against one wall: his arm had been torn from his shoulder by gunfire, his face was a bloody mask. There were two other men in the room: the assassins had all died in this quick last stand, where the GSCT officers had taken no chances. Grenades, gunfire, no questions asked, no surrender demanded. Garcia coughed again, his lungs feeling as though they were on fire. He turned away, sickness churning in his stomach.

Krwzlinski snarled something in Polish, stepping forward as the flashlight he held in his left hand picked out something on the floor. Garcia hesitated, turned back. "What is it?" he asked sharply.

Krwzlinski was standing over a gruesome, bloodied something that lay against the wall. Garcia moved to stand beside him, puzzled. "What is it?" he asked again, disgust welling up in his chest.

The flashlight beam was concentrated on a piece of destroyed flesh. It was the arm of the man lying some feet away. It had been taken off at the shoulder, neatly, almost surgically. At one extremity the fingers were curled, blackened, clawed in death. But the flashlight was concentrated on the area just below the bloodied shoulder.

"You see that?" Krwzlinski muttered.

"What?"

"The mark. The burned tattoo."

Garcia shook his head. "I don't think so. I can't make it out..."

Abruptly, Krwzlinski turned away, pushing past Garcia, making his way towards the stairs.

It was only two days later that Garcia learned the significance of what the Polish officer had seen. Garcia had his report to prepare for Interpol; he was interviewing a forensic pathologist at the laboratory to which the bodies of the assassins had been taken. The findings had been conclusive. Krwzlinski had sat there impassively as the pathologist had explained.

"The three men were all of Eastern European origin. Their ethnicity is beyond doubt. There is no suggestion that they might be of Middle Eastern origin. If you had been proceeding along the line of thought that this had been an operation undertaken by Islamic fanatics, I would consider you have been mistaken. It may be that Al'Quaeda or some other fundamentalist organisation lies behind all this, of that I cannot speculate. But the men themselves are not Asian and..."

"Have one thing in common," Krwzlinski said quietly.

The pathologist raised an eyebrow, stared speculatively at the Polish officer. "You mean...?"

"The marks on the left upper arms," Krwzlinski supplied.

Garcia turned to him, recalling the way Krwzlinski had reacted in those last few moments at the destroyed house in Argel s-Gazost. "Marks?"

Krwzlinski held his gaze steadily. "Two letters, burned into the arm. *SS*."

There was a short silence. The forensic pathologist looked from one man to the other, and nodded. "We have noted these marks."

Garcia wrinkled his nose, puzzled. "Tattoo marks... *SS*...what does this mean?"

"It means," Krwzlinski growled bitterly, his eyes darkened by long experience, "that the embers of dead men have been fanned again into flame. The rats have once more crawled out of their sewers."

Chapter One

The weather on Tyneside had a disconcerting habit of being fine and sunny and bright on those days when the pile of folders and files on Eric Ward's desk tended to reach mountainous proportions. At lunchtime on a Spring day, with the laden desktop awaiting him after a tedious morning in court, Eric was disinclined to hurry back to the office; it was more pleasurable to stroll along the Quayside, enjoy the warmth of the sunshine and watch the desultory river traffic waiting for the Millennium Bridge to tilt, making way for a Swedish naval frigate to slide upstream to a berth opposite the floating nightclub on the Gateshead bank.

Not that the stroll was entirely for pleasure: he had things on his mind and he felt he needed time, and fresh air, to order his thoughts, reach a decision on the puzzling conversation he had had the previous evening at the annual Bankers Dinner held at the Gosforth Park Hotel. Puzzling, worrying and intriguing.

His attendances at such formal occasions were not exactly a matter of necessity, but he tended to put in a reluctant appearance, not least because of the badgering he would otherwise suffer from his secretary, Susie Cartwright. "You know you should go, Mr Ward," she had insisted, hovering like a dark, disapproving cloud in the open doorway of his room at the Quayside office. "How else are you ever going to extend your range of business contacts? I've had the dinner organiser on the phone again and she wants to know whether you'll be turning up this year – "

"I always do," he protested weakly.

"In the end. But only because I keep on at you," Susie snapped. "If it wasn't for me you'd never go to these occasions, and how would the practice go on then? Dry up, like as not. And where would that leave me, with no salary to rely on? At my age, where would I find someone willing to give me a job?"

"There's always that clerk in the Crown Court," Eric had hinted. "He'd jump at the chance of making an honest woman of you."

She had glared at him, snorted, and turned away to head for the anteroom. But she'd had the last word. "So I'll get on the phone and tell the organiser you're coming, then?"

It was easier to give in, as he always did. And, though Eric was reluctant to admit it to himself, when he finally did put in an appearance he derived a certain amount of enjoyment from these occasions. It gave him an opportunity to observe some of his professional colleagues working the room, laughing loudly at inane jokes, shaking the appropriate hands, buttoning prospective clients, sidling up to the fringes of conversational groups that included chief executives of banks and building societies and estate agencies, all of whom might be useful in the development or maintenance of a legal practice in the city.

It was an activity he was disinclined to pursue, an attitude that had caused conflict and exasperation as far as his ex-wife Anne had been concerned. She and Susie Cartwright had certainly seen eye to eye on that matter at least: neither could understand why he insisted on maintaining a small criminal practice on the Quayside when there were other, more lucrative possibilities open to him. Opportunities that would come to him if he only chose to talk to the right people, undertake the necessary networking, make the appropriate noises on occasions such as the annual dinners hosted by the various professional societies on Tyneside: accountants, bankers, lawyers, company secretaries. For some years he had acted on behalf of her company, Morcomb Enterprises, and taken a seat on the London board of merchant bankers Martin and Channing, the firm in which Anne had held a stake. It was not an experience he had enjoyed, and he had discovered that villainy was not confined to petty crooks on Tyneside: there were greater frauds

perpetrated among the smooth-talking, dark-suited frater-
nity of the corporate world. Perhaps that was why he
viewed activities such as these formal dinners with a cool
detachment, an edge of cynicism.

But at least the four-course meal was good, and the
speeches relatively short, the jokes not too hoary. Neither
man seated on either side of him paid him much attention;
they were young acolytes, hanging on every word of other
more important guests across the table and Eric had little to
say. Or maybe it was the slightly rusty dinner jacket he
wore: Susie had already warned him that the jacket lapels
were outdated, to say the least. "You've been going to the
dogs since your divorce," she had added, with a sniff. "You
need a good woman to take you in hand, sort you out."
Perhaps she was right.

The final speech of the evening had been touted in the
dinner programme as a "keynote address". That meant it
would be worthy, boring and concentrating on the minutiae
of banking politics. A relief break was permitted before the
speech began; Eric took advantage of it and headed for the
bar. He stayed there, when the rest of the audience was
resettling at the dinner tables.

He ordered a cognac. He had arranged for a taxi to take
him back to the flat in Gosforth; he had a good half hour to
wait. And he'd been reasonably abstemious with the table
wine: it was unlikely he'd have problems with his eyes if he
stuck to the one drink.

He sat on a bar stool, thinking about nothing in particular, until he became aware of someone entering the room
behind him, expelling the air from his lungs with patent
relief. He stood beside Eric at the bar, ordered a double
whisky, and muttered, "Another escapee, I guess."

Eric smiled non-committally. The man was not known to
him, and he thought he had come across most of the
bankers on Tyneside over the years. The whisky drinker was
some six feet in height, broad shoulders straining at his

jacket, slim-hipped, a man who kept himself in trim with regular workout sessions, Eric guessed. His features were regular, a cleft chin that women would find attractive, an easy manner that would satisfy clients, sharp blue eyes that would inspire the confidence of a boardroom. His hair was dark, neatly parted, with a hint of grey at the temples. He had a deep suntan; he would be the kind of man who knew everybody and travelled relentlessly, as if his life depended on it. Maybe it did. *Distinguished*, would be how Susie Cartwright would describe him, Eric concluded. The man caught his glance, half-turned, smiled. Regular, expensively well-maintained teeth. He held out his hand. "We've not met. Ben Shaw."

He had an easy mid-Atlantic accent. His grip was firm and masculine in its tension.

"Eric Ward. I'm a solicitor. And yes, an escapee. But I suppose as a guest here I shouldn't really be running away from the main event."

"Any more than I should," the big man grinned, raising a conspiratorial eyebrow, "as a relative newcomer to the Tyneside scene. It's my first attendance at one of thes Newcastle shindigs, but I early on concluded that when you've been to one, you've been to them all. And somehow, the people who attend…they all seem to be the same people you've met at a hundred other such dinners."

"With the same kind of agendas," Eric agreed. He eyed his companion speculatively. "So you've not been long on Tyneside."

"About six months or so, now," Ben Shaw admitted. "I'm with the merchant bank in Grey Street. Bradgate and Savage." He paused, flickered a curious glance at Eric. "You've not had any dealings with us at all."

"Out of my league," Eric replied casually, and sipped at his cognac. "I do very little work with the merchant banks. No commercial work, in fact. I run mainly a criminal practice down at the Quayside. Pretty small beer." As Susie kept saying to him.

"But you said your name was Ward…" Shaw mused, his eyes fixed steadily on Eric. "I've come across the name… I seem to have read you've been involved in certain dealings in the world of merchant banking…"

Eric shrugged. "Maybe you've been misinformed."

Ben Shaw shook his head, certainty touching his eyes. "No, I've come across your name in some connection, in the merchant banking business." He paused, sipped his whisky, frowning slightly and staring at Eric. Then his brow cleared. "Martin and Channing…that's it, you used to have a seat on the board of Martin and Channing."

Eric looked at him in surprise. "That was a few years back. And I can't recall that I'd have done anything in those days which sent a shiver around the merchant banking world, enough to have someone I've never met recall my name."

Ben Shaw laughed, drained his glass, called to the barman and when Eric refused his offer ordered another large whisky for himself. When it arrived he picked it up, swirled the amber liquid in the glass thoughtfully, and clucked his tongue. "Martin and Channing…yes, that's it. A seat on the board…"

"In what context would you have recalled this?" Eric wondered. "As I said, I wasn't exactly up front in board politics, and I resigned some years ago. And I don't recall we ever had dealings with your firm…Bradgate and Savage, did you say?"

Ben Shaw nodded. "Yes, that's right." He flashed Eric a bright, confident smile. "But we're not a long-established firm like Martin and Channing. When you were on the board there we weren't even in existence in the UK. Bradgate and Savage is the result of a European buyout of a long-established firm that was on its last legs. German owners, looking for a foothold in the UK financial world. New finance pumped in; new business arranged; new premises in

London, and then an office up here to help finance some of the exciting new developments that have been occurring on Tyneside, the Tees and the Wear. That was three years ago."

Which hadn't exactly answered the question in Eric's mind. He decided to let the matter go: it was of little importance. He glanced at his watch. The taxi would be arriving in a little while. "So you've just been drafted in to work here on Tyneside recently. Is that due to expansion?"

Ben Shaw shook his head, a slight frown returning to his features. "No, a bit of troubleshooting, really. The first three years have gone well enough, but the board felt that a new eye was needed, to take a fresh look at some of the commitments made in the Tyneside office. So I've been going over various files, discussing various strategies..." The frown faded, and the sharp eyes returned to Eric. They held a hint of calculation. "Eric Ward..."

"The one and only." Eric glanced at his watch again. There was something in Ben Shaw's tone that made him feel uneasy. He slid off the bar stool, and finished his drink. "Well, it was nice making your acquaintance. Maybe our paths will cross – "

"On the board of Martin and Channing," Ben Shaw interrupted, "you were acting in a representative capacity."

"That's right. I – "

"For Morcomb Enterprises. That's how your name rang a bell for me. I've been reviewing our files, as I explained, and I knew I'd seen your name come up somewhere."

Eric frowned. "I thought you said your firm never had any dealings with Martin and Channing."

Ben Shaw hesitated briefly, and a note of caution crept into his tone. "That's correct, but merchant banking is a small world. And in so far as we've been seeking out new business..." He twirled the whisky glass between his fingers, thoughtfully. "When you were working on the Martin and Channing board, you were acting for the Morcomb Enterprises company, but...there was a little more to it than that, wasn't there?"

A certain coolness touched Eric's tone. "How do you mean?"

Ben Shaw touched the cleft in his chin with a hesitant forefinger. Then he pointed the finger in Eric's direction. "You were the husband of the major shareholder in Morcomb Enterprises."

Eric grimaced, and nodded. "It seems my life history has come under your scrutiny, Mr Shaw. I can't imagine why. However, I hope you'll forgive me, but I'll be on my way. I have a cab waiting."

Ben Shaw put out his hand, gripped Eric's arm in restraint. When he saw the tension in Eric's mouth he released his grip, apologetically. "Please don't be offended, Mr Ward. I've been somewhat preoccupied with business lately, there are various problems I've had to deal with, decisions to make, other earlier decisions to pull back on, you know how it is when you come in as a troubleshooter. And suddenly meeting you like this, it's made me forget my manners. Forgive me."

"It's not important," Eric said shortly and turned away.

"But it might be," Ben Shaw replied quickly.

Eric looked back over his shoulder. "To you, perhaps. Not to me, I would imagine."

"You could be wrong there, Mr Ward." Ben Shaw held up a placatory hand. "Look, you've got a cab waiting, and a bar is not exactly the right kind of place to have a conversation of the kind I would like to explore with you. I wonder whether you'd have time to call in to see me tomorrow, at my office in Grey Street?"

"I might have the time," Eric replied coolly, "but for what purpose?"

Ben Shaw hunched his broad shoulders and grimaced thoughtfully. "I wish we could have got off to a better start, but now we have met... I think we might both find it useful if you could find time to call."

Eric stared at him, puzzled. "You said you saw my name in a boardroom list for Martin and Channing. You know I acted for Morcomb Enterprises…and that I was married to Anne Morcomb. This conversation you want to have with me… It's to do with my tenure on the board, or with my ex-wife?"

Ben Shaw's features were non-committal, and yet there was a shadow of calculation still in his sharp blue eyes. "I'd be very grateful, Mr Ward, if you could call. Any time after lunch."

Eric hesitated. "I'll think about it, Mr Shaw." Then he turned and walked away to seek the taxi he had booked earlier that evening.

Eric had not slept well that night. The next morning, in the courtroom, he found his thoughts drifting back to the conversation with Shaw: there were various things about it that puzzled him. He could not imagine why his name should have leapt out for Shaw from the Martin and Channing list of board members. It could only be to do with his relationship with Anne and Morcomb Enterprises. But if Shaw's firm, Bradgate and Savage, had had no previous dealings with the merchant bankers Eric had worked with, what of importance was there to discuss? As court proceedings went on he found it difficult to concentrate, earning himself a sharp rebuke from the bench at one point when he lost his way among the papers in front of him. The young tearaway he was representing didn't seem too pleased, either. So the eventual escape to the sunshine of Wesley Square and the Quayside was a relief, and a return to the mound of files at the office an action he was not prepared to even contemplate. Susie would give him hell when he did turn up, but he was used to that. She was well-meaning, and he knew he needed organising from time to time.

But his mind was too disordered at the moment, as he paced along the river wall, and thought back to the painfulness of the last few years, the doubts, the suspicions, the realities of the break-up with Anne. Nor did he want to go back over old ground with the troubles he had dealt with in Martin and Channing days: he had left the corporate world behind him, with its wheeler-dealing, its corruption and fraud, the major scams that seemed to be a way of life, the power politics that were part of existence in that environment. It was all behind him, and yet Ben Shaw's words had dredged it up again. He wanted no part of it. But Shaw wanted to see him. And his curiosity had been whetted. More than that: he had a subdued feeling of danger in his veins. At the moment, he could not determine the reason for it. And that meant, in spite of his misgivings, he needed to go to see Shaw at his offices in Grey Street.

He walked back to the Malmaison Hotel and got a sandwich for lunch, toyed with a glass of mineral water, avoided a return to his own office on the Quayside and then walked up the hill, climbing Dog Leap Stairs, wandering slowly past Amen Corner and making his way up Grey Street. The classical curve of the street was calm in the afternoon Spring sunshine; the hum of human traffic disgorged from the Metro station at the foot of Grey's Monument was subdued, but he had an uneasy ache in his chest as he stepped through the imposing doorway of the chambers occupied by Bradgate and Savage. The eighteenth-century balustraded stairs curved elegantly to the upper floor; the walls glowed with carefully preserved early Victorian tiles; there was a cool, businesslike atmosphere to the hallway, efficient secretaries clicking their way across the parqueted floors, the muted hum of well-modulated voices, the faint smell of polish and air fragrances. The girl at the reception desk on the first floor smiled at him: her hair shone, her nails were immaculately manicured, her mouth expressed a personal pleasure at seeing him, and her accent was certainly not Tyneside. "Can I help you, sir?"

"My name is Ward. I think Mr Shaw will be expecting me."

"Just one moment, please." A quick consultation of a notebook of appointments; a slight frown, and then another smile. She flicked the switch on her desk, a brief exchange of information and the matter was concluded. "Mr Shaw will see you immediately, Mr Ward. His secretary is on the way."

So, as far as Ben Shaw was concerned, Eric considered, the matter was important.

A few minutes later he was following the slim form of Ben Shaw's secretary along the thickly carpeted corridor to the office where Shaw awaited him. He accepted her offer of coffee; Ben Shaw was already rising from behind his clean, well-swept desk, smiling, extending his hand, as Eric was shown into the room.

"Mr Ward. I'm glad you could make it after all."

Eric nodded, and surveyed the room. Booklined walls; framed copies of a Modigliani, a Turner, a Picasso; high windows; expensive, elegant, understated furniture. An oval desk, American-style notepad. On the wall an antique clock, several minutes fast as though suggesting time was slipping away faster than anticipated. A glass-fronted cupboard, a concealed bookcase with a curtain drawn across it as if its contents might be too revealing. A small silver cup on the bookshelf, a memento of a youthful rowing exploit. A photograph of young, muscular men in blazers. "University?" Eric queried.

"Cambridge. A long time ago."

Eric walked to the window and looked down to Grey Street. "Not more than twenty years, I'd calculate. You've done well in the merchant banking business."

Ben Shaw grinned. "Well enough. But it's not an easy life. As you'll know from your own experience with Martin and Channing."

"Brief as it was," Eric concurred. He had barely taken the seat proffered him when there was a discreet tap on the door and the secretary returned with a small silver tray. She offered one of the two cups to Eric, and set the other in front of Shaw, seated again behind his desk. Eric noted the barrier between them: so this was certainly going to be a business discussion. He declined the sugar, took a little cream, and then sat back, eyeing Ben Shaw carefully. "So, I'm here. Out of curiosity, in the main. But a little concerned, too."

"About what?" Ben Shaw frowned.

"About the way you seem to have been digging into my life. Isn't that worthy of concern?"

"That's not quite the way of it, Mr Ward," Ben Shaw protested. "I recognised your name...well, because I'd come across it and then I wondered..." He hesitated, gnawing uncertainly at his lip for a moment and then abruptly opened the drawer of the desk in front of him. He took out a slip of paper, glanced at it and then passed it across the desk to Eric. It was a cheque. Eric saw his name, and the amount written on the cheque registered slowly with him: fifteen thousand pounds.

"What's this for?"

"A retention fee."

"Why should you pay me a retainer when I've done nothing for you, and don't even know what you might want me to do?" Eric laid the cheque carefully on the desktop between them.

"I'll have a contract drawn up," Shaw said sharply.

"For what purpose?" Eric laughed. "This is ludicrous. We only met last night. You'll have experienced corporate lawyers to do your work for you." He nodded towards the cheque lying on the desktop. "This isn't the way I do business, Mr Shaw; and to my knowledge this isn't the way merchant banking operations are normally carried on either."

Ben Shaw drew his brows together, and fingered the cleft in his chin. He took a deep breath, and shook his head. "Merchant banking is like the practice of the law," he suggested. "Much of it is based upon mutual trust, but trust alone cannot suffice. One man's word against another...possible misunderstandings. We could proceed in this conversation, I suppose, on a non-attributable basis, an attempt to define what we each want to know, with a view to talking later. But I think a better way is to get matters on a legal footing straight away, if matters of a confidential nature are to be discussed."

"And that's what I'm here for?" Eric asked calmly. "To discuss matters of a confidential nature?"

"I explained to you last night that I'd been brought in here to Tyneside in a troubleshooting capacity." There was an edge of steel in Ben Shaw's tone, as he leaned forward to meet Eric's steady gaze. "And when I caught your name, and realised last night that you might be able to help me in certain...enquiries I am instigating, I invited you to meet me here. But our discussion is likely to touch upon sensitive issues, and confidential matters. I can't risk such a discussion on a merely casual basis. If we are to explore the issues I have in mind, I will need to establish a formal relationship between us."

"Lawyer and client."

"Precisely. Hence the retainer."

"It's rather more than I would normally expect to be paid."

"You don't know what I want from you yet."

Eric nodded thoughtfully. "So if I don't enter into this *formal* relationship, what happens?"

"We have no further conversation," Shaw replied abruptly.

Irritated, Eric leaned forward. "Hey, it was you who asked me up here: I was reluctant to come."

"When I issued the invitation last night," Shaw said smoothly, "I hadn't exactly thought through my actions. It was an instinctive reaction on my part. However, on reflection overnight, it became clear to me that I needed to clear the decks appropriately before we had the conversation I had in mind. So, do we proceed, Mr Ward?"

Eric picked up the cup of coffee, sipped it slowly. It was good coffee, freshly brewed. He wasn't certain whether Shaw was telling the truth, but the fact was he had been given enough information, enough hints to whet his curiosity. Shaw would know that. And the cheque was certainly a handsome one. Susie Cartwright at least would be pleased: she would consider things were looking up. Eric put down the cup, picked up the cheque, looked at its details again. "I reserve the right to repay part or all of this cheque if I decide I can't help you – or won't help you."

"But you agree to establish a formal relationship?" Shaw enquired.

"I accept the retainer, subject to what I've said. And that means I'm bound by lawyer-client privilege. Your affairs won't be talked about by me outside this office, or in it without your permission. Whatever you say to me will be treated in the utmost confidence." His eyes narrowed balefully. "Now what the hell is this all about, Shaw?"

Ben Shaw rose from behind his desk. He removed the jacket of his grey, well-cut suit, tossed it onto an easy chair near the bookcase. His shoulders were well-muscled from his rowing days, and his waist was slim. He began to prowl around the room on light feet, hands thrust deep into his trouser pockets, an edgy, powerfully-built man. "I told you I was called up here to troubleshoot."

"You did."

"The fact is, Bradgate and Savage have done a lot of business up here along the three rivers, in this last couple of years. Rapid expansion. And that's pleased everyone. But last year there were a few small…problems began to creep in. Some slight anxieties. So I was instructed by head office in Germany to come up here. There were a couple of dismissals. A few reprimands. But nothing too serious. Until I started going back over some outstanding financial arrangements. And I began to get twitchy."

Eric waited as the big man continued to prowl around the room.

"One file in particular concerned me. So I got all the back papers, went through all the relevant documentation, and took background information on all the parties who had had any connection with the business at all. That's when your name came up."

"My name? In what context?" Eric demanded sharply. "I've had no dealings with Bradgate and Savage."

"I told you last night. It was in the context of a seat on the board of Martin and Channing."

"And I told you that was years ago. What possible connection – "

"No *direct* connection," Shaw interrupted, nodding. "But you had a seat on the board, as a representative of Morcomb Enterprises, you relinquished it, and a new member of the board was appointed in your place."

Jason Sullivan, QC. Eric's face was stony. "You'd better give me the whole story."

"Which I now feel free to do, since we've established lawyer-client privilege between us," Ben Shaw said softly.

Eric waited, as Shaw stopped prowling, sat down behind his desk once more, took a folder from the desk drawer and consulted it before speaking. "Mr Ward, are you familiar with the Hollander Project?"

# Chapter Two

At the top of the hill there was a parking area. Eric pulled in and killed the engine. He stepped out of the Celica and stood with his back to it, leaning against the vehicle as he surveyed the scene below him. A patchwork of fields stretched out into the distance, carved by small streams edged with birch and oak, and on the far horizon there was the vague, hazy shimmering of the sea. To his left the Cheviots rose: he had walked there often, ridden with Anne in better days, and the fell country still called to him. It was a part of his past life that he missed, but there had been time to move on, to accept inevitabilities, bring order into his life.

He folded his arms, felt the warmth of the sun on his face. It was all very well trying to turn his back on the past, but it was impossible if the past rose up to confront him. As it was doing now. He thought back to the conversation with Ben Shaw in the offices of Bradgate and Savage.

"Yes, I've heard of the Hollander Project," Eric had admitted. "It's been well reported in the Press: it's being funded largely by European money, and a consortium of business interests here in the north-east. As far as I'm aware, the idea is to regenerate the coastal areas north of Amble, bring in some new light industries, electronics, software development, that sort of thing, build what amounts to a new small town with all suitable facilities, put some new muscle into the tourist industry, wipe out the deleterious effects of centuries of mining activity...the kind of thing the local politicians have supported to the hilt, for their own reasons, and the local population have gone along with because of the opportunity it gives them for employment."

"You sound as though you don't entirely approve," Ben Shaw had suggested.

"I wouldn't say that," Eric had replied carefully. "It's just that I've learned to become suspicious of large enterprises like that. Drums are beaten, politicians get up and make speeches, local worthies appear on television, and jobs are created. But I've seen what happens when a lot of money is pumped into such projects, and when a few years down the line the mainstream people involved – Japanese companies, German entrepreneurs, relocated businesses from the south – suddenly start to pull out, when the gravy train shows signs of coming to a halt and the real work has to be done... I'm not saying the Hollander Project isn't a good thing: it's just that I retain a certain degree of scepticism regarding its prospects of doing what it claims it can do." He paused, eyeing Ben Shaw. "And Bradgate and Savage are involved in the project?"

"Involved..." Shaw seemed to consider the word for a few moments. "Well, yes, though not directly. Let me put it like this. We were approached to handle some of the financing and refinancing packages. You'll appreciate that where European money is concerned there are various problems that can arise: after initial investments the money comes in only after relevant invoicing has taken place, work has to be done in advance of Brussels paying up, commitments are made. That's where we come in."

"You raise short-term finance for companies involved in the project?"

"That's one of our functions," Shaw agreed carefully, "for some of the companies involved. It's a matter of treading a delicate high wire. We prepare reports for Europe, we raise short term finance to pay for the initial outlay on the ground, and then we assist in the recovery of the promised funds from Europe. It involves the setting up of a number of accounts, under various headings, and it calls for a certain amount of...shall we say, juggling? And you know how it is: people like to deal with London because of its expertise, but they like to hold securities in Switzerland or New York."

Eric scratched his cheek thoughtfully. "You told me you were called up here to the north-east to do some troubleshooting."

Ben Shaw nodded. "I trained first as a linguist, then as an economist; finally took a Master's in Financial Management. I did a stint in Venezuela, involved in giving advice on oil revenues. Then it was New York with Schroders, then Indonesia, Gabon. I was later headhunted and I joined the European parent company of Bradgate and Savage a few years back."

Eric could guess. He was one of the younger generation the banks continued to hunger for, men who went for business rather than waiting for it to come to them. Aggressive, ruthless, broad-minded in business matters, refusing to accept tradition as a liability.

"My work has been almost exclusively in the field of handling difficult accounts since then," Ben Shaw continued, "mainly in Eastern European countries, as they've opened their borders and sought investment opportunities, but latterly in the UK. I know the form, Mr Ward, I know how these matters are handled. I've had fifteen years' experience in such matters. But there are certain fields in which I have no experience at all."

"Such as?"

Shaw looked at him, a speculative glint in his eyes. "Finding people."

Eric began to realise where the conversation was heading. "You think that this is something I can help you with?"

Ben Shaw spread his hands wide. "Initially, I wanted to discuss certain matters with you, matters of a confidential nature, to determine what fix you might be able to give me on events and personalities involved in the Hollander Project. But I instigated some further enquiries this morning, before you arrived, and I now have quite a dossier on you, Mr Ward. I learn you're not only a solicitor with experience of corporate activities; you're also an ex-policeman."

"So your original objective in talking with me has been somewhat extended?"

"You might say that, Mr Ward."

"You want me to find someone."

"Precisely." Ben Shaw's eyes glittered. "And find out what's happened to the money."

High in the blue sky above his head a kite circled, dipping its wings gently, moving elegantly on the wind currents, watching for movement in the heather, poised to drop and strike. There was something about the bird that reminded Eric of Ben Shaw: watchful, committed, alert. Eric watched the predator for a little while, then shook his head and got back into the car. He pulled out of the parking area, wheels crunching on the gravel, and then headed over the fell and down towards the valley beyond, taking the old, familiar road to Sedleigh Hall.

The curving driveway to the hall was ablaze with spring flowers, the rhododendron bushes were in bud and pheasants flew squawking their noisy, clattering protest into the undergrowth as he drove up to the main entrance and parked. He noted some work had been done on the stables since his last visit, and in the distance he could hear the steady drone of a tractor working in one of the fields of the upper meadow. When he walked up the steps to the hall he could hear the familiar sounds of curlew, wheeling and calling above the open fields.

He found Anne in the library. She was seated at the long, polished oak table, a mass of scattered papers in front of her. As he entered she looked up, rose and came forward to greet him. She kissed him lightly on the cheek. "Eric! It's good to see you. It's a while since you've been up here."

"I've been pretty busy," he replied, and glanced at the scattered papers. "As you seem to be."

She brushed a stray lock of hair from her eyes. "How are you, anyway?"

"Fine. And you're looking good," he lied.

She turned away, went back to her seat. He thought she was looking far from well. She seemed thinner; there were dark rings beneath her eyes as though she had been sleeping badly, and some of the determination seemed to have gone from her manner. He detected an edgy nervousness, quick movements of the hands that suggested tension. He moved away from her as though to give her more space, went to the windows, looked out over the sloping meadow-land that led down to the stream, and the rackety little bridge that he had replaced years ago. He had never really been much of a handyman.

"So how's your little barrister friend?" Anne asked coolly after a few moments.

Sharon Owen. It was a commitment he did not yet feel he could make. "I haven't seen much of her recently. She's been busy on a fraud case in London. And, as I said, I've been pretty busy too."

"But you've taken the chance to get away from your scruffy little Tyneside villains for a few hours to breathe some fresh air?"

He ignored the edge behind the comment. "Something like that. And to see how you're getting on."

She leaned back in her chair and contemplated matters, eyeing him carefully. He moved away from the window, took a seat to one side of her and nodded to the papers in front of her. "Morcomb Estates?"

She nodded. "The kind of stuff you could have been doing for me if you'd chosen to take up my offer. Then you'd have had a real reason to come up here from time to time."

"I told you...it's not my scene. In any case, you've got your own little male to organise that side of life for you. How is Jason, by the way?" He was unable to keep the underlying rancour out of his tone.

Her lips thinned, and she frowned. "Are you really interested?"

He shook his head dismissively. "I don't understand you, Anne. There have been warning signs enough. Why on earth you still keep him involved in your business interests – "

"Because he's able, trustworthy, and he has my best interests at heart," she flashed. "And because he *cares*!"

Eric was about to reply angrily, but thought better of it. He was not here to start raking over old ashes. She made her own decisions and always had. The fact she had never been able to understand that he wanted to go his own way professionally hadn't helped matters, but they were all old cicatrices, wounds better not reopened. "I didn't come here to quarrel."

"So exactly why did you come?" she asked, unmollified.

He tapped his fingers on the table top, uncertainly. "I told you…just to see how things were going. I heard you'd got involved with some fairly big projects, fronted by the Lord Lieutenant and other worthies."

She grunted. "You never did take to that part of my life, did you, Eric? You never understood it was part of what makes me tick, a necessary part of my background and existence. You preferred dredging around in the mud of the waterfront…" She shook her head in irritation, recognising voices echoing from their past. "Ah, but yes, we've got some big projects going."

"Like Hollander, I hear."

She glanced at him suspiciously. "Where did you hear that?"

He managed a smile. "Hey, you should know, in my business I get to hear a lot of things."

"It's not a direct involvement, really," she admitted reluctantly. "There are about twelve companies involved in a consortium, and I've been asked to take a slice of the action on the marina and construction activities. And then we've been asked to service the committee. We've been acting as a sort of banker, organising schedules, undertaking liaison work, you know the sort of thing." She gestured towards the papers in front of her. "This is some of the stuff I've had to plough through."

"So Morcomb Estates isn't actually deeply involved?"

Anne hesitated, eyeing him curiously. "Well, we've made a significant investment for fund-matching purposes, through our subsidiary Morcomb Enterprises. I'm on a few committees, and Jason has been running around negotiating various kinds of arrangements."

"Is that what he's doing at the moment?"

"What?"

"Negotiating arrangements."

She was undeceived by his nonchalance. Her eyes narrowed. "You could say that."

"So where exactly is he doing this negotiating?" Eric asked.

"He's been in Europe for the last two months. You'll be aware that the Hollander Project is largely financed by Europe. It's meant a lot of chasing up on reports, accounts, financial packages. There are banks to see, Brussels officials to persuade, money to dig out of reluctant partners..."

"So you haven't really seen much of Jason recently. With him being in Europe so much."

She leaned back in her chair, observing him with a watchful eye, searching for criticism. "I'm due to meet him on Friday, in Luxembourg. But no, I haven't actually seen him for a little while. We were intending to take a break together last week, but other things came up at the last moment here, and I was unable to join him."

"What sort of break was that going to be? A holiday, you mean?"

"Precisely that. I felt we both deserved it; things have been pretty hectic just recently." She rose suddenly, walked across the room to the false bookcase, opened the front of it and took out a bottle of whisky. "Too early in the day for you?"

"A bit," Eric agreed. "Didn't know you'd taken up the

habit."

She laughed. It was a brittle sound. "The stress of office. All those committee meetings with boring little politicians; the need to keep pompous officials on side; juggling papers around, with money going in one end and coming out who knows where. You know how it is." She poured herself a stiff whisky, rummaged around in the cupboard until she found a half-used bottle of soda water, and added a splash of it to the whisky. "I've got little caches like this all over the house these days. You think I'm becoming an alcoholic?"

"Too much control for that," he suggested. After a brief hesitation, he asked with a studied casualness, "Where was this holiday going to be? Caribbean? Bermuda? Florida?"

She sipped at the whisky and soda and shrugged. "Nothing so exotic. France. I've always been a sucker for French food, as you know. Jason and I, we'd arranged to spend a week on a boat, off the Ile de R ."

"La Rochelle."

She nodded. "But, like I said, it never happened. I got tied up." She hesitated. "So Jason went ahead on his own. He'll no doubt tell me what I've missed when I see him on Friday." She came back to the table, and sat down, pushing some papers aside and placing the glass in front of her as though making some point about priorities.

"Where did you say you'd be meeting him?" Eric asked innocently. "In Luxembourg, I mean."

"I didn't say." She stared at him, calculation in her glance. "What exactly is this all about, Eric?"

He hesitated. He was on delicate ground. Jason Sullivan had been the major cause of the breakdown of their marriage; Eric had had cause to believe he was a bad influence on Anne, and that she was in denial about his true character. The man had turned his back on a promising legal career to enter the world of business, but he had come unstuck more than once. Eric felt he was…unstable. And he was his ex-wife's lover. But he felt he had little choice other than to broach the subject with her. He took a deep breath. "You say you haven't seen Sullivan in a while."

"So?"

"There are other people who also...haven't been able to get in touch with him."

"What sort of people?" she snapped irritably.

He chose his words with care. "Professional people. Those who have been in business dealings with him."

"Clients of yours." She glared at him. "You're not very subtle, Eric. You forget, I know you pretty well. This visit of yours is nothing to do with my well-being; there's nothing casual about it. You weren't just passing by; you weren't turning up here because you missed the place. Or me. You're here to put the knife into one of my close friends, again; you're prejudging an issue!"

"What issue would that be, Anne?" Eric asked quietly.

"It's none of your damn business!" she snapped defiantly.

"But it could be," he disagreed softly. "This holiday break you had planned with Sullivan. It wasn't that you couldn't make it. My guess is he cancelled. Am I right?"

"I don't have to listen to this!"

"You haven't seen him for weeks. You'd arranged a break with him, but he cancelled. Are you really going to meet him on Friday?"

"Of course," she replied, reaching for her glass and sipping at it, calming her nerves. "You'd better tell me what this is all about."

"You haven't seen Sullivan for weeks. And I'm telling you there are others in the same situation, who are getting very edgy. They haven't seen him, and they haven't heard from him."

"What others?"

Eric hesitated. "Let's just say they're people connected with the Hollander Project."

"And you're working for them."

"I've been approached, yes." He hesitated. "If I find the enquiry gets...too close to home, raises any kind of conflict of interest, I've retained the right to pull out, back off from any involvement." He held her glance. His tone was reasonable. "I'm not here to pursue any vendetta, Anne, you have to believe me. But certain people are worried. If you know where Jason Sullivan is at the moment, it would be helpful to tell me. To set minds at rest." He looked at her carefully, reading the signs in her face. "Maybe to put your own mind at rest."

Her hand was shaking slightly as she put down the whisky glass. "I'll be seeing him Friday. In Luxembourg," she insisted. Her mouth twisted bitterly. "But if your clients want information... Well, we can't deny them that, can we?" She leaned forward, rummaged briefly through the papers in front of her, selected a sheet and passed it across to him. "His name is Mike Fremantle. He works as Jason's aide on the project administration. To satisfy your clients, you'd better talk to him, go see him at this address. Maybe he can give you the information you need. Now, if you don't mind, I've got rather a lot of work to go through."

She didn't bother to look up as he left the room.

Bamburgh Castle had been well-chosen as a site by the Normans: its walls enclosed the top of a massive precipitous rock overlooking the sea. Occupied since prehistoric times it had been the principal fortress of the early kings of Bernicia; the Normans established the castle in 1095 and from the twelfth century onwards it had become a royal castle, guarding the East March against the marauding Scots. Apart from its state rooms, it now housed a Museum of Industrial Archaeology exhibiting the work of the inventor and engineer Lord Armstrong. But many of the summer visitors came only to enjoy the sweeping stretch of the sands and wander around the teashops of the village where the Victorian heroine Grace Darling had lived. Over the years the castle had been used for a range of activities: school rooms, as an infirmary, a granary and a rest home for shipwrecked sailors, so it was not inappropriate that the great hall and chambers on the south side of the castle were presently being used to accommodate an exhibition to publicise the Hollander Project.

"I'm sorry to drag you up here," Mike Fremantle muttered, "but you seemed to suggest a meeting was urgent, and I'm going to be stuck here for a few days, with the planning and organising of this exhibition."

Eric shrugged dismissively. "It's no problem. A good excuse to get out of the office." And away from the files that, Susie Cartwright had reminded him in exasperation, still awaited his perusal.

"I'll be free in just a few minutes," Fremantle said, and hurried off to consult with the harassed leader of a group of men and women who were being conducted around the exhibition prior to its official opening. Eric wandered around the great hall, studying the artistic impressions of the new marina that was to be built some miles to the south, the printed assurances that wildlife would be preserved and protected, with stylish photographs of birds and mammals, and a wall-length painting of the housing and light industrial developments that would in due course arise along the cliffs and inlets of the coastline. It was a big project, and there was clearly some kind of selling job going on with the group that Fremantle had joined.

Eric watched him from a distance. Fremantle was a small, wiry man in his late thirties, balding at the temples. He was dressed with the precision of an accountant and his small, neat moustache attempted to cover the weakness of his mouth. He had eyes that were perceptive yet nervous in their glance; from time to time he looked back to Eric as though to make sure he was still waiting. Eric suspected the man would have preferred he vanish. When Eric had rung him, Fremantle had protested that he was extremely busy and away from the office; it was only with reluctance that he had finally agreed to meet at Bamburgh, allowing Eric to break into his schedule.

It was almost ten minutes before the group wandered away out of the great hall. Fremantle hesitated in the doorway, then came back towards Eric. He ran a hand over a perspiring brow. "Bloody local councillors. They seem to think everything has to be subordinated to their own designs and desires."

"Trouble?" Eric queried.

Fremantle grimaced. "A few planning problems. Nothing really very serious but they like to have the occasional junket, travel up here, get a good dinner from the Lord Lieutenant out of it, before they make recommendations back in their committees. Meet a few local bigwigs the same time. You know how it is."

"The Lord Lieutenant. A sort of figurative chairman, I suppose, as far as the project is concerned."

Mike Fremantle frowned. "How do you mean?"

"Well, ceremonial stuff, that sort of thing. I wouldn't imagine," Eric said casually, "he'd get to know about all the problems that inevitably attend a project of this size."

Fremantle stared at him, and ran his tongue over thin, dry lips. He glanced around the hall, as though suddenly aware of the scattering of other people in the hall, and he jerked his head towards the doorway. "Perhaps we could go outside and you can tell me what it is you want."

He led the way out into the sunshine, into the castle yard, and climbed to the walls where they could see the long stretch of sandy beach, pounded by the surging waves, blue and green, down towards Seahouses and the dark cliffs beyond. The breeze was light, but the sun was warm on their backs as they stared out to sea. Nevertheless, a slight shudder seemed to touch Fremantle. "So, what's this about? Miss Morcomb wasn't exactly explicit about why you wanted to see me. How can I help you?"

So Anne had rung Fremantle before Eric had made his own call. Eric was silent, thoughtful for a little while, until Fremantle moved nervously beside him, leaning against the stone parapet. He glanced at him. "Well, it's useful that we should meet here, really. It gives me a better idea of what the Hollander Project is all about. And that's why I needed to see you."

"What exactly do you want to know about it?"

"Background stuff, really. But not about the project itself so much, as the way it's been funded."

There was a short silence. Fremantle squinted up to the sky to the wheeling gulls that had suddenly materialised above their heads, white wings beating against the blue sky. "European money," he said shortly. "Some matching funding from the government, and from local companies."

"And your responsibilities?"

Fremantle shrugged. It did not disguise his unease. "I'm an accountant by training. I'm actually seconded to the Hollander Project by the Morcomb Enterprises board."

"So your direct employer is my ex-wife's company?"

Fremantle nodded, turning his head away from Eric as though he were fascinated by the gulls. "That's right. I've been with Morcomb Enterprises for about two years."

Eric did not recall him – but he had long since relinquished an interest in the company. "And in your secondment, what exactly is your function?"

Fremantle hesitated, shifted slightly. "Keeping an eye on financial arrangements, really."

"For Morcomb Enterprises, you mean?"

Fremantle shook his head. "No. Morcomb Enterprises have sunk quite a lot of money into the project of course, but my job is to make regular reports on cash flow, short term investments, make sure the money's coming in and out on a regular basis, chasing up contributors, that sort of thing. But my duties under the secondment lie with the Hollander Project Committee."

"Big job," Eric commented. "Lot of responsibility."

"It's not just me," Fremantle muttered, almost defensively.

"No, of course. You're working closely with Jason Sullivan on this project."

Fremantle hesitated. "That's right. He's my boss."

"You've been working with him for some time, I imagine."

Fremantle nodded. "Shortly after he took his seat on the board of Morcomb Estates."

After Eric had moved on. "So you'll be familiar with his work patterns, the way he does things."

"As much as anyone, I suppose." There was a wariness in Fremantle's tones. "Look, Mr Ward, what's this all about? What exactly do you want from me?"

The man oozed unease. Eric wondered why he was so nervous, merely at the mention of Jason Sullivan's name. "When did you last see Mr Sullivan?"

"Hey? I…I don't know, exactly. Couple of weeks I suppose."

"Is that normal?"

"How do you mean?"

"Is that how you and Sullivan work together – at arm's length, with little direct supervision and considerable absences?"

Mike Fremantle actually wriggled. "I don't see how my relationship with Jason Sullivan is anybody's business but mine, and his. We work well enough together. I don't need to see him all the time. He trusts me…" Something caught at the back of his throat suddenly and he swallowed. "We each have our own responsibilities. I don't need him on my back all the time, to do my job. He knows that."

"Even so…" Eric said gently. "It is a bit unusual, isn't it? Miss Morcomb hasn't seen him for some time. Neither have you. Has he actually been in contact at all recently?"

"Like I told you – "

"And the money...has he said anything at all about the money?"

Fremantle stiffened. On the wall in front of him his left hand contracted suddenly, fingers clawing. "What money?"

"The deficit."

A long silence grew between them. The waves hundreds of feet below beat rhythmically on the shoreline; above their heads the gulls squawked and wheeled and quarrelled. Eric waited patiently, until slowly, but with a nervous catch in his voice, Mike Fremantle murmured, "I don't know what you're talking about, Mr Ward."

Eric smiled grimly. "You haven't told the board of Morcomb Enterprises, have you? Or the Hollander board. What are you waiting for, Fremantle? Have you been given an explanation that satisfies you?"

A shudder ran through Fremantle's wiry frame. He turned his head. As he looked at Eric, his eyes were scared. "Who's been talking to you?"

"It doesn't matter. But I do have a client who's interested. At this stage no one wants to go to the police, because it might all just be a misunderstanding. The key to it all is Jason Sullivan. So, do you know where he is? I'm sure that if we could all have a little chat, things would get sorted out quickly enough, to everyone's satisfaction."

"But that's not the way it is," Fremantle blurted out. He glanced around him at the deserted battlements, as though fearful of being overheard. "I haven't dared talk to Miss Morcomb about it. She and Mr Sullivan...well, they're close. She's made it clear on more than one occasion that she's got every confidence in him."

Eric's lips tightened. "Go on."

"And my responsibilities...what am I supposed to do? I'm in a conflict situation here. I'm employed by Morcomb Enterprises, I'm seconded to Hollander, I report to Jason Sullivan, and to hell with it, I just do as I'm told, do you understand?"

"I think it's best you tell me what's going on," Eric said firmly.

"There's been nothing illegal in the arrangements we've made," Fremantle protested quickly. "It's just standard, normal practice, making the best use of money that comes in. You've got to remember, the overnight market can make a hell of a difference to what happens to an account – "

"You've been *gambling* Hollander money?" Eric queried in surprise.

"No, of course not!" Fremantle shook his head in exasperation. "Look, the first tranche of money came through from Europe, and it had to be matched with local funds. That was fine. But the outflows at this stage aren't great: we can lay off payments for some months yet. Jason and I discussed it: it made sense in our role as sort of bankers for certain aspects of the project that we should make a number of short term investments, take out favourable bonds, work the foreign exchange market, ensure that the project didn't lose money that was to be made out there. All legitimate, Mr Ward, I swear! Legitimate and…good accounting practice." He ground out the last words as though he didn't believe them.

"So what's gone wrong?"

Fremantle almost groaned. "Hell, I don't know! I've had people on my back for the last two weeks, asking awkward questions."

"How do you mean, awkward?"

"Because I can't give them the answers they want, not without talking to Mr Sullivan!"

"And Jason Sullivan is someone you've not been able to talk to for some weeks."

Fremantle was silent for a little while. Then he seemed to come to a decision. He turned to Eric. "Look, you're a lawyer, right? You got a client who's involved in this mess, isn't that so?"

"At this stage, I can't tell you who it is, but you're right,"

Eric confirmed. "And I'm prepared to treat this conversation as confidential."

Fremantle seemed almost to brush aside the assurance. He was beyond caring. "Look, the fact of the matter is we're talking about a lot of money coming into Hollander. And I did what Mr Sullivan asked. Made the overnight, short term investments, bought the bonds, easily convertible back when the need arose. On his instructions I worked the foreign exchange market, used the worldwide network. I'm good at my job, and the market's been hyperactive. So you'll understand there were elements of profits in such activity. If we were to ensure that European Fund money still came in, in the tranches promised, it was…sensible to cover the fact that significant sums had been made in the markets, with the money that had already been deposited. Not exactly hiding the money, you understand. We were just being prudent."

Grimly, Eric asked, "Where did you place the so-called profits?"

"Offshore accounts," Fremantle muttered nervously. "Labuan. A few other places."

"Signatories?"

Mike Fremantle expelled air from his lungs with a whooshing sound. "I had nothing to do with that. It was Jason Sullivan set it up. And then…just recently I got a few calls. People asking questions."

"Contributors?"

"Their agents." Fremantle's breathing quickened. "Jason wasn't around. He was wandering around in Europe, talking to people I believe, doing deals, negotiations, I don't know! So in the end I felt I ought to do some checks myself. The first thing I noticed was that the Labuan account no longer existed. It was closed about ten days ago. And I've not been able to get hold of Jason for an explanation. Mr Ward, I'm worried. I'm worried to hell. It's not my responsibility. I just did as I was told."

"Just how much are we talking about here?" Eric asked in a cold voice.

Mike Fremantle took a deep breath and shuddered. "I don't know the precise figure. But it's in excess of two million."

"Dollars?"

"Sterling."

There was a short silence as they each contemplated the consequences. Then the wiry accountant jumped as his mobile phone shrilled. He dug it out of his pocket; glared at it, pressed the button. His eyes fixed on Eric, as he listened, and nodded. Wordlessly, he handed the phone to Eric.

"Jason Sullivan?" Eric asked in disbelief.

Fremantle shook his head. "Miss Morcomb."

Her tone was cold, but there was agitation in her voice. The message was brief. "My meeting with Jason in Luxembourg on Friday. I've just had an e-mail. He's cancelled."

To Eric it was hardly a surprise.

Chapter Three

Detective Chief Inspector Charlie Spate was feeling pleased with himself. At last he felt he was being given some level of appreciation. He inspected the nameplate on his new office with satisfaction: *DCI Spate*. It was about time. Ever since he had come north to join the force he had felt something of an outsider: he knew there were views in the Chief Constable's office that he still had to prove himself after the rumours that had spread about him during his time in the Met, his closeness to some of his informants in the City, indiscreet relationships in the red light districts, but he'd kept his nose clean up here, achieved a few significant breakthroughs, and he felt he'd begun to command a degree of respect. Hence the new office.

Not that he reckoned the nameplate would cut much ice with Detective Sergeant Elaine Start. She already had formed a certain view of him, he was sure. It was clearly not one of unbounded admiration. More like a cynical knowingness. But then, on the other hand, he still wasn't sure how important her approval was to him. He had yet to work out quite what made her tick. For a while he had thought she had something going with Assistant Chief Constable Jim Charteris...

The name soured his thoughts, and took away some of his self-satisfaction. He didn't like the smooth bastard. There was a secretive side to the man; he played cards too close to his chest, didn't seem to trust his colleagues in a way they deserved. And he was on the lookout to move upwards, that was clear. So were most coppers of that rank, he guessed, away from the streets, concerned with policy and relationships, jumping like firecrackers to the sound of a Home Office directive, always on the lookout for a vacancy elsewhere, at a higher level. They were all of the same mould, but with Charteris the ambition was blatant, and considered. What suited the ACC was what counted, and the rest of the priorities could go to hell.

Priorities. It was something Charlie was going to have to raise at the morning conference he was due to attend right now. He took a deep breath, checked his watch, and set out for the conference room the ACC had designated for the briefing.

When he entered the room set out for the meeting the others had already arrived. DS Elaine Start was already seated to one side; ACC Charteris had taken his place at the head of the conference table, immaculately dressed as usual; flanking him were two men who were already known to Charlie Spate. On the right of Charteris was Joe Speakman, bug-eyed and balding, with the florid nose of a man who liked his whisky. A portly ex-miner, local politician and rab-ble-rouser, chairman of the Chamber of Commerce, he was one of the old school who insisted at elections that they stood up for workers' rights while at the same time ensur-ing they were chauffeur-driven from their expensive town houses in Jesmond to draw their allowances for attending at the council offices. To the left of Charteris was the lean-muscled, middle-aged Peter Olinger, with his unsteady eyes and discontented mouth, owner of a construction firm that had obtained regular public service contracts as a result of a judicious wooing of council committee chairmen. Charlie nodded to both men, and sat down at the far end of the table from Charteris.

"This needn't take us long," ACC Charteris began smoothly. "I've had a discussion with our two friends for the last hour or so, and I'm sure we're all now apprised of the basic facts. As I'm sure DCI Spate will acknowledge, we have had considerable co-operation from our guests, and it is much appreciated."

"It's meant a bloody mountain of paperwork," Joe Speakman grunted in the surly tone he normally adopted for meetings with the police. "And a lot of disruption." He glanced sideways to his companion, Peter Olinger. "And I know that my members, including Peter, have been put to a lot of trouble, all this checking of individual details. Peter, you want to say something?"

Peter Olinger stared momentarily at Charlie Spate then looked away: his lean features were pale, and there was an edge of strain about his mouth, a hint of anxiety shadowing his tired eyes. "Mr Speakman can talk for all his members, but the problem can be summed up in my own experiences, with my own firm. Things have changed over the years," he asserted. "When I started my construction business more than ten years ago I could rely on a steady stream of Irish labour and English tradesmen. But things are different now: the Irish have gone home to fuel their own housing boom as European funding has poured into Ireland. And wages in the building trade – the kind of wages I can afford to pay, anyway – they're bloody pitiful and certainly not enough to attract and keep good quality tradesmen."

"And it's all a load of bloody nonsense," Speakman intervened in his customary grumbling tone, "all these complaints in the newspapers about immigration. It's the immigrants who are keeping the economy functioning, whatever the media shout about. Take a look at the kitchens in the smart hotels, the porters' lodges in the hospitals, the work gangs rebuilding our public sector infrastructure. Take a look at farms, food factories, textile firms, cleaning – "

"Prostitution," Charlie interrupted.

Speakman glared at him angrily. "We should be *encouraging* immigration, not concentrating on the marginal abuses that take place as a basis for demanding all immigration should be stopped."

"There are forty thousand Eastern European workers in the London construction industry alone," Olinger added, after a short, tense silence. "Building projects in this country would grind to a halt without migrants. It's not just houses...it's schools, hospitals and roads. The labour pool is like Mr Speakman says: it's dominated by Poles – there's twenty one per cent unemployment in Poland – and Estonians, Chinese and Latvians and Romanians."

"Who've been flooding into the country. Cheap labour," Charlie Spate muttered. "That's really the underlying argument, isn't it?"

Speakman's eyes glittered coldly as he glared at Charlie Spate. "You can't have it all ways! Building is expensive. People want the cheapest price. It's not that there's a skills shortage in this country: it's simply that British people don't want to do building work because the wages are bad and they aren't prepared to work from seven to seven every day. Seven days a week." He turned his baleful glance to Charteris, seated impassively beside him. "That's why this damned campaign of harassment has got to stop. We've co-operated right up to the hilt. But enough's enough. Our infrastructure projects are grinding to halt up here in the north east, bogged down in paperwork and hassled by interference from inspections and police checks. And my members and friends, like Peter here, are struggling to complete their contracts."

"So Olinger Construction is in a bit of trouble, is it?" Charlie asked casually.

Peter Olinger's tired eyes narrowed, and he glanced uncertainly at Joe Speakman, as though seeking support. "We're just having certain cash flow problems. And we've had trouble giving guarantees over certain new contracts, because though the work's there – damn, the offers of contracts are coming out of our ears – we still can't get the workforce that we need, because of the noise that's being made with the checks you people have been instituting."

"I suppose some of your problems would have been alleviated," Charlie Spate suggested with a show of innocent concern, "if *Red Alliance* hadn't fallen at the last fence."

He felt Elaine Start's glance shift quickly to him, but he kept his own eyes fixed on Peter Olinger. The man reddened, leaned forward. "What's that supposed to mean?" he demanded aggressively.

Charlie managed a world-weary smile. "Oh, come on, Mr Olinger, it's just an observation. You're strapped for cash, you say, but the word on the street is that you put a bundle last week on *Red Alliance*. Pity he didn't make the winning post. Still running, some say. Now if you'd used some of that spare cash of yours to pump into the business – "

"This is preposterous!" snarled Joe Speakman. "We came here to make representations and expected a fair hearing. Instead we get insinuations!"

"Gentlemen," ACC Charteris soothed, "Let's calm down and stick to basic issues." He glanced at Charlie Spate, a little of his urbanity deserting him. "I don't think DCI Spate was doing anything other than having a little joke. The fact is, as I've already intimated, the Home Office had instructed us to undertake these wide-ranging checks on local industries, the reports have been compiled, the pressure is off, and I called this meeting just to ensure that we are all now aware of the position. Namely, the heat is off us; that means we can relax our checks; your business colleagues, Mr Speakman, can be released from the obligations of paper returns on their immigrant workers and continued careful background checks. And everyone can relax and be happy again."

Everyone except me, Charlie Spate thought angrily. He did not voice his opinion until some little time later, when, barely mollified and still grumbling, Speakman and Olinger had been ushered from the premises.

Assistant Chief Constable Charteris came back in and resumed his seat. He tugged at his immaculate shirt collar. His mouth was set in a thin, disapproving line. "You need to keep a button on your lip, DCI Spate. You have a tendency to speak out of turn."

"Out of turn? It needed saying! What the hell is this all about, sir?" Charlie almost exploded. "Just as we start getting some sort of control over the villains, put the frighteners on the gangmasters and use the chance to cut down on the illegals who are flooding into the north east under our very noses, you're telling us to back off!"

"I already explained," Charteris said, almost wearily. "Six months ago the Home Office asked us to undertake an exercise. Put pressure on all employers in certain targeted industries. Demand returns; check on work permits; identify immigration issues. We've done it. Background checks on workers in the hotel and construction industries have been implemented. The report has been written. I've sent it off myself. It's all done, wrapped up. Time to move on."

"And I disagree," Charlie insisted firmly. "If this survey has done anything, it's given us a raft of information and opened up a few chinks in the organisations; it's put a few shackles on people who've been making a bomb from bringing in workers who haven't gone through the proper immigration proceedings. False papers, forged documents – you know what we've uncovered. If we take the heat off now, the floodgates will open again. It's inevitable!"

"We've done the job we were asked to do, but it over-stretched our resources," Charteris replied in clipped tones. "As for ending the investigation, we don't determine policy. The Asylum and Immigration Act – "

"Has achieved bugger all! Two convictions last year! Look at that recent raid in Norfolk: sixty-three Chinese detained, one sent back to China, the other sixty-two staying here, forty of them claiming asylum. And no employers prosecuted. The Act, aw, come on – it's a joke!"

"I repeat," Charteris replied, greater heat entering his tones. "We follow government priorities!"

Frustrated, Charlie Spate glared at Elaine Start. "I notice you're keeping your head down on this, Detective Sergeant," he sneered.

Her eyes glittered murderously as she shot a venomous glance back at him. Then she took a deep breath, turned to Charteris. "DCI Spate has a point, sir. I don't go entirely along with him in his argument, but there's been one important side issue that clearly has emerged. The survey we did – putting pressure on employers – it's worked well enough. But as DCI Spate has pointed out, other things have turned up, which it would be a mistake to let go of now. We should not simply walk away from the conclusions that can be drawn from our investigations over the last six months."

ACC Charteris was silent for a little while, calming down, observing the detective sergeant carefully. Slowly, he nodded. "All right. Explain what conclusions you've drawn."

She glanced uncertainly at Charlie. He butted in: it had been his investigation. "So we've been looking at restaurants, hotels and construction industry workers. The employers have been made to produce evidence, paperwork, documents, so the Home Office can draw conclusions. But that's only one side of the picture, as we all know. We've picked up a few illegals, sweated workers who are too scared to tell us how they got in here in the first place. But as a result other things have come to light."

"What precisely?" Charteris asked in a slightly bored voice.

"The ones in the dark alleys. The drugs. The prostitutes. Things have clearly changed, sir. There's a new smell in the air, and it's a nasty one. I'm convinced there's a new thrust to the business: we're becoming the unloading point for a whole raft of illegals from Eastern Europe – Serbs, Romanians – in order to feed the darker business. Prostitution, particularly. There's a whole new network been set up and it's big business. It's well organised. And it's backed by a whole new lot of money."

Charteris frowned. He turned to look in Elaine Start's direction. He raised an interrogative eyebrow.

"It does look that way," she agreed soberly. "The whole thing now seems to be better organised, and much better financed than it has ever been in the past. The EU estimates that there are half a million prostitutes smuggled in from Eastern Europe – and we're getting a fair share of them. The operation centres on soft entry points – and the whole of the north-east coastline is pretty porous in that respect, although the main entry points are at Hull, the Tees and the Tyne. We're convinced there's a new level of organisation operating – "

"And a hell of a lot of new money underpinning the system," Charlie interrupted, repeating his point.

"Names?"

Charlie shook his head. "Only a few little guys. No point dragging them in: they'd have too much to lose if they talked to us. But we need time; give us continued manpower on this investigation, sir, so we can keep up the pressure on the ones we've got in the net and I'm sure we'll come up with results."

Charteris frowned, then shook his head doubtfully. "You'll be telling me next that it's all down to your old *b te noire* Mad Jack Tenby."

Irritation entered Charlie Spate's voice. "All right, I always thought, ever since I joined this force, that a lot of what was going on along the river was down to Mad Jack. He's an old leopard who hasn't changed his spots, even if he pretends legitimacy and has friends in high places, bought off, I've no doubt." He held up a hand as Charteris seemed to be about to respond angrily. "But I don't think Tenby can be central to this deal. We all know there's been a power shift in the controls of criminal activity on our patch. Tenby was getting old, bowing out: the young heavyweights have been coming in, taking slices of action, showing each other their muscles as Mad Jack relaxed, washed his hands of some of the operations along the river. But even that's settled down; not so many entrepreneurs riding the tracks: not so many niggling little turf wars. It's settled down because these young tearaways can see they'll do better taking orders; either that, or they know if they don't conform, they'll get taken apart. There's new muscle along the river, sir."

"Along with the new money," Elaine Start added.

ACC Charteris stretched, rose, walked slowly across to the window, stared out at the storm clouds that had been threatening to bring a late flurry of snow for most of the day. He seemed indeterminate. "You want to continue to put pressure on."

"We are surely all agreed that tackling the employers who use illegal labour is crucial in dealing with criminal gangs smuggling immigrants into the country, and cracking down on the gangmasters who exploit them. We've got to keep the investigation going, sir. Drop the background checks, fine, but let us continue to use the contacts we've made, flush out some of the more scared of our informants, see if we can't point the finger more closely at who's behind the increased number of illegals destined for the clubs in Leeds and York and Manchester, the red light districts, and the drug scams." Charlie hesitated, feeling almost helpless. "It's a bloody more sensible use of police time, than chasing up Home Office bloody surveys!"

Charteris stiffened. He turned slowly to glare at Charlie. "You've already made your point forcibly enough. However..." He locked his hands behind his back and began to pace the room. "My own view is that things will settle down. In a few months time we'll be getting a whole new raft of workers coming in, with the expansion of the European Union. Some of our present "illegals" will be legal enough then: they'll have a right to travel anywhere within the EU. The problem will fade."

"I don't agree," Charlie flashed back. "The Poles, the Slovaks and the rest of the eight new Eastern European nationals will have a right of entry, but all the latest reports stress that those countries have their own problems now of illegal immigration. The UN reckon more than ten thousand people sought asylum in Slovakia last year – only eleven individuals were granted asylum, and more than nine thousand simply disappeared from the six refugee camps set up near the Austrian border. Where are they headed for? Britain. Hell, the racket is worth an estimated four billion quid a year! It's a whole new ball game for the gangmasters!"

Charteris held up a warning hand. "All right, I still hear you about these others, brought in by the gangmasters. But let's leave that for the moment. The fact is, there's another request come from up above. The Home Office survey is concluded, but I've now been asked to organise a new investigation. We have to re-open a cold case."

"Sir?"

"The killing of Michael Podro."

There was a short silence. Charlie Spate furrowed his brow. "I seem to recollect...Podro... that case was winding up, file closed, just about the time I joined the force up here."

"Well, it's to be re-opened."

"Why?"

Charteris hesitated. "Inter-force co-operation. We've had a request... Since the killing was on our patch, we've been asked to dig again into it. Pass on any information we can raise. And...er...it has to be given a degree of priority." He paused, swivelling his head to stare at Charlie. "That means you."

"But sir – "

Charteris was clearly prepared to brook no argument. "You're the senior officer. You'll bring a fresh look to the case, since you weren't involved in the initial investigation. And I don't see how you can concentrate on the Podro enquiry as well as this continuing wide-ranging investigation into the local developments in illegal immigrants organisation. So, at least for the short term, DCI, you work on the Podro case."

Charlie grimaced. "And our leads on the new controls on Tyneside?"

"DS Start has been working with you," Charteris said blandly. "She can continue. And report to you, of course. But you're no longer hands-on with that issue, Spate. Find out who killed Michael Podro." He hesitated. "And if possible, *why* he was killed."

It was said firmly, and decisively. And there was to be no further discussion about it.

Back in his own room Charlie glared at the nameplate. His earlier pleasure had evaporated. So much for being held in respect. Sidelined on a cold case, where all the leads would have been long since dissipated, even if there had been any of consequence, while a major breakthrough was possible on a much wider operation. An operation that Elaine Start, the ACC's blue-eyed girl, was to front up. She and Charteris...he was still a little suspicious about their relationship. But maybe that was because he...

There was a tap on the door. He looked up to see Elaine Start standing there. She held a file in her hand. "I thought you might like a chat," she said hesitatingly.

He waved to her to come in. She took a seat across the other side of his desk. She crossed her legs. She had great legs. And a great bosom. He curbed his thoughts.

"You really went for it in there," she suggested quietly.

"How do you mean?"

"Speakman and Olinger."

"Ha, those tarts. They're whingers: Speakman is just interested in blustering his way around the electorate pretending he's got power, and Olinger is a guy who'll grab any cheap labour he can provided he can make enough money to indulge his real passions."

"So what was that all about, the crack about *Red Alliance*?"

Charlie grimaced. "Ah, I couldn't take that spurious garbage about looking after the workforce, fulfilling his contracts, and all that crap. Olinger, he runs a big local construction business but he's got a fatal weakness: he can't stay away from the racetrack, and he can't resist the casinos. It doesn't help that he's a bloody poor gambler by all accounts."

She smiled slightly. "I don't think it was entirely tactful to raise the matter, nevertheless."

"So when did tact begin to come into my makeup?" He caught her eye, noted the raised eyebrow, shrugged, and relaxed somewhat, grinned in reluctant acknowledgement. "Aye, well, it needed saying, I reckon. So who was this Michael Podro, anyway?" he grunted, putting the matter aside.

"I picked up the file from records. I thought you might like to have a quick look at it."

"You've read it?" When she nodded, he went on, "Well you can fill me in with the generalities. I'll go over the details later."

She shrugged. "As you like." She opened the file and gazed at its contents for a few moments. "It was a gang of young kids who found him first. It was the fourth of November. They were looking to nick some old pieces of timber, around the back of a deserted old railway shed. They thought he was praying, first of all."

"That someone really *would* blow up the politicians this time?" Charlie Spate frowned. "He'd have got support for that prayer, believe me. But how do you mean, praying?"

"He was on his knees, head leaning against an old door. He was sort of propped up. Here, take a look." She extracted a photograph from the file and handed it to him.

The man was dressed in a dirty old coat; it was a scruffy area, rubbish piled in one corner. Charlie peered at the image: a kneeling figure, highlighted by the flash of the camera, head forward, resting on the decayed wooden door of an old railway shed. "He's got his hands tied behind his back."

"That's right. He was made to kneel, wrists tied with a length of thin wire. Then he was shot once, in the back of the head."

"Clinical." Charlie eyed the photograph with distaste for a little while longer, then handed it back. "So what was the news on him?"

"Not a great deal, and nothing that was really helpful. He was finally identified as one Michael Podro, a former railway worker who had lived for years in the West End of Newcastle. He had a record, of sorts, but mainly petty theft, no muscle stuff, last conviction ten years or so back, but that was just for credit card fraud, really small stuff, said he found the card and was tempted to use it. No big deal."

Charlie inspected the photograph again. "His clothes weren't exactly Savile Row."

Elaine nodded. "He lived in rented accommodation, not the best street in the West End. Neighbours said he kept pretty much to himself. Used to drink in the Prince of Wales pub, but seems to have had no real drinking companions, at least none who identified themselves." She passed another photograph to him, one of a series taken at the mortuary, prior to the post-mortem. The heavy-shouldered body was stretched out on the slab, naked.

"Big bugger," Charlie murmured.

"That's right," she agreed. "Gone to seed over the years, of course. But what gossip the team did pick up at the Prince of Wales was that he used to be a fan of the wrestling when it was on TV, but kept shouting it was all a fix."

"Well, wasn't it always?" Charlie challenged.

"I've led an innocent life, sir," she smiled. "The point is, he went a bit further than that. Said in his day he'd have dumped any one of the muscle-bound baddies. Claimed to have been a wrestler himself."

Charlie continued to study the photograph of the man on the slab. Big shoulders, big hands. "Maybe he was telling the truth."

"It was something we were unable to get confirmation of. But then, maybe his wrestling days occurred elsewhere, out of this country."

"Why do you say that?" Charlie queried, still scrutinising the photograph.

"He wasn't English. Thick heavy accent, apparently. But no one knew exactly where he was from. It was one thing he never discussed, even when he was in his cups."

"Family?"

"He had a wife, it seems, but she predeceased him. No information on her other than she was born in Middlesbrough. But there was no great interest in the killing at the time; I mean, the investigation was soon dropped."

"Why?"

"Other more pressing business to deal with."

"Tell me about it," Charlie moaned rhetorically. "Let me see the other mug shots of the deceased."

Elaine passed them over to him, her fingertips brushing his. She had long slim fingers; he had a brief illusion, could almost feel the fingertips touching him elsewhere, caressing... He shook his head, went through each of the photographs in turn. On the head shots he noted the sunken features, the grizzled, stubby beard, the hollow eyes; he looked back to the body shots, the heavy flabbiness of a decaying frame. Then he grimaced. "Bloody hell. What are these wounds?"

"Knife cuts. Cigarette burns on the arms. Fingernails removed," she said dispassionately. "Burns on the lower legs and around the groin area."

"The poor bastard was tortured?"

"So the pathologist reckons. Some hours before his death. The report suggests he was held somewhere, tortured, then taken out and killed."

Charlie's mouth twisted in disgust. He stared at the wreck of the tortured body. "How *old* was this Podro character?"

"Undetermined," Elaine replied quietly. "But the pathologist reckoned he was well into his seventies. And he had cancer."

"What?"

"Stomach. Well advanced. The pathologist was of the opinion he had only about six months to go."

"Bloody hell." Charlie sighed and shook his head. He picked out one of the head and shoulder shots, scrutinised it. "Is this a torture wound on his arm?"

She came around the desk to stand beside him, leaning over his shoulder to inspect the mortuary shot. Her left breast touched his shoulder, and he became very conscious of her nearness. His pulse rate quickened in spite of himself. There were times when he wondered about Elaine Start, wondered whether she was up for it... He'd tried once, at the conference in Avignon, but it had been a clumsy, ill-bred attempt and she had repulsed him more than firmly. And yet there had been times since when he got the impression that she might have regretted that rejection... Who the hell really knew with women? She shifted slightly against his arm. "I don't think it's a wound," she said slowly. "It looks to me like an old tattoo of some kind."

"Maybe he was a sailor, then," Charlie suggested thickly.

She moved away, eyeing him for a moment, perhaps aware of the sudden sexual tension that had arisen between them. "Maybe. Anyway, there's nothing about it in the pathologist's report that I recall..." She inspected the notes in the file. After a few minutes, she admitted, "Well, actually there is something in the general notes, made before they started to slice the guy. But it just says: *Tattoo, left shoulder, indeterminate lettering.* Doesn't add up to much. Do you think it's important?"

Charlie tried to straighten out his thoughts. "Hell, I don't know. It would help in identification, maybe. But we've got so little on this character anyway... What puzzles me is why your boyfriend wants this case re-opened."

Her head came up; her eyes were suddenly cold. "I have no personal relationship with Assistant Chief Constable Charteris, sir."

"Aye, well – "

"And he said this was a request from above, not his idea alone."

"I never trust the brass," Spate murmured uncomfortably, regretting his big mouth. Whatever warmth had been generating between himself and Elaine Start had been dissipated by his unwise crack. He looked at her, seated stiffly in the chair on the other side of his desk. "But putting that aside, what in particular strikes you about this killing?"

"How do you mean, sir?"

He didn't like the way she kept saying *Sir*. "Well, it was hardly a casual killing, was it?"

She frowned. "How do you mean?"

"Down in the West End an old man gets into a quarrel, is beaten up, maybe. Someone who owes a grudge might take a pool cue to him. He might fall foul of some little tearaway with a knife. But all this, it's different. This killing presents a scenario, all of itself. It's a set-up."

"You mean the deliberate way it was done?"

Charlie nodded. "To start with his hands are bound behind his back with wire. Not rope, but wire. Look at the photographs: the wire had cut deeply into his wrists. He'd been like that a while...during which time they tortured him. Then he's taken out, to a deserted backwater; he's made to kneel, facing away from his killer. You said the kids who found the body thought he was praying, at first. Maybe that's what he was doing. Or what he was *forced* to do. Pray to his gods? Pray for forgiveness? Repent for what he had done? And then the manner of death. A single shot, to the base of the skull. Clean, quick, professional." Charlie clucked his tongue. "You reckon to be a film buff. So no doubt you've seen those old films of the killings in the Nazi death camps, documentaries of the Pol Pot killing grounds, the Bosnian-Serb ethnic cleansing operations."

"Not exactly my taste in films," she protested.

"Maybe so. But in those documentary reels, it's always the same. No waste of time or effort. Economical. One shot in the back of the head; the prisoner kneeling. That's what this is all about. Not casual, accidental, a quick decision taken in a hasty moment, a robbery, a mugging. It was none of those things. This was different. Deliberate. Efficient. This was a *professional* hit."

She stared at the first photograph. She nodded slowly. "I recognise that."

Charlie leaned back in his chair, locked his hands behind his head and rocked slowly. "But what interests me additionally, is *why* someone would want to torture this guy, humiliate him, make him kneel, maybe recite something, before he was despatched with a single shot to the back of the head."

"And why," Elaine Start agreed soberly, "when the victim should be an apparently harmless old man."

Charlie nodded. "At his age, and in his condition, he could hardly have been a threat to the drug barons and skimmers along the Tyne. So why would someone go to the expense of a professional hit to waste the guy?" He frowned in puzzled concentration. "Just how old did you say the pathologist reckoned he was?"

"Well into his seventies."

Charlie closed his eyes. Michael Podro had been an old man, and dying of cancer. Why the hell would it have been important to someone to torture and kill a man who would only have had a few months to live anyway? "You know," he remarked reflectively, "I can't see a professional hit like this going down without one of the big boys along the river wanting to know just what the hell was going on. Or maybe even putting on the show, for that matter."

There was a short silence. Elaine Start looked at him levelly. She could guess what he had in mind. "You're thinking of walking into the lion's den."

Charlie Spate smiled cheerfully. "Just like Albert. I don't have a stick with a horse's head handle, but I think I'll go stick *something* into the lion's ear."

"Albert got swallowed for his presumption. Whole," she reminded him.

"Yeah, but as I recall, the lion later coughed him back up. It's worth a try. After this time, everyone will be assuming the heat on Podro's killing has died down. Let's see what happens when we turn up the burners again. We'll start by having a talk with the big man himself."

"Mark Vasagar."

"The very same."

Chapter Four

The easiest way to get to La Rochelle, Susie Cartwright – all smiles since she had deposited the cheque from Bradgate and Savage – had informed him, was to take a flight from Newcastle to Stansted, and then board one of the cheap shuttle flights to the French seaport. Quickest, and cheapest: there was no point in throwing away money, was there, even if they were suddenly more than solvent in the firm account? Eric took her advice. Consequently, on the flight he found himself in the company of a mixed bag of travellers: middle-aged couples who had taken the advantage of cheap flights to the French provincial airports to purchase second homes in France; young backpackers, students, businessmen and the occasional family heading for a Spring holiday on one of the outlying islands.

At La Rochelle the airport itself was relatively unsophisticated but he carried very little luggage and was soon through to the warm sunshine on the tarmac outside. One look at the group clustered about convinced him a taxi was going to mean a long wait; some brief enquiries and he discovered the service bus stop was only two hundred yards away. The service was efficient: within half an hour he found himself in the centre of the town, and a short walk took him to the hotels on the bustling harbour front.

It was late afternoon. Eric found a single room in a budget hotel easily enough, and went straight out to take a slow stroll around the harbour with its narrow entrance flanked by the twin towers from which a chain had once been suspended to barricade the port from the predations of the English warships in the Hundred Years War. The concentration of busy caf s along the waterfront now catered for new invaders of the tourist kind. There was considerable activity in the harbour itself, some kind of boat festival in the Port d'Echouage, with music supplied by a wheezing hurdy-gurdy and crowds of schoolchildren exhibiting paintings and drawings of their view of the town. Eric was happy enough to find a seat at a caf on the Quai Duperr overlooking the scene, enjoy a drink, and think about what he was involving himself in.

He had decided to talk to Jackie Parton about it before he left. He had met the ex-jockey in the Alexandra Hotel, a seedy, somewhat run-down pub in Byker, the kind of place frequented by Parton because of the contacts he maintained there, the relative discretion of the clientele who had their own little *sub rosa* activities to get on with, and because he liked the beer. "It's a little bit out of my league, Mr Ward," the little man suggested in reply to Eric's request.

"Maybe so, Jackie," Eric had agreed. "I appreciate few of the people you know might have links into what's been going on with the Hollander Project, but for someone to just up sticks and disappear...well, there's just the off-chance that Sullivan may have used one of the networks you can tap into."

"I doubt it," Parton said reflectively. "He wouldn't need to deal with the kind of people I tangle with." He hesitated. "I mean, he's a lawyer, plenty of money, moves in different circles...I just don't see how I can really help." He sipped his beer, ruminating. "Does...does Mrs Ward...I mean Miss Morcomb...does she know what's going on?"

Eric shrugged. "She knows I'm looking for Sullivan. She hasn't seen him for weeks." He glanced sideways at the ex-jockey. He had used him as an informant, as a lead into the networks that existed along the river, ever since he had been working as a policeman. They had developed a friendship of sorts, somewhat bruised of recent years by the events in Eric's life, not least the break-up of his marriage. Jackie Parton had met Anne, liked her, and had a view about what had happened, and the reasons behind it. "The main thing is, if you hear anything on the grapevine which might have some bearing on Sullivan's disappearance, let me know."

"Aye, I can do that." Jackie Parton's glance wandered

around the room, checking who was there, putting names to faces, nodding occasionally when he caught someone's eye. "There's quite a bit stirring on Tyneside, I can tell you that, Mr Ward. The polis have been putting pressure on right across the board, a crackdown on work permits, turning up at some of the hotels for checks on the staff, hassling the cheap labour that's been coming in. There's been some scurrying around, I can tell you. You know, guys running for cover: some of the gangmasters getting out back to Rotterdam and Zeebrugge. The small ones, anyway. But there's other things happening too…"

Eric frowned. "How do you mean?"

Jackie Parton wrinkled his nose. The grimace made him appear almost monkey-like. "It's not easy to put a finger on things. Suddenly, people are kind of wary. The chatter has died down. You don't pick up the kind of crack you used to over a pint. It's as though guys don't want to talk about things. The screws are on."

"What screws?" Eric asked curiously.

Parton sighed despondently. "That's it. I don't really know. It's just a feeling I got. Of recent months, there's been some funny things going down. Unnecessary violence. A couple of beatings, a bookie getting carved. I mean, last year there was an old guy who got the real treatment… It's like there's a new wind blowing along the river, and it's got a funny smell to it. There used to be a certain security, you know, in the fact that everyone knew who was in control of business. It's not like that any more, not what is was like in Mad Jack Tenby's day. There's extra muscle moved in. There's a new edge. Something's happening; and people are keeping their heads down and their mouths shut. Some of the swagger has gone out of the guys who'd carved out their own manors, too. The hardheads are suddenly keeping quiet, looking over their shoulders, like…" He clucked his tongue ruefully, picked up his glass, drained it, shook his head. "All that's nothing to do with you, Mr Ward. And I'll do as you ask. Make a few discreet enquiries. Put some feelers out. But I doubt I'll come up with anything. This character Sullivan – he's out of my league. If he's skipped, it won't be with the help of anyone I can be talking to."

Sitting in the late afternoon sunshine on the Quai Duperr , Eric guessed that the ex-jockey was probably right. On the other hand Jackie Parton had always been a useful sounding board. But in La Rochelle Eric was on his own: he had his own planning to do. He sat there with a *cassis* in front of him, his perspective beyond the harbour limited by the Chain Tower and the tower of St Nicolas, with the Lantern Tower beyond, but he barely noticed them.

He'd had a conversation with his ex-wife Anne over the phone, pressing her for details of the holiday break that had been planned with Jason Sullivan, before Sullivan had called off the trip. She was still edgy, still in denial, insisting that there was an innocent explanation to his absence and she told him that the details of their short break had been largely left to Sullivan, but there was one thing she did remember: she could give him the name of a boat. The *Beau Soleil*. It was a start.

He began by taking a slow tour of the harbour itself, and walked down to the Vieux Port, knowing full well he was unlikely to strike lucky so soon. The inspection yielded nothing to him, nor did he find what he was looking for in the Bassin des Grands Yachts. He gave up in the early evening and decided to eat at the *Restaurant Andr :* he ordered a traditional meal of fish, and a bottle of good wine. He lingered over the meal, and ordered a cognac. As the clientele thinned, the head waiter seemed inclined to chat, if only to practise his English.

"It is a holiday you take, *m'sieur*?"

"Business."

"Ha, but La Rochelle is a place for the enjoyment of leisure! You must find time to explore and enjoy what we have to offer."

"Like sailing, maybe hiring a boat?" Eric enquired. When the waiter expounded on the immense availability of yachts and boats of all kind and description, and regular ferries to the islands, Eric waited patiently, until he was able to mention the *Beau Soleil*. "I was looking for it, down in the yacht basins, but it's impossible – so many craft."

The waiter shrugged and smiled, spreading his hands wide. "It will be like a needle in the haystack, as the English say. *Bien sur*, a problem. But in any case, perhaps this is not where you should look."

"How do you mean?"

"You should look at the Port des Minimes, at the entrance to the bay, on the south bank. *C'est le port de plaisance des minimes*. There you will find more than four thousand of all kinds of boats. It is the largest European port on the *Atlantique*."

Four thousand. Eric's heart sank. Needle in a haystack, indeed. The waiter caught his expression. He gave a shrug. "But perhaps it is not so difficult. The harbourmaster there, he will have a list of the boats. You should try there, my friend. And now, perhaps another cognac?"

At nine-thirty next morning Eric embarked on the *bus de mer*, the small, green tarpaulined craft making the short, ten-minute passage between the towers at the harbour entrance out along past the Tour de la Lanterne on his right and the promenade of the All e des Tamaris on his left, towards the Port des Minimes. As they swung into the mooring area he could see what the waiter had meant: a vast forest of masts and rigging rose up to meet him. The water-bus manoeuvred its way through the waterways past all descriptions of seagoing craft: ahead of him he could see the modern blocks of flats that had been erected to house the yachting enthusiasts, holiday lets, caf s, restaurants, displaying a bland, functional appearance in sharp contrast to the buildings of La Rochelle itself, where centuries of seafaring activity had carved out different architectural features.

It took Eric an hour of prowling around the area to find
the harbourmaster in his office. He was a short, portly, uni-
formed individual, aware of his own importance but
friendly enough, with smiling blue eyes set in a sea-tanned
face. He spoke good English – and German and Italian, he
assured Eric. His was an international harbour. "The *Beau
Soleil*..." He scratched at his thinning thatch. "There are
several such names, I am sure. And you must understand
there are three yacht basins here: Lazaret, Bout-Blanc, and
then there is Marillac...You say that this was a charter, some
weeks ago?"

"I can give you precise dates," Eric offered.

"That would be useful." The harbourmaster inspected his
registers. "Lazaret...no. And Marillac...there has been little
movement of charters there. It is too early in the year; your
friends would have not chosen the popular season, but
then, is it not better then? As for Bout-Blanc..." He was
silent for a while, poring over the records. At last he sat
back, smiled at Eric. "I think we might have found what you
are looking for, *m'sieur*. There was a charter of a yacht
under the name *Beau Soleil*. But it is not here at the
moment. The charter took the people concerned out to Ile
de R . It has not returned. It is likely that the charterer
retains the craft on the island. His name, the owner, it is
Lafitte. It is all I can do to help, I fear. But your boat, the
one you seek, I think it will be berthed at St Martin de
R ..."

"Can you tell me in what name the charter was taken?"

"I can, *bien sur*. It was in the name of Duclos."

So if it was the right *Beau Soleil*, the one Jason Sullivan
had intended to use with Anne, it had finally been taken in
someone else's name.

Eric shook the harbourmaster's hand. "My thanks for
your time."

"*D'accord, m'sieur*. Try St Martin de R ."

As he left the office and began to make his way towards

the landing for the *bus de mer* Eric glanced back. The harbourmaster was visible in the window of his office. He was
making a phone call, but when he saw Eric looking over his
shoulder, he raised his hand in a friendly wave.

Back in La Rochelle Eric found a car hire office in Quai
Valin. He was aware he could take one of the ferries across
to the Ile de R  but that would not give him the flexibility
and freedom of movement he might require. He took a
light lunch in a restaurant on the Quai du Gabut then went
back to pick up the car. He headed out of the city, taking
the road marked for the *pont-viaduc* and in a little while
found himself sweeping over the three thousand metre long
viaduct, curving high above the beaches to the island that
had once formed a regular battleground, a focal point for
the incursions of the English in the time of Napoleon.

He drove along the narrow roads past beaches and sand
dunes: the island possessed a kind of bucolic beauty with its
pine woods and vineyards, distant views of lighthouses and
church steeples, whitewashed single storey houses, with
their shutters painted grey, white and olive green, and fields
of poppies and sunflowers. The area was famous for the
oyster beds he passed, gleaming and shimmering in the late
afternoon sun. It was past four when he finally reached the
castellated stone walls of St Martin de R , its military power
only a distant memory, but still surrounded by the ramparts
that had encircled the town with rugged, crumbling, protective arms of stone, defying the English in the Hundred
Years War. He parked near the old harbour, walked up to the
bastions that looked out to sea and the distant towers of La
Rochelle, then paced slowly around the enclosed harbour.
It had once been a flourishing port; now it was lined with
restaurants frequented by the vacationers who came from
Paris for the weekends and the summer months. There were
perhaps thirty yachts in the basin; he walked slowly past
them, checking on the names. It was not long before he
found the sleek, forty-foot boat, equipped with the latest

marine technology, as far as he could see, and named the *Beau Soleil*.

There was no one on board.

He checked into a small *auberge* in a cobbled side street leading down to the harbour, and then found a caf  to take a drink, using the position as a vantage point, keeping an eye on the *Beau Soleil*. No one approached it, so eventually he gave up and took a meal at an old house that had been converted into a restaurant. From the terrace he could still command a view of the moorings and whitewashed cottages. His surveillance was fruitless: as darkness fell there was no sign of life on the boat, no lights to be seen. But he hung on, waiting until all the staff had left and he was alone on the terrace. He finally turned in, disappointed, at midnight.

He took breakfast next morning in the sunny courtyard of the house, within a walled garden with a small lawn, and cherry trees that leaned over a small fountain, splashing over white stones. When he paid his bill he made some discreet enquiries of the manager of the hotel, but the man claimed to be from Marseilles, had only recently taken over the hotel, and knew very few people in St Martin de R . "Besides," the man said with a shrug, "they come and they go, the boat people. One cannot keep track."

Eric spent the morning waiting, and watching. The sun was warm, and he took a stroll from time to time, watching old men playing *boules* in the Place de la Republique along the ramparts, still keeping the *Beau Soleil* in sight, but he was beginning to think it was all a waste of time, and he'd have to try another tack, maybe go back to the harbourmaster at Port des Minimes when he finally caught sight of some movement on board the yacht. Someone had climbed on board, and had entered the wheelhouse. Hurriedly, Eric left the ramparts, walked quickly around the harbour and made his way along the quayside to the *Beau Soleil*. He stood there uncertainly for a few minutes, until a man came out from the wheelhouse. He was middle-aged, thickset, dressed in a blue jersey and jeans. He was grey-haired, and sported a beard, russet mingled with white. There was a stained yachting cap perched jauntily on the back of his head. He looked enquiringly up at Eric.

"*Vous vous appellez M'sieur Lafitte?*"

The man smiled broadly, and ducked his head in assent. "And you are English."

Relieved, Eric called down to him, "Is it so immediately apparent?"

"One gets used to accents, *m'sieur.*"

"Could we have a few words?"

"As many as you like, my friend. The day is mine." He lifted his cap, gestured in a wide sweep of welcome. "Come on board. If it is a charter you are looking for, I have a bottle on board. It makes discussions that much more agreeable."

Eric stepped onto the deck. Lafitte pointed to a seat in the sunshine, back of the wheelhouse. "Sit there, and we will take a glass of wine together."

"I'm not exactly thinking of chartering the boat, *M'sieur* Lafitte," Eric warned. "I just want to talk about a charter you had recently."

Lafitte shrugged. "It is of no consequence. A glass of wine would suit us well, in any case." He disappeared into the cabin and emerged a few minutes later with a bottle and two glasses. "Merlot. A French chateau. None of your Australian or Chilean wines here. We must support our own industries, *n'est ce pas?*"

He poured the wine, handed a glass to Eric, and raised his own, inspecting the deep red colour with appreciation. "*Sant .*" He sipped his wine with an air of evident satisfaction, then exhaled, smiled and asked, "So what can I do for you, my friend? Are you the person who spoke to the harbourmaster at La Rochelle yesterday?"

Taken somewhat aback, Eric nodded. "News travels fast."

"In a closed community, like boat people, *bien sur.* You have been asking about a charter; the one taken by *M'sieur* Duclos."

"That's right."

Lafitte grimaced. "So many people interested... But there's not much I can tell you. On the other hand, if you have specific questions..."

Eric frowned. "The charter was taken personally by this man Duclos?"

Lafitte nodded. "By telephone from his home in Paris. A week's charter. For a friend, he said. He gave me the impression it was to be...how do you say, a romantic business? I was to be paid to take these people cruising around Ile de R , Ile d'Aix, Isle d'Ol ron...the pure air, the magnificent woods, the sandy beaches – and *les hu tres*! You like oysters, my friend?"

Eric nodded.

Lafitte grinned. "The *huitres* of Ol ron, they are the best. And for a romantic cruise, what might they do. Their aphrodisiac reputation – "

Eric was not appreciating the turn of the conversation. "You mention people."

"A couple, I was led to believe. But then at a late moment, things were changed."

"There was a cancellation?"

Lafitte shrugged. "A change in arrangements. Duclos turned up at Port des Minimes. He said my presence would not be needed: he had engaged another to run the boat. I was chagrined, *d sol* , of course, and demanded proof of this other man's ability to handle the *Beau Soleil*. It was provided. Matters were in order."

"But when the charter began, there was no woman joining the boat."

Lafitte raised his eyebrows. "Yes, that is so."

"You saw who went on board?"

"But of course. He sailed from my mooring, in my boat.

I was there. There was no woman, so it was not a cruise of romance. What a waste... There were three men. The guy who took the wheel, I think he was just a man they had hired. Apart from Duclos, there was only one other man. He was like you."

"Like me? How do you mean?"

"He was an Englishman." Lafitte paused, smiled. "But he spoke very good French, even if it was with an English accent."

"Did you find out his name?" Eric asked urgently.

Lafitte shook his grizzled head, and sipped his wine, leaning back against the gunwale. "It was not my business. My deal was with Duclos. But this other man, he was an English gentleman. You can tell, in my business. Tall; dressed carefully, with elegance. A confident man. One who would have professional standing."

A lawyer, Eric thought. A lawyer, like Jason Sullivan.

He remained on board the *Beau Soleil* for another hour, while Lafitte poured him another drink. He clearly regarded the opportunity as one to exercise his English and indulge his love of gossip. But he had little to tell that was of significance. The men had sailed out of Port des Minimes, had used the motor yacht for three days, but did not seem to have gone far and had then radioed in to explain that they were ending the charter early, and leaving the boat at St Martin de R . It was not a problem for Lafitte: he had received his money for the charter, and the boat would be safe enough at a mooring on the Ile de R until he chose to collect it again.

But his description of the brief sighting he had had of the Englishman with Duclos convinced Eric that it had indeed been Jason Sullivan. He had cancelled the projected trip with Anne, but had still used the charter, for just a few days. What the hell was he up to? And just where had he now gone to ground?

It was in a disconsolate mood that Eric finally left the

*Beau Soleil.* He had gained little, and seemed no closer to finding what had happened to Jason Sullivan, what his motives were, and where he was now staying. He checked his watch; he had had a few glasses of wine, he felt unwilling to face the drive back to La Rochelle immediately, so he decided it would be better to take a coffee in one of the almost deserted caf s along the harbour. He picked one out, sat down at a table near the water's edge, ordered a coffee.

He sat there for half an hour, turning matters over in his mind. Lafitte had been able to give him no information on Duclos, other than to furnish a first name – Georges – and a Paris address and telephone number. After the waiter brought the coffee Eric took out his mobile phone and tried the number Lafitte had given. When he finally obtained the recorded message it told him that the number was no longer in operation: it had been disconnected. He scowled at the address that Duclos had given to Lafitte. It had served its purpose in making the charter, but Eric suspected that the address would most probably be a fictitious one. If so, the trail would go cold.

He thought things over for a while. He could take a chance, drive to Paris, check out the address, but time was passing, and he was disinclined to start off on another wild goose chase. He had no idea where Sullivan might have gone, or why he had been here at St Martin de R at all. And if Sullivan had his hands on more than two million sterling, what the hell was he doing hanging around on the Charente Maritime coast anyway? Mike Fremantle had told Eric the Labuan account had been closed, the money gone from all the offshore accounts, and Sullivan had disappeared. Eric could think of no possible reason why Sullivan would even bother to be here in France, having discussions with the mysterious Georges Duclos.

People were beginning to drift into the caf -restaurant for lunch. Several of the tables near Eric were now occupied. It was time to make a move, get back to La Rochelle, check the Paris address and if that failed as a lead, there was little alternative to taking the flight back home. He'd have to pay part of the cheque back to Ben Shaw, because he felt he had achieved nothing. And he was in any case still somewhat uneasy about the whole business. He had no idea what was going on; Anne was involved and he felt protective towards her but he was not working for her, she had her own relationship with Jason Sullivan to sort out; and in addition there was something else about the whole affair that just didn't fit squarely with him. He had the vague feeling that Ben Shaw hadn't given him the full Bradgate and Savage story; there was something about Mike Fremantle that jarred with him, the man's nervousness, the hint of panic in his manner. Eric wasn't sure he wanted to carry on with the matter, in spite of his anxieties about Anne. They were no longer married; she had made a new bed for herself. This whole thing was a matter he was best left out of.

A shadow fell across his table. He looked up, squinting into the bright sunshine.

"The tables are being occupied quickly."

It was a pleasant, well-modulated voice; there was a slight American touch to the English, but the speaker was clearly French. "I'm sorry, I just stopped to have a coffee. I'm leaving immediately, if you want this table."

"Lunch here is recommended." He shaded his eyes with one hand. She was tall, slimly-built, with reddish-gold hair. Her features were clean-cut, her mouth generous. She wore a plain, white, business-like shirtwaist, and a dark skirt. As he stared at her, she removed her designer sunglasses. Her eyes were confident, friendly and dark blue in colour, almost reflective of the water lapping near his feet. She was smiling: it was a cool, easy smile. "The *aumonieres de langoustines*, in particular, are said to be quite delicious."

Eric hesitated. "I…I'm sure they are, but – "

"There is a spare seat at your table. And I hate to eat alone. Perhaps, if I took this seat, you might care to join me for lunch. Before you return to La Rochelle."

He stared at her, taken aback. Then, as she slid into the chair opposite him she extended a slim hand. "My name is Aline Pearce. And yours is…?"

"Eric Ward."

"So, Mr Ward, shall we try the *langoustines* together?"

Chapter Five

She linked her slim fingers together, supported her chin, gave a slow smile and fixed her dark blue gaze quizzically upon him. "You seem surprised."

"I don't often get asked to lunch by a beautiful woman."

She raised one elegant eyebrow. "Now it is my turn to be surprised. The English don't have a reputation for gallantry."

Eric smiled. "I speak only the truth. But I am not so much surprised, as intrigued."

The waiter was hovering. She spoke to him in rapid French, ordering for them both. He was amused by the confidence: this was a lady who knew what she wanted, and needed no permission to act. She turned back to Eric, and her white teeth flashed. "There. You see also I am decisive. The *aumonieres*, and then *loup de mer* with aubergines. And naturally I am also quite prepared to pay my own way. I invited you to lunch, therefore I order the meal, and I take the bill."

"The question is, why would you do that?" Eric countered.

"Invite you to lunch? Obviously, because I have something to gain from it."

"I can't imagine what that might be," Eric remarked easily.

"Answers to some questions."

"They must be important – or perhaps you've made a mistake, and issued an invitation to the wrong person."

"I am not in the habit of making that kind of mistake." She slipped her sunglasses back on, eyed him from behind the anonymity they supplied. "So, the first question. Why are you interested in the *Beau Soleil*?"

Eric hesitated, considering how he might respond.

She turned away. "Ah." The wine waiter was already at their side. "I think, first of all, perhaps an aperitif. *Pineau de charentes*: it is what the world drinks on the Ile de R . And then a crisp white…"

Eric watched her as she scanned the wine list, placed her order. He smiled ruefully, considering. What was the comment he had picked up earlier on the boat with Lafitte: *so many people are interested*…He sighed, understanding. "Now then, let me think. The *Beau Soleil*. Of course… Yesterday. The harbourmaster at Port des Minimes."

She nodded, a secretive smile on her lips. "The harbourmaster and I…we had an arrangement. Financial, of course. So he rang me, to tell me someone was asking questions about the boat. A small retainer. It is sufficient."

Eric nodded. He sipped at his *pineau*. The harbourmaster had been paid to inform Aline Pearce if anyone asked certain questions; when Eric was leaving him yesterday he was already on the phone, probably contacting her immediately, earning his fee. "So perhaps I should immediately counter with my question. Why are *you* interested in the *Beau Soleil*?"

"I'm not," she replied coolly. "So it is back to my question."

"I have the feeling," Eric remarked, "we're playing some kind of game."

He could not read what was in her eyes, shielded by the sunglasses, but her glance was still, fixed on him. "I can assure you, my friend, this is no kind of game," she said quietly. She was silent for a little while, looked away and began studying the other people lunching at nearby tables, but Eric knew it was a method of gaining time while she considered matters. She had no real interest in these people. Her hands were very still. Eric waited silently. Abruptly, she turned away from her perusal, finished her aperitif and leaned back in her chair as the waiter approached, uncorked the bottle of Chablis, poured each of them a glass of wine. "Perhaps we could begin once more, then, by making proper introductions, Mr Ward."

"I think Eric will do."

She inclined her head gracefully in acknowledgment. "And you may call me Aline. All right, Eric, what exactly is it that you do?"

"I'm a solicitor. I work in the north-east of England."

"A lawyer, and far from home...I see. And what would be your interest in the *Beau Soleil?*"

"Like you, I'm not really interested in the boat."

"*Touch !*" She smiled ruefully. "Then your concern with the yacht is merely in what it might lead you to, I suspect." She sipped at her wine, nodded thoughtfully. "*D'accord.* You are a lawyer. And I...I am employed by the Rijksmuseum, in Amsterdam."

"You surprise me. I thought curators would be much more..."

"Dowdy?" She flashed him a smile. "You should not accept stereotypical models. Besides, I am not a curator. I work on the investigative side. As do you... Tell me, if you are not interested in the boat itself, but maybe for someone who has used that boat...who exactly is it you seek, and why?"

Eric hesitated. "I'm not really at liberty to tell you that."

"Client confidentiality."

"Precisely."

"Then perhaps buying you lunch will indeed prove to be a waste of my professional time." She smiled, leaned back with the wine glass in her hand. "But we are here now, committed. So I suppose we might as well just enjoy each other's company?"

He was not fooled: she didn't really mean what she said. Eric guessed she was buying a little time, to think through and develop her own strategies. But he had no objection to having lunch in the sunshine of the harbour, with an attractive woman for company. So they chatted inconsequentially about the island, the impact of tourism, the beauty of the Poitier-Charente area, and when the *aumonieres de langoustines* arrived, wafer-thin crispy pancakes, Eric was able to compliment her on her recommendation. They were magnificent.

They were halfway through the sea bass and the bottle of wine, and superficially at ease with each other when she finally reached a decision. "I would like to tell you a story," she said quietly.

"Without prejudice?" he asked, smiling.

"You are a careful man," she responded, returning the smile, but there was an edge to it. "But...all right, without prejudice. I talk to you, but I accept that you talk to me only if you feel it is right to do so. My story begins in 1944."

"In France?"

She nodded. "To begin with. At a chateau occupied by a Prussian aristocrat known as Count von Sternberg. It was not his own chateau, of course: it had been commandeered by him during the Occupation, and he was not exactly a front-line soldier. Indeed, he had been enjoying quite a good war up to this point. He was living at the chateau with his mistress, and enjoying the protection of Field Marshal Goering because of the particular skills the count had developed."

"What skills would those have been?"

"Von Sternberg came from an aristocratic family, who had amassed an interesting art collection over a fifty year period. He had been brought up to appreciate art. He was a connoisseur. He had an eye. You will probably be aware that Goering had for some years been systematically plundering private collections and museums; he employed von Sternberg in order to use the man's sense of discrimination."

"Loot?"

She took a sip of her wine, dabbed her table napkin to her lips. She wore no make-up he realised, and her mouth was beautiful. "That's right. Nazi loot. Von Sternberg had chosen well on Goering's behalf: artefacts were brought to him, he selected the most valuable, they were stored at the chateau. In a way, life, the war, it passed Count von Sternberg by for three years or so. It was a pleasant existence. He was surrounded by priceless, beautiful things, he had the ear of Field Marshal Goering, and he had his mistress. But, in 1944 things changed. It became clear that the chateau – as a repository for the artwork von Sternberg had amassed – was not safe. The Allies were advancing. So Goering ordered removal of the artefacts. Count von Sternberg was to make the necessary arrangements. But, like most of the Nazis, he was a careful man. He first compiled a full catalogue of all the holdings."

"Maybe he didn't trust the men who'd be carrying the works to safety," Eric mused.

"Or maybe he wanted to protect himself in case he had to face Goering's wrath at some future occasion. Or maybe he was just being *German*," Aline remarked with a faint smile. "Anyway, the holdings were packed up, to be transported to a new home, near Konigsberg. But, in the bustle, the coming and going during the arrangements for the removal, there was an oversight. The catalogue was left behind."

"Careless."

"It made little difference, perhaps. Von Sternberg must have had his own copy, one presumes. However, he retreated with the loot, under Goering's orders, to a large private house outside Konigsberg. Then, within months, almost overnight, his world crashed about him. While Hitler was congratulating Skorzeny on his taking of the Citadel in Budapest and telling him of the F hrer's last desperate throw of the dice – the projected offensive in the Ardennes – the Russians burst into German territory in the east. In October, the Russian Army under General Tscherniakowski broke through into East Prussia. They were headed directly for Konigsberg."

"Time for von Sternberg to move again, then," Eric suggested.

"That's so. But now there was a real problem. When von Sternberg received the new instructions from Goering the roads were full of refugees fleeing in panic from the Russians. They had heard the stories of the behaviour of the Russian soldiery. The murders, the mutilations, the rapes. The German army was in retreat. Count von Sternberg had received his orders from Goering to move the artwork he had been storing, but he now found that was easier said than done. There was the possibility of damage. There were problems of transport. Suddenly, Goering's orders didn't carry their earlier prioritisation. And Count von Sternberg dithered. He got some of the artefacts away. But the bulk of the art collection was still at the mansion when a forward unit, a Russian platoon, arrived. You know what they were like, some of those men."

Eric nodded. He had read all about the fears of the German population when they heard the Russians were coming. The devastation that had been caused in Russia was about to be visited on Germany. "What happened to von Sternberg?"

"He tried to get out. But he had left it too late. The speed of the Russian advance was bewildering. The platoon caught him on the road. They didn't ask too many questions. They strung him up from the nearest tree. Then they went on to the mansion and they found his mistress. She was raped several times, before they cut her throat." She grimaced. "They weren't actually Russians. Russian Army, yes, but the platoon, it seems, was made up of Latvians, Poles – men who'd been dragged into the war, natural haters."

"Auschwitz was manned by a lot of people like that," Eric agreed soberly. "Ukrainians. They were reckoned to be like animals; almost worse than the SS."

"Full of hate and violence," she nodded thoughtfully, "but also ignorant. They ransacked the mansion. Took the obvious things like silver and gold, broke up a great deal of it, stealing items for themselves. Who knows what they really took and what was destroyed in that chaos? But they also vandalised a lot of stuff. Part of the collection consisted of a series of classical paintings. Because they depicted nudes, some of these ignorant soldiers who had perhaps never seen a naked woman, took the pictures, tore them apart, cut out the nudes and actually used them as pin-ups in their armoured vehicles. Think of it, Eric: wonderful works of art, paintings that would be almost priceless on today's market, cut up to adorn the inside of a tank."

Eric eyed her curiously. "How do you know all this?"

She toyed with her glass, shaking her head slightly. "It's largely a matter of record. The Americans rolled into France. They used Count von Sternberg's commandeered chateau as a group headquarters. And after they had settled in, someone found the catalogues. Nothing could be done immediately, of course, but in 1946 the State Department carried out an investigation. They checked through the lists that von Sternberg had kept on behalf of Goering, so they were aware of just what had once been held in the chateau. They learned about the move to East Prussia. It was early days after the war and at that stage the Russians were in a relatively co-operative mood. They even helped trace the unit, the group that had hanged Von Sternberg. It had later been cut up in an action in some woods near Gumbinnen, most of them killed. But, incredibly, even after that length of time the authorities managed to locate the remains of some of the unit's burned-out vehicles, some still with small pieces of the canvases, pieces of the artwork in the wreckage. The fragments were preserved, a deal was struck with the Russians and the American investigators were able to return some fragmentary items to the museums from which they'd been looted in the first place. The Rijksmuseum included. It took years, of course but, incredibly some of the more sturdy artefacts were actually recovered."

"And when the Cold War started?" Eric asked.

"Co-operation ended. Consequently, most of the Sternberg holdings were lost to view."

"But you know more or less what was lost," Eric murmured, "because of the catalogue found by the Americans at the chateau."

"That's one thing one could always say about the Nazis," Aline Pearce commented drily. "Their bookkeeping was immaculate."

"You used the word *lost;* you didn't say *destroyed*. So, when you emphasise lost to view…" Eric queried. "Do you imply that some of the works are still out there somewhere?"

She nodded vigorously. "That is precisely the case. We have no real idea what actually happened after the army unit acquired the works of art, but it's clear that somewhere along the line a number of pieces from the Sternberg collection were brought together. There have been rumours of reprisals being made against individuals, executions having taken place in 1946, soldiers who were suspected of looting. But it wasn't until the seventies that some of the loot actually began to surface again."

"Where?"

"Romania, to begin with. Then, over the years odd items that had appeared in the catalogue came up for sale in other Eastern European countries. There was no chance of any agreements, no way to get in to find the truth because of the iron grip of the Communists, but from time to time an item would come up for purchase."

"To go into private collections, no doubt," Eric commented grimly.

She nodded. "But then, in the last decade things have changed again, and there's been a concerted attempt on the part of Western governments to try to recover looted art that had been sold to private collectors. That's included works held by von Sternberg. A lot of looted artworks are impossible to recover, because there's no way the claimed provenance can be discounted. But the works in the Sternberg collection were well documented, and the original owners from whom the Nazis looted the pieces were known. The result has been the recovery of a number of important works of art, for the museums that had originally purchased them."

"I've no doubt the private collectors will have put up a struggle," Eric suggested.

Aline's smile was grimly appreciative of the comment. "You can be sure of it. And some have successfully resisted all attempts to make them give up the looted items: they say they bought them in good faith. It is particularly difficult to get back works that have been sold to Japanese collectors. Whereas in many Western countries the laws allow recovery, if it can be proved that it was looted art, the Japanese have a different view. Provided the new owner can show he did not actually know the artwork was stolen in the first instance, he can very quickly gain ownership of it, under Japanese law."

"And this is the investigative work you're involved in?" Eric asked. "The recovery of artworks that were lost almost sixty years ago?"

She smiled again, but now there was a hint of weariness at the edge of her smile. "Sounds crazy, doesn't it? After all that time… But it's important and, well, the work becomes obsessive. I've been doing it now for five years: not for my employers, the Rijksmuseum, not directly. A special group was formed three years ago, funded by the major museums, and supported by the State Departments. Much of the work is undercover, boring, frustrating, and ends in failure. But every so often…" She paused, her glance flicking up to his. Her eyes, he decided, were a midnight blue. "You've heard of Paolo Vasari."

"Vaguely," Eric conceded. "Mediaeval painter."

"He painted *The Adoration of the Magi*, among other

things. It's a well documented painting. It was owned by the Rijksmuseum. It was looted in 1942. It was catalogued in the list kept by von Sternberg. Quite a small painting, really. But priceless."

"A word somewhat over-used," Eric suggested, "and perhaps meaningless."

"If the painting came on the market today, a private buyer would not expect to pay less than thirteen million dollars."

Eric grimaced thoughtfully. "But who would buy it, if in the end it would have to be handed over to the rightful owners, the Rijksmuseum?"

She shrugged, her glance still on Eric. "There are such men. And also, one has to be rational about such things: what would the Rijksmuseum itself do? It would have a choice: pay a sum of money for its return – not thirteen million dollars, maybe – but certainly an impressive amount of money, in order to recover the work. Refusal to do so, to negotiate, would perhaps result in loss of the painting for ever. Calling in the police might frighten the seller. It could even result in its destruction."

Eric nodded. He finished the wine in his glass, leaned back in his chair and looked around at the harbour. The caf s and restaurants were crowded, the sun was shining, people were smiling, laughing, enjoying themselves. It was all a far cry from sixty years ago, war-torn Europe, chaos, death, the clouds of destruction rolling across the land. He nodded again, slowly. "Yes, I see your point. In the circumstances, the museum would pay. Negotiate, at least. Or maybe..." His glance slid back to the attractive woman facing him. "Or maybe, they'd present themselves as being *prepared* to negotiate, pay a price, enter the haggling phase, while at the same time...employ people to determine the location of the work, maybe bring in the police – "

She shook her head. "Not immediately. Such matters are too delicate to allow police involvement. Not until the artefact itself is safely in the museum's keeping, or under its control."

"I can see that… This painting, by Vasari. You mentioned it particularly, but it was just an example?"

She smiled enigmatically. "*The Adoration of the Magi*? No, not just an example. The painting's been lost for sixty years. But…" She turned, retrieved the small handbag she had hung from her back of her chair. She opened it, took out a small photograph. She stared at it for a few seconds, then handed it to Eric. "This is the Vasari. This picture was given to us two months ago, as an earnest of good faith."

Eric gazed at the photograph and frowned. "How do you know it's the original?"

Aline took back the photograph, stared at it again as though it held a particular fascination for her. "It's been authenticated by experts, checked against our own photographs at the museum. As far as it can be. Of course, before the museum could ever agree to hand over money, it would have to be absolutely certain that the artwork itself is really the original, not a fraudulent copy. But we have been told there is a number stamped on the back of the canvas. It is the same number that we find in von Sternberg's catalogue. German efficiency again. There is more than a strong chance that the Vasari in the photograph is the original."

"And it's up for sale. It's out there in the market place."

She put the photograph back in her handbag, and nodded. "Just that."

Eric regarded her quietly for a little while. "An interesting story. A Vasari that was looted in 1942, disappears for sixty years, it suddenly reappears, apparently, to be sold at a negotiated price…fascinating. But what relevance does this story have to you and me sitting here in a restaurant at St Martin de R ?"

She hesitated, clearly still uncertain of how far she should go. But in a sense he knew she had already made the decision. "Contact was made a little while ago with the holder of the Vasari. We are in negotiation, and discussions have started. But only over the phone. It is hoped that there will be a face to face meeting later this week. Matters will hopefully progress further then, the actual Vasari will be produced and a proper authentication can take place. But I have serious doubts about this."

"How do you mean?"

She made a little sound of annoyance in her throat. "We have some experience of these matters. It is almost unknown for an approach to be made by the person actually holding the art. Such people know they are on the fringe of an illegal transaction and will always be reluctant to expose themselves, sometimes even refusing to do so, even at the last moment. No, we are always dealing with agents, with middlemen, and our problem is that this is unreliable. If we are to achieve our ultimate objective, we have to deal with the holder of the work of art, not his colleagues, his agents, his front men, his employees. There are signs that the man we are dealing with is nothing more than just such an agent. We will talk with him, of course, but what we really want to find out is the identity of the shadow behind him, the man who actually has his hands on the Vasari itself."

Eric nodded in agreement. "I understand your point. But..." He held her glance calmly and deliberately. "You and I have both approached the owner of the *Beau Soleil*. But we also agree that neither of us is really interested in Lafitte, or the boat."

She nodded. "The man who has made contact with us about the Vasari, he is the man who actually chartered the *Beau Soleil* a few weeks ago."

"His name?"

"His name is Georges Duclos." She turned her head, raised a hand, beckoned to the waiter. She ordered two coffees, and two cognacs. Eric waited, impassively.

"As soon as an identification was offered, we naturally checked the address he gave us in Paris. It was put under surveillance. It soon became apparent that it was little more than what you call an accommodation address. But we had to be sure. So…" She gave a little shrug. "We made certain arrangements, so that the concierge looked the other way, and we gained entry to the apartment. It was empty. The phone was disconnected. If Duclos had used the apartment, it would have been some time ago."

Eric smiled. "Illegal entry. Bribing a concierge. Paying a retainer to a harbourmaster. I can see why you're not yet talking to the police."

"Discretion is essential," she said sharply. "If we involve the police at this stage, there is the possibility of information being leaked, our negotiator disappearing, the painting being destroyed in a panic, or the offer being withdrawn and made to others who would be only too pleased to take the risk and place it in a private collection"

"Your point is made," Eric said gently. "But you've stretched your discretion: you're telling *me* all about this."

"You are a lawyer. You understand about discretion: you have to live with it. Besides, I have a feeling that perhaps we have an objective in common. So I take a chance, I make a decision."

Eric nodded. "So who is this man Duclos?"

"As far as we can make out he is a businessman who operates out of offices in Geneva, London and Berlin. He has some kind of *entr e* to committees of the European Union, has acted for various clients in the submission of plans for European funded projects, but he is somewhat difficult to pin down. An entrepreneur, certainly, and we suspect one who has assisted in certain frauds perpetrated in the name of the Common Agricultural Policy – "

"I've always assumed that's a national pastime," Eric remarked drily.

She ignored the comment. "And he is also known in the art world as a dealer, an expert in his own field, and a financial consultant. The main thing is, he moves around a great deal. The Paris address was merely a blind cul-de-sac. We can't even be sure the man talking to us is the real Georges Duclos. But what we're pretty sure is that he is a front man; we think he is not the man who holds the Vasari itself."

"The shadow behind him," Eric murmured.

"So," she said with a degree of finality. "You were not interested in the *Beau Soleil* itself, you questioned the harbourmaster at La Rochelle about the charter, you discovered it was Georges Duclos and you have now questioned Lafitte, its owner, as I already have. My question is, who *are* you really interested in?"

The waiter was approaching with the coffee and cognacs. Eric was silent, considering the matter thoughtfully. He gained the impression Aline Pearce had been frank with him, but in return there was only so far he could go. He had a client to protect: the reality was that lawyer-client privilege could be dispensed with only by his client, Bradgate and Savage. He sat mulling over the matter for a little while until at last Aline leaned towards him across the table. "Maybe I should give you some assistance: provide the answer for you. You only want to find Georges Duclos, because you want to know who was with him on the boat."

He stared at her. "I…I am seeking someone, on behalf of my client."

"An Englishman." She nodded, not waiting for confirmation. She hesitated, then went on, "I should tell you further, all the signs, from comments made by Duclos, hints we've picked up on, the surveillance we've managed so far, limited though it is, it all suggests to us that the Vasari is maybe in France, or possibly somewhere in England, and the shadowy person behind Duclos is an Englishman." She picked up her coffee, sipped at it, but her eyes never left Eric. "And I am beginning to believe you know just who that Englishman is."

Eric took a deep breath. He had a brief flash of Anne in his mind, in denial and yet unhappy, unwilling to believe

anything was wrong, and yet uncertain because of her failure to maintain contact with her lover.

Bloody hell, he swore under his breath. What the hell had
Jason Sullivan got himself into now?

Chapter Six

At the end of their discussion, Eric and Aline had reached no formal agreement, but they understood each other. They had concluded they were looking for the same person: the man who had accompanied Georges Duclos on board the *Beau Soleil*. It was clear that Aline suspected Eric already knew the identity of the mysterious Englishman; Eric guessed that his best chance of finding his quarry lay in joining forces with the woman from the Rijksmuseum. They agreed to meet the next morning at La Rochelle. Eric drove back over the viaduct to the mainland and checked back into his budget hotel near the waterfront. She came around to see him after breakfast the following morning. She looked fresh, her eyes were sharp, and her mouth was determined as they walked out along the Quai Duperr towards the Lantern Tower, gaunt under a lowering sky.

"Why do you think Duclos chartered the boat?" Eric wondered.

Aline Pearce shrugged. "I don't think it was of great significance. We have been seeking Duclos; I believe he has felt the pressure. It's highly likely he was aware that he was under surveillance. And your mysterious Englishman seems to want to retain his anonymity. It would have seemed a good idea to use the boat, if he was so reluctant to have discussions with Duclos that might be overheard too easily. Private conversations are facilitated if you are sailing..."

Eric had his doubts about the explanation. The charter had been planned originally as a holiday break for Sullivan and Anne: matters must have been moving quickly for Jason Sullivan to cancel that arrangement, and go with Duclos alone.

Unless Anne knew about what was going on...

"So what's the next step?" Eric asked, reluctant to dwell on the thought.

Aline Pearce stopped, leaned against the railing to look

out over the harbour mouth. The *bus de mer* to Port des Minimes was heading out on its regular, brief journey; further out they could see the assembly of pleasure boats, small yachts swinging in the breeze, sails flapping as a scudding wind freshened, driving them offshore. "The meeting," she said. "My colleagues are setting it up. Duclos rang last night and confirmed the arrangements. The location is agreed: Poitiers. The time and place is still being negotiated." She hesitated, glanced at him. "You will appreciate that in matters such as these it is as well that one does not act alone. There are so many...dangerous possibilities. And my employers have a view, that as a mere woman..."

He caught the hint of irony in her tone. He smiled. "They've provided you with some muscle?"

She laughed. "It is something like that. It is a standard arrangement: what you might call rules of engagement. I have two colleagues who will be making the contact, meeting Duclos, and only when it is deemed safe will I be called in to make expert judgments about what the man has to sell." She eyed him with a hint of mockery. "I could have argued that you would be with me when I met Duclos, but then, I would not expect to be entirely safe in the hands of a lawyer." Her eyes sparkled. "I mean, of course, that lawyers are not usually men of muscle."

He had a brief image of things he had met, and done, in the alleys and back streets along the Tyne, in the days when he had been a young policeman on the beat, but he was disinclined to tell her of those days, or suggest he should take a more up-front role. "So you are still convinced we should work together."

"It seems we seek the same man," she suggested. "Consequently, it could be a matter of mutual support and advantage. You might be able to tell me if I am being...conned?"

So it had been agreed. Two hours later, when another message had come through, they were on the road to Poitiers. The meeting had been arranged.

As they sat in the car, waiting, Eric was very aware of the light hint of Aline's perfume. She was an attractive woman, confident, decisive and businesslike, but she demonstrated also a softness of touch and word, and an odd vulnerability on occasions. It was possible this was merely a matter of manipulation, her way of getting what she wanted in a masculine world, but he doubted it. He had asked her about her background – her father had been a Canadian, and she had been educated in the United States, but her mother had been French, and her career was being built in the museums of Europe. What was soon clear to him, when she introduced him to the two men – Montfort and Leclerc – who were acting as her minders, was that she was very much in charge of the operation, and that they held her in considerable respect.

So perhaps the air of vulnerability was indeed a shield she had deliberately raised to hide the true toughness of her personality. In either event, Eric was intrigued.

They were parked within sight of the asymmetrical towers of the Cath drale St Pierre. Eric glanced around at the rest of the people thronging into the area. A small party of Japanese tourists were being escorted around the cathedral precinct and were presently being lectured to by their guide, in front of the large, thirteenth-century fa ade. Behind them, Eric could see the burly figure of Montfort seated on a bench under the trees; the slighter frame of Leclerc was out of sight, at the corner of the Rue Arthur. The other benches were unoccupied; a pair of lovers were entwined, leaning against one of the trees: there was a man seated on the wall in front of the Eglise Ste Radegonde, munching his way through a baguette with a deliberate concentration, a paperback in his free hand, and a young mother with two children was walking slowly towards the ramparts that overlooked the river far below. Two elderly men were engaged in a heated conversation in front of the cathedral, and time was passing: they had already been waiting for half an hour past the appointed rendezvous time.

"I must see what's happening," Aline said with a sudden impatience and got out of the car. Eric watched as she walked towards Montfort: he rose from the bench as she neared him and they had a brief conversation. As they spoke together, Leclerc appeared from the street corner and hurried towards them. He had a note in his hand. He offered it to Aline. She almost snatched at it, read it and then shook her head angrily. She came walking slowly back towards the car. Eric got out to meet her.

"He's nervous," she said quietly, but he caught the edge of frustrated anger in her tone.

"Nervous about what?"

She shrugged. "About meeting us. Surveillance, maybe? Suspicions about what we have in mind? The police? *Merde*, I don't know." She glared about her, frowning, as though checking to see if Duclos was in sight. "An urchin gave this note to Leclerc, so Duclos must have seen us, picked out Leclerc. What the hell is he playing at? He's skittering around like a frightened cat. Anyway, he's changed the rendezvous. Now, it's two o' clock, in the open-air caf at Marche Notre Dame." She glanced irritably at her wristwatch. "That's an hour from now."

"Where is the market place?" Eric asked.

She glanced past him and nodded. "Just a short walk down there, beyond Notre Dame le Grande." She sighed, looked around her to the fa ade of the cathedral. "At least he didn't suggest Buck Mulligan's Irish Pub."

Eric laughed at her woebegone expression. It broke the tension. "It does exist, you know – serving the inevitable Guinness, of course." She grinned ruefully, shook her head. "He's watching us, I'm sure of it. They're always nervous, these people, but he's picked the rendezvous, it's out in the open, and he's got the advantage of us. He'll be around here somewhere…but quite why he's so touchy, I don't know. Maybe watching out for the police. Or something has spooked him. Anyway, we can only do what he asks."

They had an hour to wait. There was no point in immediately rushing to the rendezvous so they decided to remain in the area of the cathedral, stroll along the battlements overlooking the river, sit in the sunshine in the Parc de Blossac for a little while. Leclerc and Montfort kept their distance; they were watchful, Eric noted, and he wondered why they thought trouble might erupt. Georges Duclos, it seemed, was not the only one who was nervous. He and Aline had little to say to each other: they occupied themselves with their own thoughts. And Eric wondered again about just how much Anne might be involved in this whole matter.

Some fifteen minutes before the appointed time they made their way down to the market place. The caf terrace was fairly busy but Eric and Aline found a table near the edge of the terrace, under a red sunshade, ordered coffees and settled back to wait. Leclerc and Montfort took a separate table, some little distance away from them. A few people left the caf , two more tables were occupied, and then a few minutes later Eric saw a man in a grey suit approach the two minders. He was of medium height, with thinning hair and a neat moustache that gave him an air of fussiness. He was clearly unhappy, his hands waving as he spoke vehemently to the two men. They replied to him but he shook his head violently, gestured around at the caf , and stabbed an admonitory finger at Leclerc. Montfort put a hand on his arm, but the man in the grey suit shook it off, turned, and made his way towards the table where Eric and Aline sat.

He grabbed a chair, pulled it under the shade of the red umbrella and sat down. He was perspiring freely. His eyes ranged angrily from one to the other. "You are not discreet," he muttered viciously.

"You are Georges Duclos?" Aline enquired in a cool tone.

He glared at her, then snapped a glance in Eric's direction. "Who is this?"

"My legal adviser," she replied smoothly.

"Legal adviser, thugs, what sort of game do you think this is, *madame*? You are not discreet. You are too obvious. I had expected a certain degree of care – "

"The choice of rendezvous was yours, Duclos," Aline interrupted severely.

"And it had to be in the open," he snarled, "because of the incompetent way you do business. I have been aware that there have been attempts at surveillance; I know you have entered the apartment in Paris. What is it you want? You think I am a criminal? I've no doubt you've already informed the police. And I'm not fooled by your attempts to scare me."

"Why should we do that?" Aline queried innocently, raising her eyebrows.

"To force down the price," Duclos snapped. His eyes were never still, shooting nervous glances around at the nearby tables. He watched as two brawny young men in shirtsleeves, talking loudly, took a table some feet away, calling for *cassis*. "This is not the way to behave. I am trustworthy; I am acting for the good of everyone; but this sneaking around, the surveillance, the following in cars – "

"I don't know what you're talking about, Duclos. I assure you – "

"No matter," he interrupted, still eyeing the two men nearby. "We go now."

"Go where?" Aline asked.

"To my car. I drive." His glance slid to Eric. "You stay here. Along with those other two thugs."

Aline smiled, and shook her head. "That's not the way we do business, my friend. You expect me – a mere woman – to go in the car with you, to an undisclosed location, leaving my companions behind?"

He frowned at her, tugged at his moustache in a nervous gesture. "I am alone. I am trustworthy. We cannot do business here."

Her tone was scornful. "And I am not prepared to do business in the way you suggest. If I go anywhere, it will be in my car. My lawyer stays with me, and my companions over there – to whom you have already spoken – will follow behind."

"That is not possible!" Duclos was becoming even more agitated. "It is only you I speak with. It is you who will be demanding the authentication, is it not? If you come with others, how am I to trust you? You could force me to hand over the merchandise. I am no fool!"

"And we are not in business under the conditions you suggest," Aline Pearce replied calmly. She picked up her coffee cup, took a sip of the thick, black liquid.

"This is an *impasse*," he growled.

"It need not be," Aline replied, setting down her cup. "At least we have now made contact face to face. And we can now take the first steps towards authentication. Only after that can we talk about prices."

"I have sent you the photograph," he complained in a querulous, frustrated tone.

"Hardly enough to form a decided view," she insisted. "Come, *m'sieur*, you surely do not expect negotiations to be carried out without some more decided provenance being offered? Or perhaps a sight of the merchandise itself?"

Silence fell between them. Duclos lowered his head, thinking. He was still clearly nervous. Eric glanced at the two men seated nearby. They were young, muscular, shirt-sleeved, both with hair cropped close to their heads – students it would appear: twenty-five per cent of the population of Poitiers was made up of university students. They seemed at ease, talking in desultory fashion, eyeing up the girls who were walking by.

"This provenance you talk of," Duclos muttered. "I cannot show you the...work itself. It is not in my possession."

"I had assumed you were an agent for the Englishman," Aline admitted.

The man's eyes widened. "How did you know – " He hesitated, glanced at Eric, then frowned. "I am acting on behalf of a friend. I cannot show you the work itself. But it is possible…if you were to meet him, he can persuade you, but we must be discreet. If you come with me – "

"No."

Duclos wriggled in his seat. "Then we must make arrangements. You…you will come to the address I give you. You may bring these men with you. But only you…" His nervous glance slid towards Eric. "Only you and your lawyer may enter. Those other two," he insisted, jerking his head, "they stay outside."

Aline considered the proposal thoughtfully. She glanced uncertainly at Eric, but he guessed the uncertainty was feigned. "I suppose this could be possible. But I am concerned, Duclos, that all this could be nothing more than a wild goose chase. You have given us nothing, other than the photograph. You could be wasting our time. Who is this man you are working for?"

"Helping," Duclos muttered. "I am merely helping a friend. And you do not need to know his identity. The work itself is enough."

"And you give me no more information on its provenance. So why should I waste any more time on this matter?"

"You have the number stamped on the back of the painting," Duclos said sullenly. One of the two students had lit a cigarette: Duclos watched the blue smoke exhaled, curling into the air. "That should be enough for you to know we are serious, and this is not a fake."

"The number could be added to anything. All you needed to know was that the painting had a number, stamped on the back sixty years ago."

Duclos was irritated, annoyed that his honour was being impugned. "Then if I give you a name, will that suffice to convince you? *Grabowski!* Is that enough?"

Aline stared at him without expression. "The name means nothing to me."

"Pah!" Duclos stood up. "I am dealing with amateurs! Enough! I have made my offer." He dug one hand into the pocket of his jacket, took out a small card. "Here. If you remain interested in doing business it must be at this address, at ten o' clock tonight. If I can persuade my friend to come. He has already become concerned that arrangements have had to be changed. I will try to persuade him. If not...hah! And as for you...you make your own choice."

He glared at them, turned and walked away across the square, to vanish around the corner of Rue Notre Dame.

Several other people were leaving the caf ; one of the two students had already gone, his companion inspecting the slip of paper on which their bill had been printed.

"What do you make of it?" Aline asked.

Eric shrugged. He had seen sad little men like Duclos before. Negotiators, jumpy at every wrong sound, worried at every turn of events. "The man's nervous; scared even. But if you want things to proceed, I think we'll have to go along with what he suggests."

She took a deep, contemplative breath. "Our training, our experience, it tells us we do not go into cars without back-up assistance, and we do not put ourselves into the hands of someone we do not know." She glanced at him ruefully. "And that applies to male investigators as well as women."

"He's agreed I can be with you," Eric reminded her.

"A lawyer, with attitude." She smiled. "I suppose it will have to do."

"And the provenance matter? The name he gave you – Grabowski?"

She shook her head. "It means nothing to me. So who can tell if it is important?"

The ancient street was cobbled, the entrances to the houses dark, doors studded with iron; tall-storeyed buildings loomed above them threateningly. Leclerc and Montfort entered the narrow street with them, but Aline told them to wait at the corner. A bell tolled back in the heart of the church quarter; distant clocks took up the chiming in the darkness. The windows of the houses in the street were shuttered: from some of them occasional chinks of light gleamed through to illuminate the roadway fitfully, puddles glinting among the cobbles from the recent light shower of rain.

Aline led the way, peering at the numbers on the doors. Eric was not impressed with Duclos' choice of rendezvous: the area was run down, crumbling in the decay of centuries, the walls peeling and desolate in their appearance, few signs of habitation, the cobbles underfoot ill-set, so that he stumbled twice as they walked the length of the street.

"We must have passed it," Aline muttered irritably, and they turned to retrace their steps. A flashlight glittered at them from the corner of the road: Leclerc, checking on their progress, advising them he and Montfort were still there.

Aline walked slowly back along the road, heels clicking on the cobbles. She paused uncertainly, peering at the plate on the house to her left. "I think this must be it."

Eric stepped back, looked upwards at the house. It was three-storeyed, marked with a general air of desolation. No light gleamed from any of the upper storey windows, and everything was dark on the ground floor. Aline glanced at him, then stepped forward. There was a small bell-push: she pressed it and they heard faint chimes from deep inside the house.

They waited. There was no answer, so she pressed the bell again. When there was still no reply, she hesitated uncertainly, then put one hand against the door. It swung open slowly, heavily, creaking a protest under her touch. It was unlocked, and unlatched. After a momentary hesitation she began to step forward but Eric put one hand on her shoulder, warning her to wait. He had memories of nights like this, under a different sky. Drab houses down by the River Tyne, enveloped in darkness, a narrow corridor that smelled of urine, and crack cocaine, an atmosphere that was redolent with danger. "Wait."

He stepped back into the centre of the narrow street and waved his arm. Leclerc and Montfort caught the signal and came quietly down towards them.

"Duclos said only you and I were to go in to meet him," Aline protested.

"So why isn't he answering the door?" Eric queried grimly. "You wait here."

She shook her head. "No." She turned to Leclerc and Montfort. "You two wait here at the doorway. We'll check things out." She held out her hand and with reluctance Leclerc surrendered the flashlight to her. The hairs bristled on the back of Eric's neck as he stepped into the darkened hallway of the ancient house.

He felt along the wall for a light switch. He found it, depressed it. Nothing happened. Aline flicked on the flashlight: the hallway was narrow, dilapidated, with damp wallpaper curling from above the door. To their right was a small room, its door open. An office for a concierge, but it had not been used in years as far as Eric could make out. Together they walked along the corridor, inspecting the rooms on the ground floor. None of them had been occupied in a long time; none of them held any furniture.

"Are you sure this is the address Duclos gave you?" Eric asked.

"I'm sure. As you saw, he is a cautious man, and he must have thought this place was safe."

"Apart from being about to fall to pieces," Eric muttered. "We'd better look upstairs."

Neither of them was inclined to call out, he noted. He could hear the heavy, tense breathing of Leclerc and Montfort at the doorway; Aline shone the torch up the stairs and the floorboards creaked under his tread. As he began to ascend he saw the reason why there was no light in the hallway: the bulb that should have been swinging from its socket had been removed. There was no telling when it might have happened.

Halfway up the stairs there was a window to the alleyway at the back of the house; it spattered suddenly with a light touch of rain. One of the panes was broken, and he could hear a faint whistling as the wind in the dark world outside began to rise, moaning slightly through the aperture. Through the window he caught a glimpse of a rusted, iron fire escape.

Eric had a bad feeling about this venture. The house seemed dead, an ancient tomb, hiding the secrets and sorrows of generations until at last, exhausted, it had no more secrets to accommodate. Or maybe it did have one last secret to hold. They reached the first floor, and the floorboards no longer echoed to their tread. There was a strip of carpet running the length of the hallway, threadbare but serviceable. Three doors ran off the corridor. The first was open. Aline shone the torch into the room and dust danced in the air. It was empty, a pile of rubbish accumulated in the corner, the wreck of an armchair, a collapsed table. They moved on.

"Ah!" Aline was unable to prevent the sound, as something scuttled away from them, to vanish at the end of the corridor. "What was that?"

Eric could guess, and something cold touched his stomach. He stood still, listening, and thought he could hear a faint creaking sound. He held out a warning hand to Aline and she stood stock still, her breathing coming harsh and anxious. He imagined he could almost hear the beating of her heart. He extended his hand, took the wavering flashlight from her, and for one brief moment caught the red gleam of the eyes of the rat in the corner before it vanished into the crumbling wainscoting. Aline grabbed his arm; her fingers were rigid as she clutched at him.

"Duclos can't be here waiting for us," she whispered. "This must be the wrong place. It's a mistake. This place hasn't been lived in for years."

Which might have been why Duclos had suggested they met here, Eric thought grimly. And there were rats here. They might have been attracted by something. He stepped forward to the second door and pushed at it with his left hand. The door swung open slowly. There was a strange, ammoniac smell in the air. A familiar odour from the experiences of his past: urine. The beam of the flashlight picked out the same kind of detritus they had seen previously in the other room, the same kind of shambles of discarded, useless furniture. Except for the table. It stood squarely in the centre of the room. A jacket had been placed upon it, crumpled: the jacket of a grey suit. Beside the table was a chair, overturned. But the beam picked out something else, suspended, swinging slightly. Eric knew now what the creaking sound had been. And he knew what had attracted the rats. He backed away, pushing Aline out into the corridor. "That's enough."

"What is it? What's the matter?"

"Stay here," Eric ordered fiercely, and stepped back into the room. The shoes were at his waist level, polished, gleaming; the white shirt was stained with vomit, the trousers with urine; the man's hands hung limply down by his side. His head was at an odd angle, facing away from Eric as he stepped forward flashing the beam of the torch up to the man's face. Staring eyes; a tongue that was blackened, forcing its way between the exposed teeth, lips bared in a hideous grimace. The thin rope that had strangled him was attached to a hook in the ceiling. The weight of the body still caused a slight swinging, and the hook, loosening in its timbers, creaked in a gentle, rhythmic protest.

In spite of his warning, Aline came into the room. He heard her gasp, then stifle an exclamation. She came forward, put a shaky hand on his arm, before turning to call out down the stairs to the two men below. Moments later, Eric heard the thunder of their feet on the stairs.

"Is it...is it Duclos?" Aline asked tremulously.

"It's Duclos."

"But why...he'd arranged to meet us here...why would he hang himself like this?"

As Leclerc and Montfort came rushing into the room Eric put his hand over hers. It was cold.

"Maybe he didn't," he said quietly.

Chapter Seven

"So I think it's time you talked to me, Anne."

As he sat facing his ex-wife across the long table in the library at Sedleigh Hall, Eric thought back briefly to his earlier discussion with Aline Pearce two days ago in Poitiers. It had gone against the grain, but Eric and Aline had agreed it was the most sensible thing to do, to avoid getting drawn into a matter in which they would lose control. Neither of them was prepared to get involved in the police investigation that would inevitably follow the discovery of the hanged man. Aline was concerned that her own work in trying to get hold of the Vasari would be compromised. "You think I am obsessive?" she asked belligerently. "You believe I think of nothing except my work?"

Eric shook his head. "A man is dead. We're not equipped to discover the circumstances of his death, or the reasons for it. Suicide, or murder, it's best left to the police. Let them handle it. But if we do get involved, it means your search will get bogged down in protocol and procedures, endless interrogations, and I've certainly no desire to spend months here in France failing to answer the questions that will surely be thrown at me."

It was the kind of attitude he would have decried years ago, an attitude that would have infuriated him as an investigative policeman. Ethically, as a solicitor, it also bothered him. But times had changed, life had changed, and there were questions he wanted to ask back in Northumberland.

"So what do we do?" Aline had asked.

"I'd suggest Leclerc should phone in anonymously, direct the police to the house. And then stay out of the way. As for you…if you want to continue your search, I think you should come with me to England. The trail has gone cold here. My guess is it's there we'll both find the answers we want."

She had thought it over for twenty-four hours. He had

not seen her during that time.

And now Eric sat in the library at Sedleigh Hall: Anne, white-faced, staring at him, still defiant, still unwilling to accept the suspicions that haunted her. "Talk about what?" Anne demanded in a tone of exasperation, even though he saw the shadow of uncertainty lurking in her eyes.

Eric retained his patience. "Talk about Jason Sullivan, and what you know about him, what he's been doing these last few weeks, and what you know of his whereabouts."

She shook her head vehemently. "I've already told you all I know, Eric; there's nothing more to explain."

An edge of anger crept into his tone, in spite of himself. "You don't seem to realise what you're getting yourself into! I want to know the full story. Don't you realise how serious all this is? I didn't feel I could explain to you earlier, but I've been retained to find Sullivan because there's a small amount of some two million pounds involved."

Her eyes widened. "What are you talking about?"

"That's the amount of shortfall on the Hollander account."

She sat up straighter in her chair. Her voice was shaky. "That can't be so!"

"You told me to go see Mike Fremantle, Sullivan's aide," Eric insisted impatiently. "I did just that, and he confirmed to me what my own client suspected: that there's money missing – a hell of a lot of it!"

"But it can't be anything to do with Jason," she insisted stubbornly, shaking her head. "There must be some other explanation."

"According to Mike Fremantle Jason is the person responsible for the movement of that money. He needs to explain things. We can hardly find another explanation if we can't even find him to start with." Eric eyed her sourly. "Do you really know what he's been up to? Are you aware he's been siphoning money out of the European funding to salt away in offshore bank accounts?"

She shook her head. Her mouth twisted angrily. "I can't believe that. That's not the way it is. You're getting it all wrong: imputing dishonest motives. All right, I did know something about it. Jason explained all that to me, months ago, when he started doing it with Mike Fremantle's assistance. The system he set up, it's quite legitimate: it's just a way of making sure that money held for short periods of time can be productive, gain interest, take advantage of fluctuations in exchange rates – "

"Whether it's legitimate is one thing; ethical is another," Eric interrupted heatedly, annoyed at her defence of the man he was seeking. "Can't you see that the important thing is what's happened to that money! Fremantle may have helped him set it all up, but Fremantle is running scared himself now: he tells me the money has disappeared out of the offshore account – and just like you, he can't find out where Sullivan has gone. The thing is – are you telling me everything you know? Do you really not know where Sullivan is hiding?"

She didn't like the word: she flared. "He's not *hiding*! I'm sure there's an explanation for all this. He's been in Europe for weeks on other business. I explained it to you: he's chasing around at the Commission, negotiating, dealing with officials! And if he has changed the offshore accounts, I have every confidence that Jason had good reason to move the money."

There was a short silence between them; she was breathing quickly, her eyelids narrowed as she stared at him, still defiant, but the shadow of anxiety still lay at the back of her eyes. Eric took a deep breath, fighting for control, infuriated at her blindness, then nodded slowly. "All right, then tell me all about Georges Duclos."

"I don't know the man!" she flashed, too quickly to be believable.

"You must have at least heard of him," Eric insisted. "He was involved with the trip you'd planned with Sullivan."

"Not to my knowledge!"

Eric eyed her in open disbelief. "The boat was actually chartered by Duclos."

"I wasn't aware of that," she replied sullenly, shaking her head. "I left the arrangement to Jason."

"But it wasn't to be just a pleasure trip, was it?"

She stared at him, hesitating; there was a nervous edge to her tone. "I told you...we were going to take a break together..."

Eric shook his head. "I don't think so. A certain pleasure, yes, but I think there was a business angle to it."

She was silent, thinking. At last she sighed, looked up at him, shrugged. "All right, he told me that we could take a trip, have a break, because he expected to conclude an important commission that he was negotiating in France. He didn't tell me what it was, but he was excited about it, and we hadn't seen each other in a while, it was weeks in fact, with the work he was doing for Hollander in Europe, so I didn't question him too closely. I had no need to. And then he cancelled the trip...You're now telling me he went ahead with the charter?"

Eric nodded, but he remained unconvinced she was telling him everything she knew. "He took off with Georges Duclos. Are you sure he told you nothing about this...commission? Nothing at all?"

She shook her head vigorously.

He took a deep breath. "And if I tell you that Georges Duclos died a violent death, you'll still go ahead with your story?"

All trace of colour slowly seemed to seep from her features. She licked her lips nervously, staring wildly at him. "Dead? You mean he's been murdered?"

"I didn't say that," Eric replied in a level tone. "It was a violent death, but I didn't hang around to investigate."

"You *saw* him?"

He nodded, leaning forward. "Georges Duclos is dead: I

saw him hanging by the neck. Maybe it was suicide, maybe not. But what is certain as far as I'm concerned now is that Sullivan was involved in a piece of business with Duclos, and if I had any sense I would have gone straight to the police with what I discovered in Poitiers. But I stuck my neck out for you, Anne, in doing that. I'm still sticking my neck out – and if I find that you've been holding out on me, keeping back any information you've got on that bastard Sullivan, I swear to you…"

His voice died away helplessly. Threats were useless: misplaced loyalty to Sullivan, or ignorance was making her keep her counsel. And what he had said was not strictly true: part of the reason why he had walked away from the house in Poitiers was that he wanted to protect his client Ben Shaw, at Bradgate and Savage.

And help Aline Pearce as much as possible.

But when he left Anne behind at Sedleigh Hall, having got no more information than he had arrived with, his mind was in a turmoil.

On his return to Newcastle Eric called in at his Quayside office and dealt with some of the files that had been accumulating on his desk. Susie Cartwright came in to see him and gave him a list of telephone messages she had been holding. He went through them with her: most of them could be dealt with later, there were a few fairly urgent calls he'd need to place in connection with clients who were due to appear in court the following week, and there was a brief request from Ben Shaw to contact his office, so they could arrange a meeting to consider what progress Eric might have made in the matter that concerned Bradgate and Savage. Eric was not sure it was a meeting he wanted to contemplate just yet: he had too much on his mind. And he was certainly disinclined to mention to his client the death of Georges Duclos.

He had arranged to meet Aline at her hotel in Gosforth later that evening. After due reflection, he decided to call

Jackie Parton also, to arrange a meeting. He telephoned Aline's hotel when he had finished dealing with the more urgent matters on his desk, and suggested they take a meal together. She joined him in the hotel foyer and he drove her down to the Quayside to dine at the Red House. It was noisier that he would have wished, and the food could have been better.

"Not up to the standard of the Ile de R ," he apologised, "but since you're here in my home town I thought you might at least be entertained in one of the oldest quarters of the city. We're alongside Bessie Surtees' house – the woman who was castigated socially for eloping with a coal merchant's son."

"What's special about that?" she enquired.

"The coal merchant's son eventually became Lord Chancellor of England. While his brother became an admiral."

"Romantic." She did not seem particularly impressed, nevertheless, but for the moment it took her mind off darker things. For a little while at least. Even so, there were some things that could not be avoided. "I've been in touch with Paris," she muttered eventually.

"Leclerc?"

She nodded. "He and Montfort reported back, without saying anything about Poitiers, other than that the meeting had been aborted. To all intents and purposes, the trail has gone cold, the Vasari trade is in abeyance, and we are pursuing further enquiries." There was a worried look in her eyes as she glanced at Eric. "It seemed the best thing to do: I didn't want my own superiors starting to get excited too much about the decision we made."

Eric shook his head: they were both getting into deep water. "Have you heard anything about the police investigation?"

"The newspapers have reported that the body of a man called Duclos has been found in Poitiers. The police are said to be treating the matter as suspicious, but to date they have not declared it murder."

It was only a matter of time, Eric guessed. He had not really discussed it with Aline, but in his view it was highly unlikely that Duclos had killed himself. Not when he was on the edge of, as he thought, concluding an important financial deal. He sighed. "And I've got no further yet with discovering the whereabouts of the Englishman you and I seek."

"You have not given me the confidence of divulging his name yet," Aline remarked quietly.

Eric hesitated, thinking. He had a duty towards his client to maintain confidentiality; he felt an obligation towards Anne. But he was now involved with Aline Pearce, a man was dead, and there seemed little point in prevaricating further. "I think the man you're looking for is called Jason Sullivan. He's a lawyer."

She raised an eyebrow, snorted mockingly. "Another one!"

"Also," Eric added after a short pause, "he works for my wife. Or rather, my ex-wife."

She was sharp: she had caught the slip of the tongue, and the correction, and she was quick enough to read something more into his tone of voice. "He works for your ex-wife…and that means there is a further complication?"

Eric grimaced: there was no mileage to be gained in keeping the matter from her. "I believe he is also her lover."

She watched him for what seemed an age, saying nothing. He was unable to read what was in her eyes, but her voice was soft when she said, "He is the reason your marriage ended?"

Eric shook his head. "No. Well, partly. It was more complicated than that."

"Is it not always so?" she agreed, with sympathy. She kept her eyes fixed on him for a little while, in calculation. "But your wife is not your client."

"That's right," he asserted. "I'm looking for Sullivan on behalf of someone else, and I won't go into that because of client confidentiality. But Anne – my ex-wife – is involved to the extent that she and Sullivan are lovers, she was supposed to be on the *Beau Soleil* with him until he cancelled; he's disappeared, I'm not sure whether she knows more than she's telling me…"

"Wives can be like that…and so can ex-wives. With perhaps more reason." She mulled over the situation for a little while. On a nearby table some students were noisily drinking a toast to the successful outcome of an inter-university rugby match; a middle-aged couple muttered to each other about the disgraceful behaviour of the young. "They are noisier here, than the ones we seemed to see in Poitiers," she considered quietly." There was a short silence. "I've wondered about that. Those young men seated near us, at the caf  in the Marche Notre Dame. They arrived just after us; they left when we did…"

Eric nodded. The suspicion had lurked at the back of his mind. Georges Duclos had been convinced they were being indiscreet; he seemed worried that they were all under surveillance. Duclos had hurried away after agreeing to meet later; it was not impossible that he had been followed from the caf . One of the two young men had disappeared as soon as Duclos walked away from Eric's table. But there was no real evidence…just suspicion.

Aline sighed, dispelling the dark thoughts. "But I am now here in England with you, you still don't seem to know where this man Sullivan is hiding, and I'm not clear what steps we now take to go further."

"When we're finished here," Eric replied firmly, "we'll be meeting someone. I'm hoping he'll be able to help us to some degree."

"I hope so. The delights of Newcastle," she smiled, sliding a glance in the direction of the carousing students, "are considerable, but I'm interested only in tracking down that

Paolo Vasari. Well, not only that, but..." Her voice died away. She gave him a quick glance, but said no more.

A little while later, Eric paid the bill and they made their way out to the Quayside.

Somewhere along the river a ship's siren moaned. It was a lonely, distraught sound and Aline Pearce shivered slightly as Eric locked the car and gestured towards the dark building at the corner of the street. The area was rundown; factory closures, the loss of river traffic and shipbuilding along the Tyne had each played their parts over the years, and while other areas of the river front had seen some regeneration, new high rise apartment blocks, scattered industrial developments, the pub known as The Hydraulic Engine stood grimly at the edge of a largely deserted roadway backed by crumbling terraced houses and a sloping hill where a few scrubby trees remained as a reminder of demolitions that had never been seen as a forerunner of regeneration. Even the lights from the pub itself seemed subdued, as though overcome by the generally decayed air of the neighbourhood. As they paused at the door, with its garish, painted glass insets, Aline looked at Eric quizzically. "You are showing me some more local colour?" she asked.

Inside the smoky lounge they were met with odours of stale fish and beer. An old woman sat in the corner by the empty fireplace, a glass of dark ale in front of her, contemplating a future as bleak as the cheerless grate. There were no other occupants: from the public bar beyond they caught the raucous shouts of laughter that seemed forced, out of keeping with the faded wallpaper. "Darts match," the barman explained as Eric approached the bar counter. "Second in the league, if we win tonight. What'll you have?"

"I'll have a half lager. And a glass of red wine."

The barman's eyes widened slightly as though surprised at his temerity in bringing a young woman into the lounge, even more so if she drank only red wine, and there was a short delay as he wandered along the shelves of stock.

"Shiraz do?"

Eric was gratified that there was a choice, but in reality there was not: it was the only wine the barman could offer. As the barman poured a generous glass of wine, Eric asked, "Jackie Parton in tonight?"

"He is that. Watchin' the darts." He cocked an eyebrow. "Won a few bob in the old days, on horses he took past the post. You know him?"

"Who doesn't?" Eric replied, smiling slightly.

"Aye, Jackie's well enough known round about. You want a word with him?"

"In his own time."

Eric walked back with the glasses, set them down. Aline eyed hers with a degree of suspicion that he did not find surprising, but when she sipped it she seemed agreeably impressed. She glanced around her, taking in the air of seediness and dilapidation. "In small French towns there are cafes and bars that are not unlike this," she suggested. "They are used almost exclusively by lonely, middle-aged men, who talk about old times that were never good times."

"And futures that would be worse." Eric looked around him, at the decayed room, the shabby furniture. "Yes, it's not much different, I suppose, from the myriad *Bars de l'Union* that one comes across." He failed to add that it was the kind of pub that Jackie Parton frequented regularly, not just as a matter of choice. It was in places like this that the ex-jockey picked up the kind of information that over the years had been extremely useful to Eric – the reaches along the river that seemed to harbour men who had information to impart, casually, or for payment.

It was only a matter of minutes before Jackie Parton came into the lounge, chuckling at something that had been said back in the bar. When he caught sight of the woman seated with Eric his smile faded and some of the ease deserted him: he was generally uncomfortable around women, Eric had noted, and now he adopted a slightly formal air.

"Hello, Mr Ward."

"Jackie…this is Aline Pearce. You've got a drink?"

"There's one half-downed in the bar, with me mates." He hesitated, and then slid into a seat beside Eric. "I got a message you wanted a chat, like." He cast a doubtful glance towards Aline.

"We're working together on the matter I told you about," Eric explained, keeping it brief. "Have you picked up any leads at all?"

Parton was clearly puzzled about Aline's presence, and was nervous about talking openly while she was there. He shrugged doubtfully. "I told you before, Mr Ward, there wasn't much chance of me picking up any news, because…the man you wanted traced, he wouldn't be using the kind of people I mix with."

"I just thought there might be something you'd come up with. So there's no whispers at all?"

The ex-jockey screwed his eyes to narrow slits. "Not really. But things are a bit touchy right now along the river. People aren't saying too much about anything: there's a kind of nervousness in the air."

"You told me earlier you thought something was happening."

Jackie Parton shook his head doubtfully. "Not so much happening, exactly – more a waiting for things to happen. People are like holding their breath; there's new muscle coming in, and the squeeze is being put on a few of the young wild lads who think they can carve out new territories."

"Drugs?" Eric asked curiously.

"Nah, there's that, but the emphasis doesn't seem to be on that side of things. The gangmasters – you know, the guys who were placing the illegals in jobs, or sending them south – they more or less faded while this police pressure was on these last few months. Now the coppers are easing off, there's a rumour the gangmasters are on their way back, but it's not the ones who'd established themselves over the last few years."

"New people?" Eric asked in surprise.

"So it's being said."

Aline Pearce leaned forward, curious. "Gangmasters? Illegals?"

Jackie Parton regarded her soberly. "The British polis have sealed off the Channel Tunnel pretty effectively these days: they've stationed officers in France, co-operating with the French coppers. But further north up here, things aren't so tight, and organisations are pulling in people from China, the Middle East, Morocco, and Eastern Europe, to work illegally. It's big business. They're filtering them through the northern ports with forged documents: some get intercepted, claim asylum, and when they're rejected they just fade into the black economy. The North East has become a major reception and distribution point. The trade almost stopped recently while the polis put the screws on, but from what I've picked up there's a whole new ball game about to start. New people; new faces; new muscle." Jackie turned back to glance at Eric. "A lot of guys are running scared, like. I'm not talking of normal, here. There's something bad in the air."

They were all three silent for a little while. Aline, with a quick glance at Eric, suddenly asked, "Does the name Grabowski mean anything to you?"

Jackie Parton frowned thoughtfully, then shrugged. "Not right off. There's plenty around these days with foreign names: never seen so many Latvians and Poles and all sorts coming into the Tyne and Wear. You got some kind of context for this name?"

She shook her head. "Not really. It's a name Eric and I picked up..."

Eric eyed the ex-jockey thoughtfully. "Aline has her own reasons for wishing to trace Jason Sullivan," he explained. "The name Grabowski has come up, so if you do hear it around..."

"Aye," Jackie sighed, and began to rise to his feet. "But like I said, I never expected to be able to find anything out about Sullivan, and to be honest, asking questions at the moment about anything, it makes people shut their mouths like traps. Every rabbit's looking over a shoulder for the ferret, if you know what I mean." He hesitated, thoughtfully. "But I tell you one thing. I'm not the only one who's been asking questions."

Eric's interest quickened. "How do you mean?"

"You asked me if I could find any trace of Jason Sullivan. There's someone else doing the same thing."

Something cold touched Eric's stomach. "Who?"

Jackie leaned forward, knuckles on the table. "He gives out his name is Frank Dennis, but he's no Geordie, by his accent. I'm told he sounds more like a bloody German. He reckons to be a private detective, but no one I've talked to has ever heard of a guy with that name, in that line of business, around here. So he must be from out of town."

"And he's trying to trace Jason Sullivan?"

"Seems so. He's discreet; he treads light, *gans* canny. But, he's certainly been asking around."

Eric frowned. "But you don't know who he's working for?"

The ex-jockey shook his head. "No news on that."

"What's he look like?"

Jackie slid his hand into the pocket of his windcheater. He extracted a wallet; from it he took out a photograph. It was a blurry, grainy image of a man seated on a bar stool. The lighting was poor; the photograph had obviously been taken surreptitiously. The subject was perhaps in his thirties, burly, with dark hair cut short. His profile gave an impression of ruggedness; at some stage his nose had probably been badly broken. Eric shook his head. "He rings no bells for me."

"Keep the photograph. I got it for you. Just in case your

paths cross." Jackie stood back, nodding to them both. "I'd better get back to me pint." As he moved away he glanced back over his shoulder. "But you know...there's you, Mr Ward, and Miss Pearce...and this Dennis guy. Your Jason Sullivan, he's suddenly become a very popular man, hey?"

Chapter Eight

Charlie Spate's ego was bruised. The fact that he had been instructed to delve into the killing of Michael Podro meant that he felt he had been sidelined, but since he was still expected to maintain an oversight of the police investigation into the organisation of illegal entrants in the area, he used this as an excuse to hold more than just a watching brief. It also meant that he could insist that Detective Sergeant Start reported to him on a regular basis.

He was perversely annoyed, nevertheless, when she came into his office on the Monday morning with the comment that she had taken it upon herself to do some work on the Podro killing in her spare time, over the weekend. He glowered at her for a few seconds.

"I thought you'd been instructed by Charteris to concentrate on the illegals," Charlie muttered.

She stared at him, raising a challenging eyebrow. "You're complaining, sir? I thought you might appreciate a little help on the matter."

She knew Charlie's enthusiasm about the Podro investigation was not great. His scowl deepened and he shifted uncomfortably in his chair. "So what've you got?"

She stood in front of him in his office, a bulky ring binder clasped to her bosom. "I went to see my dad this weekend," she explained. "Haven't seen him for a while: since my mother died he's been living alone in a cottage up at Bolam, you know, near the lake country park. It's nice there: he can go for walks, used to do a bit of shooting but that's not possible since the new gun laws came in. It's the innocent guys like my dad who suffer then isn't it? The bloody villains can still get their hands on whatever shooters they want."

Charlie waited impatiently, not sure where this was all going.

"Anyway, we went for a walk in the woods around the

lake, and we got to talking about the past and then he told me something I'd really forgotten. He was a bit of a sportsman in his younger days, before he got married. He did quite a bit of wrestling: north regional champion or something. I was never really interested, so it had sort of slipped my mind. But we got talking this weekend and somehow or other we got around to the topic."

Charlie ostentatiously stifled a yawn. "There's a point to all this, is there?"

She smiled, in confidence. "Oh, yes, there certainly is, sir. You see, although it was the wrestling he was interested in, he used to do a lot of weightlifting in the gyms, to make sure that he put on the necessary muscle and poundage to compete. And he got to know quite a few people on the circuit here in the north."

"So?"

Her eyes glinted in triumph. "One of them was Michael Podro."

There was a short silence. "Your father knew Michael Podro?" Charlie muttered. "I don't believe it."

"Hasn't seen him for years," she countered, "but my dad knew him back in the seventies. Shortly after he came to this country."

Charlie Spate leaned back in his chair, frowning. His glance fixed on the ring binder she still clasped close to her bosom. "You got more to tell me."

"Not a great deal. But what I've got is interesting. As a young man, my dad was working in the gyms, and he followed the competitions, local, national, and international. He even kept a scrapbook at the time, going back to the '68 Olympics. He's got some quite interesting cuttings: kept them over the years in this ring binder." She opened the binder, moved to stand beside him, turning over the pages. Her left breast touched his shoulder lightly, leaning against him. "This is my dad when he was thirteen; here's him in the regional club side. And this one, it's an action shot in the trials for the national squad. That's him on his back with his legs in the air." She shook her head, smiling. "He never made it that year."

"I still don't see where you're going on this," Charlie growled. He had never had the slightest interest in weightlifting.

"Well, this is the really interesting cutting, sir." She jabbed her finger at a team photograph, taken from a national newspaper. "He went to Yugoslavia that year, on an expenses-paid tour, and he took this cutting from a local newspaper."

Charlie peered at the yellowing cutting. A group of burly men, smiling at the camera, taken in an hotel reception area. "Who are they?"

"My dad met them in the hotel. They were putting on an exhibition. They were on a preparatory tour, before going to the Olympics in '68."

"So?"

She touched the photograph lightly with her index finger. "This man here, in the front row. My dad says that he's the person my dad knew here in the north as Michael Podro."

"How can he be certain?" Charlie asked suspiciously.

"My dad met Michael Podro in the local wrestling club in Newcastle. They had a common interest; they got to talking. And when my dad mentioned he'd seen the '68 Polish Olympic team , and had an old cutting of them, Podro got all excited. He told my dad he was one of the team; my dad took this ring binder into the club; and Podro identified himself on the photograph."

Charlie looked again at the cutting. There were no names to identify the individuals. "Podro could have been just boasting."

"Why would he do that? He was talking to a fellow enthusiast; he was excited at seeing a memory of his own past." Elaine Start hesitated. "Anyway, the name on the team sheet apparently wasn't Podro."

"How do you mean?"

She grimaced. "The weightlifter changed his name when he came to England. And he wouldn't tell my father what his original name was."

Charlie scowled. "So, this is all very interesting to your father, I'm sure, but it doesn't really get us very much further. You say Podro, according to your dad, adopted a new identity when he came to England. Why would he do that? Just to make his name easier to pronounce for the English?"

She shook her head. "No. It was because he was a defector."

There was a short silence. Charlie stared at her in puzzlement for a little while. "Under what circumstances did he defect?"

She shrugged. "The conversation with my dad was a long time ago; it was the only discussion of its kind; and soon afterwards Podro stopped turning up at the club and my dad lost touch. But as far as he can recall, Podro hinted that he had been a member of the Polish Olympic team, but never actually went to the Olympics. He defected to the West, and took a new identity. But the fact he was in that team means we now have two lines of enquiry you could follow up, sir. There'll be records of these old teams; and there will very likely be newspaper stories about defectors to the West…"

"And you think this might give us some kind of lead to his killing, all these years later?" Charlie queried.

She stared at him evenly. "You don't seem to have any other leads, sir."

Charlie Spate had to agree with that. He gestured towards the ring binder. "All right, you better leave that with me, and I'll get Records to start some checking." He allowed a hint of gratitude to leak into his voice. "I appreciate that you broke into your weekend to take this matter up."

"It was a coincidence," she admitted. "I'm not interested

in weightlifting myself. I can think of better things to do with my time."

Her glance held his, tantalisingly. He could not be sure, but he felt she was mocking him, issuing some kind of veiled challenge. But he had to be careful: he remembered the rebuff in Avignon. And he also remembered the reasons why he had been forced to leave the Met, and come north.

She handed the ring binder to him, and he slipped it into the drawer of his desk. She nodded, and turned to leave, then hesitated, looked back to him. "You see the news this morning, sir?"

"What about?"

"Your gambling friend, Peter Olinger. One of his warehouses went up in smoke."

Charlie's eyes widened, and he grimaced thoughtfully. "Is that so? No one injured?"

"Seems not. But from what I hear on the grapevine, there seems to be a view that maybe it wasn't an accident."

Charlie was silent for a little while, mulling it over. Elaine Start waited, but when he appeared to have ignored her presence she made to leave. He stopped Elaine at the door, just as she was closing it behind her. "Hold on a moment… You know, most of a copper's work is based on graft, hard work, toil, you know what I mean?"

"I do."

"But there's a place for instinct too."

She shrugged.

"So I've got a feeling in my water. This warehouse fire, maybe we ought to go down, take a look at it."

She waited, eyeing him. "You mean both of us?"

"We know from the returns we've had that Olinger has been using a lot of foreign labour in his construction business. All right, we didn't find any illegals as such, though there's always the chance that some of the documentation had been forged."

"We found no proof of that, sir," she warned him.

"I accept that. But he has been using foreign workers from Eastern Europe, we know there's a flood of these people coming in, and this warehouse fire... Hey, you came in here this morning with a coincidence; let's run with my gut instinct. Why not?"

"Nothing to lose," she suggested carefully.

And there was a bonus, Charlie thought triumphantly: he'd get a ride out with Elaine Start on a bright sunny morning.

Smoke still drifted from the firehose-soaked piles of timber and rubbish in the yard. The warehouse was situated on the Gateshead bank of the river, and three fire engines had been called to control and eventually subdue the blaze. The black oily smoke had curled along the river, fading slowly in the still air of the morning. A small group of sightseers still hung about on the Newcastle bank near Wesley Square and on the Millennium Bridge, watching proceedings. A discussion with some of the security firemen at the gateway to the site informed Charlie Spate that the conflagration seemed to have started in the early hours of the morning; an alarm had been raised by the night watchman, but the fire had quickly gained hold, spread throughout the building and consumed its contents quickly. Timber stored in the warehouse had burned rapidly, but the fire brigade had prevented any spreading of the fire across the river, or along to the adjoining buildings. Charlie and Elaine Start left the car in the side road leading down to the riverside; stepping back as a blue Jaguar nosed out into the main road and headed east along the river. Charlie hesitated, staring at the car as it disappeared around a bend in the road and then the two police officers wandered around the edge of the site, unable to enter while the hard-hatted crew still worked at clearing the area. They were standing near the entrance when they saw two men emerging, engaged in deep discussion. Elaine glanced at Charlie, raising her eyebrows, and he smiled wolfishly.

"Mr Speakman," he called, raising a hand in greeting. "And Mr Olinger."

Both men seemed startled momentarily, to see him standing there. Then, with a degree of reluctance they came forward. Speakman was frowning, his heavy brows knitted suspiciously. "What are you doing here? You investigating fires these days? Nothing better to do?"

Charlie smiled expansively. "No, just happened to be passing, that's all, and heard about the fire. But I could say I'm a bit surprised to see you here, Mr Speakman. You're not tied in with Mr Olinger's business, are you?"

Peter Olinger's eyes were wary, as he glanced at his companion. "We have no business connection, but Mr Speakman is here as a concerned friend."

"And I represent the chamber of commerce," Speakman growled. "We'll offer all the help we can."

"Like with the insurance claim, hey?" Charlie asked cheerfully. "I guess you were well insured, weren't you, Olinger?"

"I don't need to discuss my business affairs with you," Olinger replied frostily. The atmosphere was souring fast.

"Oh, don't get me wrong," Charlie pleaded insincerely. "I mean, it's good business sense to make sure you cover contingencies like fire insurance, particularly when things haven't been going too well for you, with labour problems and all that sort of thing. I mean, when you're strapped for cash, an insurance payout can come in very useful."

There was a loaded silence as the two businessmen glared at Charlie Spate. Icily, Speakman ground out the words. "Just what are you implying, Chief Inspector?"

Charlie spread his hands wide in a placatory gesture. "Hey, I'm implying nothing! I'm just saying I'm sure a businessman like Olinger here will have protected his back." He grinned disarmingly. "Just as well none of your foreign workers were in there when it went up, though, isn't it?"

"There was no one on site," Olinger growled, "except the

watchman."

"And maybe the guy who torched the place," Charlie advised.

"You've no proof – "

Speakman laid a warning hand on Olinger's arm. His eyes glittered menacingly. "I think DCI Spate is trying to wind you up, Peter. I don't think we need pursue this discussion any further. We have nothing more to say about the matter. The appropriate investigations are already under way. We are certain it will turn out to have been an accident."

Charlie nodded. "Yeah, spark from faulty wiring, that sort of thing. You just can't get the labour these days, can you? Particularly if you buy in cheap."

Olinger opened his mouth to say something but thought better of it; he turned, brushed past Charlie, and the portly, pompous Speakman followed. Charlie watched them as they walked back to their car. The two men got in, the car disappeared along the river road. Elaine Start sighed deprecatingly. "You were pushing things a bit there, weren't you, sir? Any more of those heavy hints and they'd have been justified in yelling blue murder to the ACC."

Charlie Spate grunted. "I haven't finished yet. Did you notice that Jaguar that was turning out of the side road when we arrived? We weren't the only ones who came along to see what had happened here at the warehouse."

"Jaguar?" Elaine Start frowned. "I noticed it, but it didn't ring any bells..."

Charlie Spate grinned. "It was chauffeur-driven. But in the back was an old acquaintance of ours. Mark Vasagar." He raised an interrogative eyebrow. "Do you think maybe we should pay a call on him now, to trade impressions about what happened here in the early hours of the morning?"

"Are you sure that's a good idea?" Elaine queried doubtfully.

"Didn't we agree we ought to pay a visit some time to Mad Jack Tenby's heir? As to whether it's a good idea, I've never seen discretion as a suitable bedfellow," he countered.

Twenty minutes later they arrived at the large house on the private estate outside Newcastle, where Mark Vasagar was known to have purchased a house. The houses were modern, security-camera observed, with large manicured gardens, and doric columns outside each front entrance. They were pretentious, expensive, and boastful of their owners' perceived views of themselves. When they arrived Charlie clucked his tongue thoughtfully: parked beside Mark Vasagar's Jaguar was the car in which Speakman and Peter Olinger had driven away from the destroyed warehouse.

Charlie whistled a merry tune between his teeth. "Now what have we got here? Looks like Vasagar turned up at the warehouse to invite our two friends round for a coffee," he suggested joyfully. "Here's a meeting to warm the cockles of your heart. Let's go join them."

He began to get out of the car. Elaine Start put a restraining hand on his arm. "I don't think this is wise."

But Charlie was beyond discretion. He marched up to the front entrance, and she followed reluctantly, slamming the car door behind her. He rang the bell: the chimes echoed deep in the house. When the burly manservant with the battered features opened the door, Charlie was leaning against one of the Doric pillars. "Detective Chief Inspector Spate," he announced, and stepped forward. For a moment the man seemed about to resist him, raised a hand, but then stepped aside uncertainly. Charlie strode into the vast hallway. Mark Vasagar was standing at the foot of the stairs, staring at him. "See from the car outside that you got company," Charlie called out. "In the lounge, are they?"

Tall, lean, good-looking and confident, the dark-eyed, Sri Lankan-born businessman hesitated, then managed a thin, wolfish smile. "Mr Spate... Nice to see you again. Yes, I have company. How can I help you?"

"Business, is it?" Charlie asked, walking across towards

the lounge doorway. Vasagar's glance slid past him to Elaine
Start, moving hesitantly into the hallway, and shrugged.
Charlie stood in the doorway of the long lounge area. It was
expensively furnished, deep easy chairs and settees in gold
brocade, thick carpet, heavy drape hangings at the window.

The two men seated in the room looked up at him, and
there was a brief, shocked silence. Then Speakman
exploded. "What the hell are you doing here? Did you follow us? This is harassment!"

Charlie spread wide innocent hands. "Hey, don't get so
excited. I didn't know you and Mr Olinger here were on
your way to see Mr Vasagar. I had some things to talk over
with him; it's just coincidence us meeting here again." His
glance flickered over Peter Olinger. "And after you had all
this trouble this morning, too."

Speakman stood up. His plump face was red with anger.
He gestured towards Peter Olinger. "Our business here is
finished, anyway. Peter, come on, let's go." He strode past
Charlie, brushing against his shoulder with an angry delib-
eration. He nodded to Vasagar. "We'll take your advice,
Mark. We'll be in touch with you again."

White-faced, clearly shaken about something, Peter
Olinger followed Speakman into the hallway. The door
slammed loudly behind them. Mark Vasagar stood watching
Charlie Spate, a hint of amusement in his dark eyes. He
brushed back an errant lock of his smooth black hair, and
flashed Charlie a confident smile. "You seem to give rise to
strong emotions in people, Mr Spate. But as Mr Speakman
suggested, our business is finished, so perhaps you'd like to
come through." He extended an elegant hand towards the
lounge. "Can I offer you both a drink?"

Charlie grinned at him, and swaggered into the lounge.
"I'm sure you'll have a superior malt I could be persuaded
to partake of. Detective Sergeant Start, she'll decline. She'll
be driving." He glanced at her and was immediately aware
of the hostility that was starting to simmer in his companion at the remark: he enjoyed a certain juvenile triumph in

it. Vasagar walked across the room to an ornate mock Louis Quinze drinks cupboard, and poured two glasses of whisky, making no comment.

"I'd appreciate a glass of mineral water, if it's not too much trouble," Elaine Start said coldly. Vasagar smiled at her, nodded, opened a small bottle of Perrier, poured the contents into a cut glass tumbler and handed it to her. He brought his own and Charlie Spate's drink towards the chief inspector, now settling himself comfortably in one of the easy chairs. Elaine perched herself grimly on the arm of a settee, distinctly ill at ease. Vasagar seemed unfazed by their presence, leaning against the wall, observing them.

"This will be the first time you've been to this house," he suggested.

"We tried your office first," Charlie explained, "but they said you'd been out all morning. Of course, you were down at the riverside earlier, at Olinger's warehouse."

"Ever since I was a child in Sri Lanka, I've been fascinated by fires," Vasagar commented smoothly. "And, of course, hearing it was the warehouse belonging to Mr Olinger – "

"You thought you'd go around for a look-see. So he then came around here, tapping you up for financial help, then?" Charlie interrupted. "Him and his mate Speakman?"

There was a short silence. Mark Vasagar's eyes were lidded; he was cool, his lithe body relaxed, unmoved by the contempt in Charlie's voice. "They came to discuss business matters; I offered to help where I could."

"Like getting Olinger some illegals on cheap rates to help his business get back on the rails?" Charlie asked, sipping his malt whisky with an air of detached appreciation.

Vasagar seemed to uncoil himself like an elegant snake from his posture against the wall; he wandered into the middle of the room, seeking a chair that would suit him. He smiled at Elaine, seated himself on the settee where she leaned, and then turned slowly to look at Charlie. His tone was enigmatic. "The comment you'd just made, Mr Spate, it's as though you seek to provoke me in some way. What could you possibly mean by the suggestion...unless it was a joke?"

Charlie clucked his tongue. "I'll tell you what the joke is, Vasagar. I been chasing Mad Jack Tenby ever since I came to Tyneside, never convinced he'd given up his old ways. But the joke's been on me: while I was looking at Tenby, you were sneaking in by the back door. Do a deal with him, did you? Use his contacts, his gangmasters, his middlemen, for a percentage of the return?"

Vasagar shook his head disdainfully, fully in control. "I've no idea what you're talking about, Mr Spate."

Charlie frowned, demonstrating his lack of conviction. "I been up here long enough on Tyneside to know what makes the place tick. It used to be Mad Jack, until senility and a desire for respectability caught up with him and he found life easier hobnobbing with the elite, the rich, the so-called powerful, and half-bent coppers." He smiled thinly. "You know we recently lost some of our senior officers to early retirement, of course."

"Times change, people move on," Vasagar remarked non-committally.

"While villains remain villains," Charlie offered. "But the trouble is, for a guy like you to come in and build a really tight ship you got to have time. And from what I hear, things haven't been going too well."

"In what respect, Mr Spate?"

"The grapevine tells me things aren't...settled along the river. The whisper is out that there's a degree of nervousness around...people waiting to see which way the cat is going to jump."

"What cats are you talking about? You speak in riddles, Mr Spate." Vasagar extended a lean arm, consulted his wristwatch pointedly. "I will need to get to the office soon. Just what exactly did you want to discuss with me?"

Charlie lifted his glass, inspected what remained of the

liquid. "Well, you were down at the warehouse, so I was just wondering whether you ordered it to be torched."

There was a short, pregnant silence. Something flickered deep in Vasagar's eyes, but after a moment he smiled broadly, and confidently. His teeth were very white in his lean, dark features. "Me? Why on earth would I get involved in such activity?"

"Hey, who can say? But you were fast enough getting down to the Gateshead bank and then Olinger came straight around here, with his back-up Speakman, from the chamber of commerce."

"I also am a member of Mr Speakman's organisation. We businessmen must stick together at difficult times like this, help each other."

"That's what you do with the illegals, is it? Help out your fellow businessmen?" Charlie chuckled. "Must have been a bit difficult recently, with the way we been nosing in, demanding documentation, checking for forged documents."

Mark Vasagar was silent, his dark eyes fixed on Charlie. He sipped at his whisky, then set the cut glass tumbler down on the table in front of him. "Would there be anything else you might wish to raise with me?" His tone was cool and confident. "As you know, I'm always eager to assist the police in their investigations."

Charlie nodded. "How much is Peter Olinger in to you for?"

Vasagar raised an eyebrow. "I don't understand – "

"Aw, come on, he's known to frequent your casinos, your night clubs, quite apart from his ventures at the racetrack. Did you torch the warehouse to help him get some insurance, so he could pay off his debts to you?"

Mark Vasagar leaned forward, picked up the glass again, finished the drink, and smiled at Elaine, seated stiffly at the edge of the settee, staring coldly at Charlie Spate. "I think you'll have to forgive me now, but I really must be leaving.

I'll see you out…"

He rose. Charlie finished his drink slowly before rising. He led the way out, saying no more. The door closed behind them with a firm thud.

As they walked back to the car Elaine Start muttered, "Well, that was quite a performance."

"Yeah, pretty cool, wasn't he?"

"I meant you. *Sir*. What on earth did you hope to gain by that kind of confrontation?"

"These gorillas need their cages rattled from time to time," Charlie growled as he slid into the passenger seat.

"Did you really think that kind of rattling will be in any way productive? If he looked worried, it escaped me! And you've got nothing by way of evidence to back up any of the statements you made in there!" She started the car, began to turn in the wide driveway. "And you sure as hell gave Speakman grounds for complaint."

"Hey, you're along just to drive. So do that," Charlie ordered ungraciously.

She would not be gainsaid. "Putting pressure on, and following through with the investigation into illegals coming in through the Tyneside gangmasters is my task," she muttered through gritted teeth. "Your intervention hasn't helped. I understood you were concentrating on the Podro murder."

Assistant Chief Constable Charteris seemed to hold a similar view. He was standing in the doorway of Charlie's office when they returned to headquarters an hour later. He had his hands on his hips. His mouth was twisted brutally; his eyes were red-rimmed with anger.

"What the bloody hell do you think you've been up to?"

# Chapter Nine

Susie Cartwright was very positive about the matter when Eric returned to his office on the Quayside next day, after a morning in court dealing with a knifing in a West End nightclub. She stood in his doorway as he dumped his briefcase and sat down behind his desk, nodded towards the blue-covered desk diary open in front of him. "He insisted that I check your diary, and he fixed a time when he would call in to see you here." She pursed her lips in disapproval. "He left me with the distinct impression that he felt you've been avoiding him, Mr Ward, so in view of the size of the retainer that he's already paid you, and I've already banked, I thought it best to comply with his request. He'll be here at three-thirty. Sharp. His words."

"Ben Shaw?"

She nodded.

Eric groaned. A meeting with the man from Bradgate and Savage was the last thing he wanted right now: there were still too many questions left unanswered, and he had yet to make sense of what the hell was going on. But he was unable to criticise his secretary: she was quite right. Ben Shaw had every reason to insist on a meeting.

He was able to mollify Susie to some extent by rapidly clearing away some of the mounting pile of files on his desk before Ben Shaw arrived for his appointment.

"You're a difficult man to get hold of, Ward, and I need to be brought up to date," the big banker muttered as he eased himself into a chair in front of Eric's desk. "I gather you've been off to Europe, and I need to know what you've found out."

Eric hesitated, uncertain how far to go in his account. He contented himself, finally, with explaining the meeting he had had with Mike Fremantle, at Anne's request, and consequently with the harbourmaster at La Rochelle, and with the owner of the *Beau Soleil* on the Ile de R . When he finished, Ben Shaw shifted his bulk in the chair in obvious disappointment. "Is that all you've got? No further trace of this man Sullivan?"

Eric shook his head. "He chartered the boat, went off for a few days with a man called Duclos, and then just disappeared again. I...I managed to trace Duclos, had a word with him, but he was unable to give me any clear leads."

He made no mention of finding the dead body of Duclos. He was also conscious that he was saying nothing about the part played by Aline Pearce and the negotiations over the Vasari, but he felt such information merely blurred issues, and had nothing to do with the brief he had been given by Ben Shaw: find Jason Sullivan. But suspicion stained the banker's eyes as though he guessed Eric was holding something back; he leaned forward, fixing Eric with a doubtful stare. "Are you sure this is all you can tell me?"

"More or less. I've still got feelers out," Eric replied feebly. "But at the moment – "

"You've spoken again to your wife? You've pressed her for information?" Ben Shaw demanded.

Stiffly, Eric replied, "She claims she has no idea where he is."

"And you believe her?" Shaw demanded with a sudden anger.

Eric was silent for a moment, holding the banker's glance. "I told you at the beginning, Mr Shaw, that this assignment is not greatly to my liking. I also said that if I felt any conflict of interest arising, personal or otherwise, I'd give you back your cheque. The fact is, I'm still uneasy about a number of things, and if you feel I'm not serving your best interests, I'd be only too happy to pull out of this whole matter."

Shaw leaned back in his chair slowly, reining himself in, calming down with a deliberate effort. He ran a hand over his forehead, brushed the greying hair at his temples, inspected his fingertips. "Look here, Ward, you must realise

I find myself with a problem. If I'm pushing things, it's because I'm being pushed. Our financing of the Hollander Project is under pressure; every day that goes past makes it more difficult for me to satisfy enquiries; there may be a very good reason why this money has been...moved. But I need explanations, fast."

"It's as I explained to you," Eric replied coolly. "I spoke to Mike Fremantle, the accountant who's been working with Sullivan. He's nervous, he's scared, but he confirmed how the money's gone missing. He insists it was nothing to do with him. And he insists he's no idea where Sullivan is. But if you want to talk to him yourself..."

Ben Shaw gestured angrily with his left hand, dismissing the suggestion. "It's best I stay well clear of these people. I need to find that money, and that means finding Sullivan first, get an explanation before the whole thing blows apart. And get the money back. I'm employing you to do the digging: I'm not qualified to start cross-examining accountants on the policies they've been following under another's direction." He paused, considering things for a while, fingering the deep cleft in his chin in a characteristic gesture. Then he frowned suddenly, as a thought occurred to him. "The name of this man you say you spoke to, the one who chartered the boat with Sullivan."

"Georges Duclos," Eric said uneasily.

"The name rings a bell..." Ben Shaw's blue eyes glittered suspiciously as he flicked a glance to Eric. "Did I not see a report...a man of that name has been found dead?"

"You have wide sources of information, Mr Shaw."

"I'm a banker," Shaw snapped dismissively. "This man Georges Duclos had a financial background in Europe. The grapevine... Do you have any information about how this man died?"

"No," Eric lied.

"Is it the same man? The man from the boat?" Shaw pressed.

"It may well be," Eric prevaricated irritably, "but that matter is something for the French police. And I have no information to offer them. I'm just concentrating on what I've been asked to do: I'm looking for Jason Sullivan."

After Ben Shaw had gone, Eric felt certain that the banker did not believe him. Yet, oddly enough, Shaw still wanted to retain his services for Bradgate and Savage.

Eric met Aline Pearce for lunch at The Blue Moon, in a side street near the Quayside. It was a small, discreet restaurant, much frequented by businessmen, and it was a little too small to indulge in an open and frank discussion of the problems they were facing. But the lunch was enjoyable, even if their conversation was constrained, and later they walked along the Quayside as the pale sun sent dancing lights on the dark waters of the Tyne. On the Gateshead bank, there was still activity on the site of the warehouse that had been burned down a few days earlier. They walked onto the Millennium Bridge, leaned against the parapet and watched the workmen clearing the site.

"So," Eric asked, "is there any more news from your colleagues?"

Aline Pearce frowned, and shook her head. "I'm expecting a call this afternoon, but I'm beginning to feel that it was a waste of time coming here with you to England. If your ex-wife is unable to give you any information, and we've no idea whether this man Sullivan has actually returned to England, I think we are merely waiting for things to happen…"

Instead of making things happen. Eric agreed with her point of view. But the thought of her going back to France left him with an odd feeling of reluctance. "My client's been on my back," he offered, "and I had to lie through my teeth to keep him off the Duclos business."

"You didn't tell him about me, and my interest in Sullivan?" she asked quickly. "You'll be well aware, Eric, that the need to maintain discretion over these delicate negotiations is paramount if we are to recover the Vasari."

"I kept you out of it," Eric soothed her. "But to be honest, I don't know that I want any continued involvement in any of this business. It's all too close to home, and we don't seem to be getting anywhere. Sullivan could be running around almost anywhere in Europe, or even elsewhere. I don't see – "

There was a buzzing noise, Aline's mobile telephone. With a hurried excuse, she stepped aside, checked the phone. Eric leaned against the railings and stared down into the dark waters of the Tyne: he felt dissatisfied, disoriented. He felt he had got into difficulties both emotionally and professionally, and could see no way out. He glanced over his shoulder to Aline: she was pacing slowly along the bridge, back towards the promenade, the mobile phone close to her ear, listening, saying nothing. She stopped some twenty yards away from him, the line of her body tense, then slowly she turned, staring back at him. She lowered the phone, clicking it off, and slowly made her way back to stand beside him at the railings.

"That was Leclerc," she offered quietly.

"News?"

She frowned thoughtfully. There was a puzzled look in her eyes. "They want us to close down."

"Close down? What do you mean?" Eric asked in surprise.

She linked her arm in his suddenly, pulled him away from the railing and began to walk briskly away from the bridge, back towards the Quayside, and along the promenade, as though the pace of her movement would accelerate her thought processes. There was a hint of anger in her voice. "They damned well want us to bring an end to the negotiations, end the search for the Vasari. The chicken-hearted bastards...what the hell is going on?"

"I don't understand," Eric said. "Who are you talking about?"

Fiercely, she said: "Leclerc reported to the committee overseeing the negotiations, the committee to whom I'm seconded from the Rijksmuseum. They in turn made use of certain contacts in the hierarchy to instigate enquiries into Georges Duclos. And the results came back very quickly."

"What's happening?"

"It seems the death of Duclos is not going to give rise to any overt police investigation. It is to be reported as suicide," she said, through gritted teeth

"The circumstances hardly make me believe that makes sense. I don't see how – or why – Duclos could have killed himself," Eric insisted.

"The matter is closed," she snapped. "The French authorities have issued a statement. Duclos was in financial trouble; he was depressed; he killed himself while the balance of his mind was disturbed. It is over. And the negotiations over the Vasari are to be ended. I'm to have my contract concluded. I'm to return to work at the Rijksmuseum."

Eric shook his head. "I don't understand."

"Neither do I!" she flashed angrily. "Except that the committee, ah, well, it's a politicised group, you know what I mean? They depend on links in the hierarchy, European diplomats, ministers of state in Brussels and Luxembourg, and for some reason they're running scared. The death of Duclos, maybe, or something that's been said to them, a hint dropped...what do I know? But it's to be ended!" Her grip tightened on Eric's arm, fingers digging into his bicep. "It'll be the death of Duclos, it must have scared someone off. But we could be getting close, and this faint-heartedness...I'm pretty certain Duclos was acting merely as an agent, and my instincts tell me he was acting on behalf of this mysterious Englishman, this Jason Sullivan that you are pursuing for your own reasons! Or if he was not acting for Sullivan, at least this man Sullivan knows something about the whereabouts of the Vasari. He is *involved*, I'm sure!"

She stopped suddenly, swung around to face him, her

eyes blazing. "I can't do this Eric: they can't do it to me! I've lived, breathed, driven myself over this Vasari negotiation. I'm committed to it; I've spent so much time on it, and just when it seems I was getting close to a resolution, to finally getting my hands on the Vasari I'm being told to stop, close it down, walk away from it. I can't do it, Eric. I can't!"

Tears of fury and frustration glittered on her eyelashes. Gently, Eric took her hand, led her across to a bench, and sat down beside her. "Tell me exactly what Leclerc told you on the phone."

She was silent for a little while, fighting for control. "It seems, as I said, that Leclerc made his report to the committee, omitting to mention that we had actually found the body of Duclos hanging by the neck. He merely stated that Duclos had not kept the second appointment. And he gave the committee the only other lead we have: the name Grabowski."

"So?" Eric prompted.

"He heard nothing for a few days. Then everything moved very quickly. It seems that the committee had asked Interpol to seek out information on this name Grabowski, and the response was almost immediate. Leclerc was called in. It was an embarrassing meeting. The committee was clearly not pleased with the instructions that had come down to them from higher quarters, but were unable to do anything about it. Leclerc was to step down to other duties; my contract was to be ended; the negotiations for the Vasari were to be concluded, and no further action was to be taken to discover the whereabouts either of the painting itself, or of the person who might be in possession of it."

"But why?"

She grimaced. "Because the matter is being taken care of by other hands."

"What's that supposed to mean?" Eric demanded.

"It is a matter for active pursuit by Interpol. And by

national criminal investigative agencies."

Eric shook his head in bewilderment. "You're being warned off. The death of Duclos is being hushed up, and Interpol demands that the Vasari negotiations are to end...I don't understand what's going on."

"Neither do I," Aline replied bitterly. "But it all revolves around the name Grabowski. As far as Leclerc was able to discover before he was summarily told to proceed to other duties, this man Grabowski – if it is the man who was linked with Duclos – was a defector to the West some years ago. Leclerc was able to find out little about it all, but it seems that a new interest has suddenly been kindled in this man's history. One of the committee, the one who made the approach to Interpol, feels humiliated by the whole thing so was perhaps a little indiscreet in explaining some of it to Leclerc, angry that our own investigations are to be closed down. But it's something to do with a Cold War defection, a link to Riga, and an investigation that's ongoing. And we are to step aside, and forget all about what we've been doing." She stared at him, her eyelids damp with furious tears she fought to control. "So what are you going to do?"

"Me?" Eric was taken by surprise. Slowly, he shook his head. "I don't see what all this has to do with me. They might be able to tell you to shut down *your* operation, but strictly speaking that's nothing to do with me. I'm working for a private client, I'm looking for Jason Sullivan – albeit somewhat helplessly – and that work still has to go on. Your controllers have no influence over me. So, to all intents and purposes I'm still going on."

"Let me help you," she demanded fiercely.

"But you've been told – "

"To hell with what I've been told! Do you think they can just tell me to back off, and then really expect me to walk away from an important investigation like this? If they want to close down the investigation, that's their business, responding to official pressure, but that doesn't mean I have to meekly crawl back into the woodwork and let all my chasing around become just a lot of wasted effort!"

"You've had your contract ended," Eric reminded her quietly.

"So what?"

"You have to return to the Rijksmuseum."

"I've been working solidly for two years," she flared. "I'm entitled to some leave. I'm not giving up on this matter, Eric! And we have a common objective: to find this man Sullivan. You need him for your purposes; I need him for mine. I'm not going to be sidetracked now when I've put in so much work. We have the same thing in mind, so why should we not continue to work together?"

He could see no valid reason why not. He nodded, aware also of a certain tingling of pleasure and relief that Aline Pearce was not about to disappear from his life. "Let's get back to my office, and talk this through, develop a plan of campaign. And first of all, you'll have to tell me *exactly* what Leclerc has told you."

"Now I've always reckoned that, pound for pound, it was Jimmy Wilde who was the best of 'em. Aw, I know there was talk in the fifties of Sugar Ray Robinson as bein' the best the ring ever did see, and back in Wales there was always a big followin' for Tommy Farr, they reckon he really beat Joe Louis in his prime, but if you talk to the old 'uns, they'll always tell you it was Jimmy Wilde, and I go along with that. Pound for pound, that is."

The old man looked even older than his seventy-plus years. His features were raddled, his large nose a mass of broken veins from the drink that had still not managed to kill him, and his rasping voice sounded as though it came out through a crow-like sound box. He had been a big man in his prime, but his body had shrunken, the flesh had leached from his bones and the skin hung on his face in folds, seamed and dry. Yet his eyes were still bright, and his memory sharp.

"Naturally, I was always a fight fan – not a bad fighter myself – but strictly fairground stuff," he croaked. "I did a few bouts here on the Town Moor in the old days, at the Hoppings, but there was never the same kind of hunger for the noble art as we used to call it, not around here. So when the few places that still operated closed down, there was only the gyms, and the wrestling dens that I could spend time in. Not the same thing, of course, and not like it was back in the valleys, but it was okay, I suppose. And that's how I came to meet Grabbo. That's what we used to call him. Grabbo."

Jackie Parton's glance flicked towards Eric. They were seated on the worn, imitation leather bench of the decrepit billiard hall, beside the old man. He came in every day, it seemed, just for the stale smell of sweating men labouring over the pool tables, paunchy, yesterday's men, reliving dreams and destroyed destinies, recollecting triumphs of almost mythological proportions that had never been. Jackie had tried to explain when he had rung Eric at the office.

"He's an old Welsh miner called Meredith, who came north in the sixties, for work in the pits. He's lived in Benton for the last forty years, and he's falling apart physically, but he's got a memory as sharp as razor wire. For some things anyway. And it seems the name Grabowski rang bells for him. I'd been asking around, as you wanted, and his name came up. His memories, they may be faint, but it's all I've been able to come up with."

Eric had agreed that they should meet the old man as soon as possible. When they walked into the decayed public billiards hall above the steel-shuttered fa ade of the garage below there was a certain whispering that surged around the shabby-carpeted room as the middle-aged players caught sight of Aline Pearce. There was a feeling of resentment in the air as she walked in, a woman in a seedy, male, smoke-filled atmosphere, but they had insufficient energy for protest, and a few minutes after Jackie, Eric and Aline walked in, they had all gone back to their desultory games, soon forgetting the insult that she represented in their masculine stronghold.

Eric leaned forward, almost touching the old man. He caught the odour of old sweat and stale beer as he stared into the old man's rheumy eyes. "So, Mr Meredith, this man you call Grabbo. When was it you came across him?"

The old man cackled, displaying to Eric a few decayed, yellow teeth. "Hey, you think I'm too beat-up to remember, don't you? You look at this bag of old bones and you think I got nothing left upstairs. But it ain't true." He cast a leery glance at Jackie Parton. "For instance, I can remember the first winner young Jackie here rode at the Town Moor. That's a way back, ain't it!" His mouth wrinkled ruefully. "Course, there's things happened yesterday I don't recall too well, but you ask me about thirty years ago and I can remember, clear as a curlew's call on the hills above Nant Cesyg."

"The man called Grabbo," Jackie Parton prompted.

The old man sighed, dragged back from images of his childhood in Wales. "Aye, well, it was when my local club, where we used to still have a boxing ring for youngsters, it was when the club closed down and the local wrestling federation – they was supported by a grant from Scottish and Newcastle Breweries, you know – it was when they took over. There was quite a few promising wrestlers around in Benton in those days, and the club went well for a while. That's when this character we called Grabbo turned up. A big lad, he was, heavy, and had a go at the wrestling but he always admitted he was just fillin' in like, keepin' hisself fit, because his real skill was in the weightlifting. He was a bit wild, you know, in his attitude to the opponents. Seemed as though he wanted to throw them out of the ring. No science, like, really. Brute force. And he had a bit of a nasty side, I tell you. It was like he had a kind of cold, vicious drive in him. Conditioned, like. *Trained*. Used his elbows on more than one guy's face. That's why he was told to leave the club, in the end. Too violent. Never saw him after that. But when he was in the club, we used to have a few drinks together, in the pub around the corner."

"How long ago was this, Mr Meredith?" Aline asked.

He ignored her, refusing to accept her presence. He continued to address himself to Eric. "It would be about 1970, as I recall. And I was always happy to have a drink with him. He didn't have any friends, like, really, and he was always the one pushing the boat out and I didn't have much of the ready at the time."

"How do you mean?" Eric asked curiously.

"Well, I was out of work, and he was always flush, you know? Always had plenty of cash on him. Never minded buying the drinks."

Eric glanced at Jackie and frowned. He turned back to Meredith. "So what was his job?"

The old man leered at him. "Hey, don't ask me, boy. We called him Grabbo because of his wild wrestling style, and his own name wasn't easy to say, being Hungarian or whatever he was, a refugee or something, but I don't think he had no job; just cash in the pocket, like. But that was probably because he was friendly with the bloke up at Sherstone Manor."

There was a short silence. Aline leaned forward, seemingly about to say something but then subsided at a glance from Jackie Parton. "Sherstone Manor?" the ex-jockey asked. "You talking about the place in Gosforth that was pulled down years ago to build a block of flats?"

"Aye, that's the place," Meredith nodded. "There was a judge or something living there. Grabbo knew him, so he said. And from what I could gather, I reckoned the judge was slipping him a few quid, regular like. Enough to make sure Grabbo didn't need to do no work. Then in the nineties they pulled down the property. Construction company; property development or something such-like. But the developer got it wrong, made a hash of the site, there was some kind of argument, lawsuit or something about dodgy workmanship, concrete not up to specification, or asbestos or something, I don't know."

"And what happened to the previous owner?" Eric asked.

"The judge?" The old man wrinkled his alcohol-ravaged nose. "Aw, he was long dead by then. He popped his clogs just about the time Grabbo got thrown out of the club." There was a short thoughtful pause. "In fact, come to think of it, it was exactly at that time. The night Grabbo got banned, he was in a foul mood, and got very violent in the ring. Maybe it was because the Sherstone Manor guy had just cashed in his chips. Maybe it was because Grabbo knew that his money box had just got slammed shut. *Duw, duw, bach*, it was a long time ago, what do I know?"

"How did he die?" Eric queried. "This judge?"

"The way all lawyers ought to go," Meredith cackled, gap-toothed. "The knacker's yard. Hell, I don't know; wasn't really interested. When a lawyer goes, don't we all raise a glass and ask no questions? Now then, Jackie Parton, where was that bottle you promised me?"

There was nothing more to be got out of the old man. In the street outside, Jackie Parton raised his eyebrows and shrugged deprecatingly. "It was a long shot. The only whisper I've got on Tyneside of anyone knowing someone called Grabowski. I don't know whether it helps in any way."

Eric glanced at Aline and shrugged. "I'm not sure, Jackie. But it's the only lead we have."

"So where do we go from here?" Aline asked. Eric glanced at her. He was concerned: since Leclerc had told her that the Vasari negotiations were to be discontinued she had seemed preoccupied, worried. Each time they had met there had been an edginess about her: it was as though she had something on her mind, something she wanted to tell him but was reluctant to do so. He had asked her about it, but she had been quick to dismiss the idea that there was a problem. He wondered whether she was having second thoughts about taking the route she had decided upon, working against the wishes of her employers.

"We need to get our heads buried in newspaper and other local records," Eric replied. "See what we can find out about the owner of Sherstone Manor, and maybe discover what connection there was with this man Grabowski."

"We don't even know whether the person that Meredith is talking about has any link at all with the Duclos connection," Aline muttered doubtfully. Eric was inclined to agree: it all seemed very tenuous and he could see little prospect of it leading them towards finding Jason Sullivan. But otherwise they were at a dead end.

A door banged behind them. The old man was emerging, the bottle of whisky that Jackie Parton had given him clutched tightly to his chest. He grinned at them. "You're awright, Jackie, me lad. At least you gave me a bottle. The other bastard, he gave me nothin'."

Jackie Parton turned, stared at the old man for several seconds. "The other bastard…who are you talking about?" he asked quietly, after a quick glance in Eric's direction.

"The other guy who was asking me about old Grabbo."

"When was that?" Eric asked quickly.

The old man shook his head and began to shamble off away from them. "Hell, that was ages ago. A year maybe? Longer, I think. Maybe two years. I tell you, I got short-term problems with my memory. But it was a good while ago." He stopped suddenly, cocking his head to one side as though listening for birdsong in the darkness. "Ah, yeah, and there was something else, I almost forgot. I told that other feller though, a year or so ago. Grabowski, Grabbo we called him, his first name was Michael. And after he left the club, he sort of just disappeared, faded from the scene, you know what I mean. After the judge died. Maybe he moved away, I dunno. I never run across him again, after that. But

Michael, yeah, that was it. Michael Grabowski. Wild bugger that one, in the ring. I used to have the feeling, watching him, that he could have killed, easy as anything. Maybe done his share of killing, in the war. He had the hands...and he had the mind. Aye, a wild bugger that..."

Chapter Ten

"How are we getting along?"

Eric leaned back in his chair, rubbed his hands over his eyes, willing away the dull ache that was affecting them and gestured to Aline to take a seat beside him. For two days he and Aline had been ploughing through old newspaper files. Eric had called in some favours: some years ago he had acted for the managing editor of the newspaper in a libel action and had got the case against the newspaper thrown out. Now, he and Aline had been given access to the local press archives, along with some assistance from one of the office boys – who had done the fetching and carrying of dusty old volumes – in the dingy, dusty back room in the basement of the offices in Grey Street. They had had little to go on, and the consequence was that the process had been slow and drawn out. While more recent documents had been computerised, the editions they were seeking belonged to a different, non-computerised era.

Aline put a hand gently on his shoulder. She seemed to have come out of her earlier reserved, worried mood: getting down to some graft had clearly revived her, and cheered her up. She had been out of the archive room for a few hours following up another possible lead. He smiled at her now, and shrugged. "Well, it's slow, but I've discovered an obituary for the man who owned Sherstone Manor which makes it clear he was no lawyer. He was no judge. He was called John Jarvis, all right, as we both discovered, but he was a career diplomat, a civil servant."

"So you think Meredith was wrong in his information?" Aline asked, leaning her hip against the side of his desk.

Eric shook his head in doubt. "Difficult to say. Maybe he was right about the Sherstone Manor connection, but just got confused regarding the owner's background. An old rubber-head like Meredith, maybe he wouldn't know the difference between a lawyer and a civil servant anyway."

Eric sighed, closed the files in front of him. "But I've had enough for the moment, sneezing over all this dust. What say we get a cup of coffee somewhere and bring each other up to date?"

Aline was quick to agree.

A cool breeze swept up Grey Street from the river. Eric walked with Aline down to a small caf in the Bigg Market; he would have preferred to sit outside on the small terrace under the awnings, to help clear his head after the hours spent poring over old newspaper files, but he saw Aline shiver slightly, so they went inside.

"We warm-blooded French are not used to your northern climate," she said, half-smiling ruefully.

"I'd have found it too cold outside as well, after a few minutes," he admitted. "But I just needed to get the dust out of my lungs and nostrils. I like the musty smell of old newspapers, but there are disadvantages, crouching over those decaying papers." He ordered two coffees, and then sat opposite her. She had been looking tired, and somewhat disconsolate and she was clearly still smarting from the decision to close the Vasari negotiations, and worried about her future. Or maybe she was concerned that she and Eric were getting nowhere fast in their investigations. He smiled at her, slipped a reporter's notebook out of his pocket. She opened her handbag and took out a similar small book.

"Snap," he said.

"I beg your pardon?" she asked, puzzled.

"Forget it. Which of us to start?"

She looked up as the waiter came forward with the coffees. When he had set them down and returned to the counter she nodded to Eric. "You first."

He nodded. "Fine. Well, as I said, the owner of Sherstone Manor seems to have spent his working life as a civil servant, mainly in the Diplomatic Service. From *The Times* obituary I gathered he was Cambridge-educated, served as a major in Intelligence during the Second World War, mainly because he spoke several languages, as well as Russian in which he had graduated at university. He acted as an interpreter during the Nuremberg Trials, still in uniform, which maybe is how Meredith got it wrong, because Jarvis was then working with the Judge Advocate's Department, but thereafter he returned to the Diplomatic Service. Clearly, he had proved his worth to the Civil Service mandarins, because he was promoted and from then on remained in Europe, stayed in Eastern postings as a cultural attach at various embassies."

"For cultural attach read spy?" she asked.

Eric shrugged. "Who knows? During the Cold War intelligence officers were given all sorts of titles, mainly spurious. But he remained in Europe until about 1965, when he returned to London duties. After that, there was only one short posting back to Berlin before his early retirement from the service in 1970."

"How old was he then?" Aline asked.

"He was approaching sixty: regulation retirement age, but it seems he went a little early. But he didn't get to enjoy a long retirement. He died in 1975."

"Natural causes?"

Eric shook his head. "It was a car crash, in Scotland."

"Ha!"

"What?"

"I'll tell you later."

Eric eyed her for a moment, then nodded. "Okay. He was up there on holiday, it seems. A lonely road. He hit a tree. Killed instantly. From the details that appeared in the files, it seems it was an accident, no other car involved. It was late at night: maybe he'd been drinking. The police reckoned there were no suspicious circumstances, and wrote it all off. There was an obituary in *The Times*." Eric frowned thoughtfully, and sipped at his coffee. "Odd thing, though. No mention of it in the obituary, but he had never been awarded any sort of gong."

"What is that?" she asked, eyes widening. She had attractive eyes, he considered.

"John Jarvis had worked in overseas postings in Eastern Europe for years. He had reached the level of Assistant Secretary. He had a good war record, and had all the right connections socially and professionally. It's common for people like that to be honoured when they reach retirement, or shortly before. They get an award, a knighthood, an OBE, whatever. It's almost guaranteed, if you spend your time in the service. But he ended up just plain mister." He caught her eye, still puzzled. "That's it. No award. No gong, in common parlance."

"Like a *L gion d'Honneur*. I must remember the idiom. So would there be any reason for this omission?"

"Has to be one," Eric conceded. "But I've turned up none. All I can assume is that he blotted his copybook in some way, crossed someone in the hierarchy, so that he was blackballed – " He saw the look in her eye again and held up a hand. "Blacklisted. Anyway, the fact is, he didn't receive what his fellow civil servants would, in normal circumstances, have deemed to be their just deserts, their rights. The obituary made no comment, as I said, but there's something odd about the situation, I believe. However, I've been able to dig up nothing about it." He sipped again at his coffee. He had tasted worse. He glanced out of the window. A man was standing on the pavement outside, casually looking in. Their eyes met briefly, before he moved on. "So, that's all I got on our friend Jarvis. Your turn, now."

She nodded and flicked open her notebook, checked the shorthand scribbles she had made, and then looked up. "The suggestion from your newspaper manager friend that I should contact the local genealogical society was a good one. They were very helpful. They have a quarterly magazine which contains articles about members' genealogical interests, and I was able to interview one old gentleman – Mr DeLancey – who had compiled an article some years ago for the magazine, on the history of Sherstone Manor. It was completed just before the house was demolished, but it was a project that he had been working on for quite a long time. He had even interviewed Mrs Jarvis about it."

Eric raised his eyebrows. "There was no mention of Jarvis having been married, in the obituary. Again, that's a bit unusual."

Aline smiled faintly. "Some families like to keep their private lives just that. Private. Anyway, I was able to read the article and interview its author. It was interesting. Mr DeLancey was able to tell me that the manor house was owned by John Jarvis, certainly, but it had not come to him through his own family. It was previously owned by the family of Jarvis's wife. A dowry on their marriage, it seems."

"A dowry? I didn't think that sort of old-fashioned idea was still going on."

"We are talking here about the 1930s, Eric. Mrs Jarvis was previously Andrea McBrayne. She was an only daughter; her father had an engineering business near the Clyde. When John Jarvis married Andrea – they met when they were both students at Cambridge – her father presented the couple with the house in Newcastle, as a wedding present."

"So this was the Scottish connection you said you'd come around to," Eric suggested.

"Not exactly," she demurred. "John Jarvis and Andrea McBrayne were married in 1935, and there was one child but it died in infancy. There were no children thereafter. But when the author of the article was talking to me, he had a certain glint in his eye. Mr DeLancey is an old man now, and likes his glass of whisky in the afternoon. I think it loosened his tongue, somewhat. And he told me something which seemed to amuse him, but something which he did not think appropriate for publication: he had never put into the article when he wrote it for the genealogical magazine." She cocked her head to one side. "A family scandal, no less."

"Most families have them. And I understand that quite often genealogical research tends to reveal rather more than the researcher is looking for." Eric glanced out of the window again. Something stirred at the back of his mind, irritating him. Then he tried to concentrate once more on what Aline was saying, even though he was beginning to wonder whether this research was going to take them any further forward.

"From what Mr DeLancey was telling me, there was a certain stiffness in Mrs Jarvis's manner when she talked with him about the house. When he interviewed her, her husband was in Poland, it seems: he was still in the Civil Service then, and Mr DeLancey never got to meet him."

"He wouldn't need to, if all he was doing was researching the history of the house itself."

"Which dated back to 1640, apparently. But although DeLancey was interested mainly in the house, he had also carried out genealogical research into the families who had lived there. And then, later, after both Mrs Jarvis – she died in 1969 – and Mr Jarvis had passed on, he was curious about who would claim the estate. Bearing in mind both were only children. And had had no progeny."

"So who did come into the inheritance?"

Aline would not be rushed. "It's a rather romantic story, really. Whatever the circumstances of the Jarvis marriage – maybe the loss of a child pushed them apart, or maybe Jarvis's absences during the war caused a rift – what seems to have happened was that Sherstone Manor was used for military purposes during the 1940s, and Andrea Jarvis returned to Scotland for the duration. It was during one of his visits to see her that John Jarvis must, presumably, have met the other, younger woman."

"Ah." Eric cocked an eyebrow. "And something happened?"

Aline smiled. "Mr DeLancey has the view that an affair began. One that was to be of some long standing. He told me he had checked the records. The woman was a nurse, working in Scotland. She gave birth to a son, some years later, in 1953. Or, as my interviewee put it, she was delivered of a bastard son."

"Who was adopted by Andrea Jarvis?"

Aline shook her head. "Certainly not. There was a maintenance agreement: John Jarvis paid for the child's education and so on. But clearly, Andrea would not countenance the child coming to live at Sherstone. After the war, Sherstone Manor was returned to the Jarvis family, she moved back in about 1956 and John Jarvis also settled back there. Jarvis retired, his wife died, and then he was killed in a car accident."

"In Scotland."

She nodded. "Not a simple holiday, one can guess. More likely he was visiting a son."

"Born on the wrong side of the blanket," Eric murmured.

"*Excusez-moi?*"

Eric sighed, shook his head, and smiled. "So do we know the name of this son, or his mother?"

"Mr DeLancey could not remember the name. It was only gossip he had picked up, which was not relevant to the article. Nasty things in the woodshed...you see, I am familiar with *some* of your English idioms," she smiled. "But he says he can talk to some people in the society, and if I go back maybe he'll find me the name from local records." She hesitated. "I'm not sure it's important."

Eric sighed. "I think maybe you should follow it up, in case it provides us with another link."

"There is one other thing Mr DeLancey was quite certain about. Jarvis was not a wealthy man in the first instance, and when his wife died, he was not enriched from her family. His father-in-law's business on the Clyde had got into difficulties after the war, with the collapse of the shipping industry; he had entered into unwise investments and left little to his daughter. So Sherstone Manor was the only thing of value John Jarvis had when he died."

"Yet our drunken friend Meredith tells us that Jarvis certainly had enough money in the 70s to make contributions to the lifestyle of a wrestler in Benton, who went by the name of Grabbo among the locals." Eric finished his coffee in a thoughtful silence. He glanced at his watch. "I think I'd better get back to the office: I've got a living to make and Susie will be having my guts for garters if I don't get some work done on the files she's holding."

"Guts for garters. You English have colourful expressions. I am finding this trip most useful for my language skills," Aline said dryly.

Eric grinned in acknowledgement. "Anyway, we need to find out whether there really was a financial link between our mysterious wrestler and John Jarvis. If Jarvis was supporting him financially, why was he doing it? And if Jarvis was just living on a Civil Service pension, what would possess him to part with regular sums? Aline, I think you're right. We might find a link, if we can determine who Jarvis's assets went to. While I'm at the office I can get Susie to do some checking for me. If John Jarvis left a will, it will be a public document – and Susie has strings she can pull which might get us a quick sight of its details. If he didn't make a will, there's the letters of administration..." He nodded, pushed aside his coffee cup. "I'll get Susie on to that. Meanwhile, when are you due to see your genealogy expert again?"

"Tomorrow afternoon."

"Then we can meet again after that, and compare notes." He glanced at his own notebook. "Now then, what else have we got about the man Meredith called Grabbo? I've combed the local newspapers, and I've come across nothing, not even in the small sporting print. The man may have attended a wrestling gym but he doesn't seem to have entered any competitions."

"What about records of membership from the gym

Meredith was talking about?"

"I've had Jackie Parton check it out. The club closed down years ago, the records were never kept, or if they were have disappeared, and although Jackie's done a trawl among old members, for most of them it was too long ago, and he was never around all that long anyway. So if Meredith's acquaintance Grabbo was really the Grabowski mentioned to us by Duclos, we don't seem to be much nearer finding him."

Aline hesitated, pursing her lips. "Meredith told us the man was strong, a wrestler, but not a skilled professional one. He also told us he thought his friend was Hungarian – "

Eric laughed cynically. "I wouldn't rely on that. He seemed a bit vague about the Hungarian origin. Certain he was foreign, but I wouldn't pin hopes on his accuracy about the Hungarian nationality. My guess is that any nationality west of Wales, except the English, would be a vague blur to old man Meredith."

Aline nodded. "Yes, but it occurs to me that the fact the man was foreign might be the link to Jarvis."

"How do you mean?"

"Jarvis was a Civil Servant. He spent most of his working life in Eastern Europe. Meredith says his Grabbo was Hungarian. No job, but money from Jarvis. The thought occurs to me…it was the sixties, the Iron Curtain had come down, Jarvis had numerous contacts in Europe. Perhaps it was not Jarvis money that was keeping Grabbo in funds."

"I don't follow," Eric said slowly but there was a germ of an idea growing in his mind.

Aline regarded him steadily. "Jarvis had worked in Intelligence and in the Diplomatic Service. Perhaps, when he was back in England at the end of his career, he still had one more service to provide."

"A conduit for funds for someone he had known in Europe," Eric breathed. "Funds he was passing on, from another source."

"It still happens today," Aline offered quietly. "Men who provide a service are in turn provided with a safe location, funds to keep them alive... It was the sixties, the Cold War..." She stared at Eric uncertainly. "I think I should talk to Leclerc."

Eric frowned. "Your colleague in Paris? He's off the investigation. The whole thing's been closed down. He's been put on other duties."

"But he is an old friend. And I know that he is as angry at what has happened as I am. Like me, he has devoted much time and energy to the Vasari negotiations. He is as frustrated as I am. He will be more than happy to help me, I am sure of it. He still has people he can talk to, people who can help us if the requests are seemingly innocent, unconnected with the Vasari negotiations."

"What are you going to ask him?" Eric queried, still doubtful.

"I'll ask him to use his contacts to find out if there was anyone called Grabowski who left the Eastern Sector for England, when John Jarvis was in his last posting to Germany."

Eric nodded, considering the matter carefully. "It's worth a shot...provided it doesn't get you into hot water with the Rijksmuseum, or the committee. You've already been warned off."

She regarded him soberly. He seemed to detect a shadow in her eyes, a hint of guilt. "I'm pleased at your concern. But I think Leclerc and I, we can handle this with discretion."

She preceded him as they walked out of the caf . She took a deep breath, seeming to shake off some of her depression, as though his acceptance of her research efforts had given her a renewed confidence. At the door she leaned forward, and kissed him on the cheek. It was a surprising, but pleasurable experience. "I'll see you tomorrow," she said.

He watched her walk away for a few seconds as she made her way back up the hill to Grey Street, before he turned and went back down to the Quayside, and his office. But there was something else still on his mind, a shadow in his memory, an image he could not fix with any precision. But it niggled at him, an irritation in his mental processes.

Susie was relieved to see him: she spent an hour in his office going over various files, checking correspondence, taking instructions regarding phone calls from clients, and was discreet enough not to press him too hard in view of the mood he was in. The extended work in the close confines of the newspaper archive room had given him a headache, and the old familiar signs of stress and overwork were emerging, the needle-sharp prickling at the back of his eyes, a slight blurring of vision. She was not surprised when he abruptly ended their meeting and told her he'd be going home.

Back at the flat in Gosforth he made himself a meal, and opened a bottle of wine. After he had eaten he relaxed in an easy chair, listening to some Dvorak, eyes half-closed, a glass of wine in his hand. Gradually the pain washed away, but he was still unable to seize on the thing that was worrying at him, the shadow at the back of his mind. He thought back over the events of the last week or so, going over each meeting, each conversation, trying to recall in sequence each detail. It was when he lingered over things that Jackie Parton had said to him that finally the recollection moved sluggishly to the front of his consciousness. He reached for his wallet, opened it, took out the grainy, indistinct print, the photograph that Jackie had given him.

Frank Dennis, Parton had told him: the private detective who no one seemed to know on Tyneside. Eric stared at the print, scanned it closely. He could not be certain, because the photograph was far from clear. Nevertheless, he was more than half-convinced that he had seen the man in the grainy print. Standing in the window of the caf  where Eric and Aline had taken coffee. He could be wrong, it could be a coincidence, and yet as he studied the photograph Eric became more and more convinced.

He had seen the man in the photograph outside the caf , and for a brief moment their eyes had met.

Next morning Eric was due in court. He was forced to set aside all thoughts of the search for Jason Sullivan while he concentrated on the matter in hand: a girl arrested on suspicion of involvement in an armed robbery at a trustee savings bank. She had been kept in custody, interviewed eight times, and kept in a detention room. No caution had been given until the eighth interview and she had been in a distressed condition. It was Eric's argument that admissions she had made in that last interview should be excluded as inadmissible, on the grounds that it had not been made voluntarily, by reason of oppression.

"Having regard to her personal characteristics, the fact she had not been allowed to see any of her family, the number of interviews conducted, the period of time involved and her being shut up in a detention room, it is quite clear," Eric summed up, "that her free will had been sapped. Our contention is that, looking at it subjectively, it cannot be said beyond reasonable doubt that there was not oppression of my client."

The detective inspector whom Eric had earlier examined stared stonily at him as he finished his summation. His own feelings were clear, and Eric knew they were commonly held among the police. Eric Ward had been one of them, but now he had crossed over, he was on the other side, and that meant he was the enemy. It was something Eric had come to accept with a certain stoicism.

The rest of the day dragged on in court: a customs and excise case against a client who'd been arrested on a booze run to France; the mugging of a seventy-year-old woman by two youths who were already well known to the court as well as Eric; a reckless driving case, a burglary, possession of an imitation firearm in a corner shop robbery. At the end of the day Eric felt exhausted and drained; depression set in as he sat in his office and stared out of the window, asking himself yet again the question others had asked him: what the hell was he doing with his life? Maybe Anne had been right all along; maybe Susie Cartwright was correct in her views, maybe he ought to drag himself out of the rut he had dug for himself. There had to be better things to do.

Then the name Frank Dennis came back into his mind, and the brief image of the man standing outside the caf , peering through the window. Eric wondered whether he ought to tell Aline Pearce about it. After some consideration he decided to say nothing: it might worry her unduly, and in any case he could not be absolutely sure that the man had been the one in the grainy print given to him by Jackie Parton.

Back at the flat he showered, changed his clothing and called to meet Aline at her hotel as they had prearranged. A light evening meal around the corner from the hotel was planned. First, they had a drink in the hotel bar and discussed the results of her second meeting with the elderly Mr DeLancey.

"He was in good form," she explained, "and quite excited about what he had learned, bringing up to date the article that he had written on Sherstone Manor years ago. From discussions with colleagues in the genealogical society he found out that Sherstone Manor had been sold to a property developer after the death of John Jarvis. The developer had demolished the house completely, thus ending a three hundred year old history to the annoyance of the society – they had actually started a campaign to save it – and then the site had been used to build a block of flats."

"We more or less knew that already, from Jackie Parton," Eric suggested.

"That is so," Aline conceded, "but what we didn't know was that there was a close link between the property developer and the construction company. It would seem that the owners of Sherstone Manor were in financial difficulty after the death of John Jarvis – "

"By owners, you mean the heirs of John Jarvis."

"That's right. It was clearly felt that if the best value was to be obtained from the manor house and its land, property development was the answer. A purchase was arranged: Sherstone Manor was bought by a company called Tenby Holdings Ltd, and the construction company..." she checked her notes, "which was called Belville Construction Ltd, was employed to erect the block of apartments."

"So who made the sale?" Eric asked.

"One moment, please." Aline took a sip of her gin and tonic, and went on, "It was not long after the building was completed, and the initial tenants were installed, that complaints started to be made about various things: damp, shoddy construction, breaches of the building regulations. Mr DeLancey was quite gleeful about it, because the society had opposed the whole venture from the start. Large amounts of compensation had to be paid, the property itself was resold at a loss and no one who had been involved in the whole development came out happy, financially speaking. Not Tenby Holdings, not Belville Construction."

"So it was all a great loss," Eric agreed, "but that wouldn't have affected the heir to Sherstone Manor, if he or she had made the sale to Tenby Holdings."

Aline smiled knowingly. "Ah, but there we have it. DeLancey was quite amused by it all, as I said. He considered it was a case of chickens coming home to roost." She smiled again. "An idiom I recognise. You see, he was able to tell me that the sale to Tenby Holdings must not have been quite straightforward. He suggests that the property was sold at below market value, in consideration of Belville Construction, as a new company, being given the contract to build the apartment block."

"And does he suggest a reason for that?" Eric asked cautiously.

Aline nodded. "It was the owner of Sherstone Manor who set up Belville Construction. It was his way of establishing a business, and obtaining financing."

"But in the end it all came to nothing."

"Ended in tears," she agreed.

Eric raised an eyebrow, gave her a calculating glance. "And now you're going to tell me that the owner of Sherstone Manor, John Jarvis's heir, is long dead and gone and our trail ends abruptly."

"To the contrary," she said. "He is still operating, successfully it seems, on Tyneside. And still in the construction business. When your secretary manages to get the details of the will of John Jarvis I think we will have confirmation that the owner of Sherstone Manor, who sold it to Tenby Holdings, was the illegitimate offspring of the liaison between John Jarvis and a lady called Rose Olinger, in Dunfermline."

"Who was a young man in 1975, and wanting to start out in business," Eric said thoughtfully. "So he raised finance by bringing in Tenby Holdings, set up his own construction company to do the work, and made a cock-up of it. And this man's name would be...?"

"Peter Olinger," Aline said.

"So," Eric mused, "I wonder if he's ever heard of a man called Michael Grabowski?"

"Michael *Podro* Grabowski," Aline corrected him. "According to the records of the Polish Olympic team, that was his full name."

Eric's eyes widened in surprise. "Leclerc?"

Aline nodded, smiling, pleased with herself. "He was on the phone to me this morning. His contacts were extremely helpful. It seems that Michael Podro Grabowski was a member of the Polish Olympic weightlifting team preparing for the 1968 Games. But Grabowski never took part in the Games. He disappeared, in the months before the

Games were held."

She closed her notebook triumphantly. "It seems he defected to the West."

Chapter Eleven

Charlie Spate waited for the call in his office. Elaine Start would also be waiting, he guessed: they had both been invited to a meeting with the Assistant Chief Constable, Jim Charteris. Charlie hoped that the ACC would be in a less violent mood than when they had last met.

The dressing down he had given Charlie a few days earlier had been unprecedented. Red in the face with frustration, waving his arms in fury he had stomped up and down in his office while Charlie had stood rigidly facing him, keeping his mouth tight shut.

"What the hell do you think you're playing at? You think I *like* making bloody apologies to people like Speakman and Olinger? You think I enjoy trying to cover up things for you with the Chief Constable? What the hell is the matter with you? In the first instance, I told you to leave the illegals investigation to DS Start, and what do I find? You been sticking your nose in! Secondly, I tell you to concentrate on the Michael Podro killing and what have I heard? Bugger all, except for one thin, measly report that I was embarrassed to pass on to the Home Office! And now I get people screaming down the phone at me because you've been harassing Speakman, and Olinger, poking around a warehouse fire on the Gateshead bank, marching into the private premises of a citizen like Mark Vasagar – even if we know he's bent – and just generally making an arsehole of yourself! Don't you realise there are procedures we have to follow? Don't you realise we got to tread on eggs at times? Don't you realise that if the Chief Constable gets on my back, I'm going to get on yours? I'm telling you Spate, you'd better sort yourself out! I'm tired of your insubordination, your general attitude, and the way you think you can ponce around and disobey every rule in the bloody book! You were in trouble in the Met a couple of years back and you had to move to save your career – everyone bloody well knows that. Well, I'm telling you now you're getting into trouble up here as well and the sooner you sort yourself out the better it will be for everyone. Or you'll be out on your arse. Again!"

Charlie had had the good sense to say nothing in his own defence, partly because he was forced to admit that most of the things Charteris were saying were true. But inwardly he was seething: results were never obtained by pussy-footing around, in Charlie's view; Charteris had to grease up to the Chief Constable and that also meant keeping important people happy. But too much of that kind of behaviour had led to the downfall of the last Chief Constable, who had got too close to the bigwigs, and found that investigations were being compromised. Charteris maybe was largely right, but at the same time Charlie had no intention of changing his ways. Tone things down a bit, maybe, he confessed reluctantly to himself. But if he saw a criminal jugular to sink his white teeth into, he was going to go for it. That was his nature: the nature of the beast.

Brave thoughts, he suggested sourly to himself, as he sat brooding in his office. But if he ever got his hands on Speakman and that weasel Olinger in the right situation...

There was a tap on the door, and Elaine Start looked in. "We're on the boards," she said.

ACC Jim Charteris seemed a different man as he introduced Charlie to his guests. He had cast off the cloak of fury in which he had challenged Charlie. It was as though there had been no difficulties between them, no bawling out. Charteris was calm, friendly, almost gracefully detached as he completed the introductions. He was the smooth operator, out to impress, in charge of his men. Charlie, still smarting from the dressing down even if it had been days earlier, found it difficult to respond other than gruffly. Not least because he didn't like the look of the men seated beside Charteris around the conference table. He'd seen their kind before.

The older man from the Home Office had all the precision of a finely honed razor blade. His features were sharply defined, his chin clean-shaven. His diction was clipped, his accent cut-glass, his attitude lofty and superior, and he clearly had every confidence in his ability to hold an argument, dismiss a non-sequitur or detect an ambiguity in any argument. His memoranda to his minions would be marvels of detailed summation; his decision-making swift, and his advice to Ministers of the Crown accurately drawn and as immaculately presented as he himself was in his dark, pin-striped suit. His thinning hair was carefully brushed, every hair seemingly in place, the deep-set eyes under his satanic eyebrows slightly mocking, his thin lips pursed in an insincere smile. His name was Singleton, and he had brought an underling with him who would be considerably lower in the pecking order, and intended only as a supporting act to the main event, Singleton, to deal with boring details. And to act as a witness, of course. He had been introduced as Dobson, in typical Civil Service manner: younger, balding, bespectacled, he had something of the air of an academic about him. He wouldn't last five minutes in a real job, Charlie thought sourly to himself.

After the brief formalities were concluded by Charteris, Singleton immediately addressed himself to Elaine Start. "Now you will be the young lady who has been conducting the investigation into the documentation of workers in the various industries." He smiled at her in a patronising manner. "We are extremely grateful for the effort put in. You see, the investigation we asked to be carried out was in preparation for the new legislation which shortly comes into effect – section 8 of the Immigration and Asylum Act, calling for basic document checks by all employers using immigrant labour. This will make it harder for illegals to get jobs using fake documents."

He clearly thought himself something of a ladies' man: it came across in his winning, insincere smile and his unctuous manner. Charlie knew that kind of approach would not wash with Elaine Start: she was beginning to bristle already.

"I don't think matters are that simple, sir," she contended. "We are continuing the checks, though on a somewhat reduced scale because of the problems we foresee with the gangmasters – "

"Ah, yes, I gather that some concerns have been raised about these so-called gangmasters, and their activities." Singleton glanced at Charteris, smiled, and shrugged slightly. It was a vaguely dismissive gesture. "It is appreciated that there is concern but we really have to take that issue in its context."

DS Start's tone was careful, and controlled, but it held an underlying edge. "By context, I imagine you mean issues such as the fact that the gangmaster controls every aspect of the workers' lives: using fear and intimidation, shoving the workers into squalid and overcrowded conditions, hot-bedding them so that as many as eighteen people are forced to occupy six beds in a twenty-four hour period?"

Singleton's patronising smile froze, then slowly faded. A hint of irritation crept unbidden into his tone. "Hot-bedding. An interesting term: I must add it to my lexicon. I hear what you say, DS Start, but by context I meant the fact that the Government has to look at the situation rather more broadly. We cannot be simplistic. We cannot get bogged down by localised situations. It has to be remembered that the people we refer to as gangmasters have operated in this country as legitimate contractors for more than a hundred and fifty years. We have been aware of the kind of problem you mention raised in agricultural areas such as Lincolnshire and Norfolk, and we are dealing with that in new legislation – "

"But what about the gangmasters up here?" Elaine Start interrupted, clearly getting angrier by the moment at what she saw as a dismissive attitude. "Human trafficking is closely linked to drugs and prostitution and it seems to many of us up here that you're turning a blind eye to the most basic issue that we have to face – never mind the agricultural areas down south. We all know these people, the ones who are involved in and making huge profits from their activities – most of them have records as long as your arm, for violence and drug-dealing."

Singleton no longer looked on her as an attractive young woman. She was an opponent, to be ground into submission. His tone was cold, his eyes colder. "Proposals have been made by Private Members Bill for a regulatory system for gangmasters. The Government remains undecided about the merits of a statutory licensing system for such people, though naturally it is keeping the matter under review."

"And ignoring the fact that these same gangmasters are bringing in illegal immigrants, and thereby defeating the controls that have been set up."

ACC Charteris shifted uncomfortably in his seat. Charlie Spate glowed. This was a woman after his own heart. He didn't have to say a word. Singleton had got Elaine Start's dander up, and she wasn't about to let him off the hook too easily.

The civil servant's thin nostrils flared in disdain. "We are not standing still on such matters. As far as illegal immigrants are concerned we are thinking of introducing a new criminal offence of trafficking people into the UK for purposes of exploitation."

"*Thinking* about it," she snapped in derision, "while every day there are hundreds of prostitutes pouring in from Eastern Europe and China to work in virtually slave conditions throughout the northern cities!"

ACC Charteris felt it was time to intervene. He leaned forward, slightly red in the face. He fixed Elaine Start with a warning eye. "I think the point has now been made, DS Start, and I'm sure Mr Singleton will have picked up on it. No doubt he'll be able to take your views back to the Home

Office."

Charlie noted that Charteris did not go so far as to align himself with those views. He was keeping his options open, and his nose clean. Career man to the last.

"The purpose of this meeting, is, in fact," Charteris continued, "not to do with the illegal immigrants issue. Mr Singleton thought it might be as well if we were all brought up to speed with the other enquiry that we were asked to instigate." His glance slid coldly towards Charlie. "The one DCI Spate is heading up."

Charlie shuffled his feet under the table, and scowled. "We've not been able to get very far with the Podro investigation. It's a cold case, we've been able to find very few leads – "

"As was apparent from your report," Singleton interrupted smoothly, regaining his control now he was no longer under fire. "But there have been some recent developments that have come to our attention at the Home Office, and there were some significant matters mentioned in your report, sufficient to persuade us that perhaps we had better have a discussion about the reasons for the enquiry in the first instance. It might enable us to proceed more quickly hereafter, and more efficiently." He raised one eyebrow, and held Charlie's glance. "From the report it is clear that you consider this to have been a planned killing, by a professional gunman, and you opine that it might be a gangland matter. Though it seems you have found no connection between Michael Podro and the local underworld."

"That doesn't mean to say – "

"One thing we can clear up immediately," Singleton continued, overriding Charlie's response. "Your report mentions a marking, a form of tattoo on the dead man's shoulder. It has considerable significance, and gives legitimacy to our opening up a wider range of enquiry."

"We weren't able to identify the mark," Charlie muttered defensively.

Singleton's smile was thin. "But our experts were. It's the mark used by an organisation known to us. Clearly, an attempt was made at some time to remove the mark. It had, perhaps, proved to be an embarrassment. But our experts were able to identify the original tattoo. It consists of two letters. *SS*."

There was a short silence. Charlie stared at the civil servant uncomprehendingly. "*SS*...are you trying to tell me that this man Podro was a member of the SS, the notorious *Schutzstaffel*. Are you saying he'd been a bloody *Nazi*?"

"Far from it." Singleton's companion, Dobson, spoke for the first time, his tone eager and enthusiastic. But he subsided immediately, as Singleton glared at him for being so bold as to speak without invitation, then turned back to Charlie.

"As my colleague says, he was not a member of the Nazi party. The tattooed *SS* does not refer to the *Schutzstaffel*, the elite Nazi Protection Squad. Their tattoos merely reflected their blood groups. No, it is in fact a reference to an entirely different organisation, though one arguably equally as ruthless in its attempts to achieve its objectives as were the Nazis. No, the letters *SS* are an abbreviation: they stand for the words *Solis Sacerdotibus*."

Charlie stared at him, uncomprehending. Singleton smiled superciliously. "*Solis Sacerdotibus* was the motto of the members of the Order known as the *Fratres Milicie Christi de Livonia*."

The silence in the room lengthened. Singleton sat back in his chair, a pleased smirk on his face as he contemplated the incomprehension in the faces of the three police officers. "The mark on the shoulder of Michael Podro," he murmured at last, "goes back to the early years of the thirteenth century."

"*What?*" Charlie snapped in bewilderment.

"The year 1202, in fact," Singleton offered blandly. He

glanced sideways to his companion. "Perhaps it is appropriate that my colleague Dobson should go into the detail. He
has made a study of the Order."

A hint of eagerness touched Dobson's eyes. This was
clearly something that enthused him. "It all began with
Theoderic van Trenden, in 1202, who later became Bishop
of Estonia."

"Are we going to have a history lesson here, sir?" Charlie
protested, but Jim Charteris held up a warning hand.

"I'm sure we have all heard of the Knights Templar,"
Dobson continued after a slight hesitation, unsettled by
Charlie's interruption. "They were established in 1114, to
guard pilgrims in the Holy Land, some have said. Others
would contend they had different motives. But in any event
they consisted of a group of warrior monks, in their origins.
Now, in 1202 Theoderic van Trenden established a kind of
offshoot of the Templars. The establishment was actually in
accord with the General Chapter of the Knights of
Clairvaux but schism soon occurred between the Pope and
the Order itself. The Pope's permission was conditional on
this being an independent command – "

"Detail," Singleton interrupted warningly, "but not too
much detail."

Dobson, nodded, swallowed, and continued. "The Order
of the *Fratres*, the Brothers of the Sword, was established as
a military order. Its declared purpose was to pursue the crusade in the Eastern Baltic region of Livonia. But it soon
became the first "Order State" in history, when Theoderic
sought from the Bishop of Riga a third part of the territory
of Livonia, that part not already converted to Christianity.
Permission was granted and consequently the Order came
to hold one third of Livonia and Lettia from the bishop in
return for defence against pagan attack. The Order itself,"
he began to digress, "was a Templar-inspired rule redolent
with the usual symbols of cross and sword; they indulged in
secret rituals; they were professional holy warriors, and

they – "

"Dobson…" Singleton warned.

Dobson quivered, and went on, subdued. "They were also lords of land, because of the Bishop's agreement. They became extremely powerful and wealthy. They established their headquarters on the banks of the river Rige but by the year 1287 their purpose had really ceased to exist, and they were absorbed by the similar Order of Teutonic Knights. This meant a more rational, institutionalised process of succession, so that one competent male warrior leader was simply replaced by another on death. There was never a head of the snake to strike off, so to speak. It simply grew another. But even though the organisation was absorbed, it never really died. It retained, within the Order of Teutonic Knights, its own separate identity throughout the Middle Ages. These particular individuals, this group within a group, used the identifying motto *Solis Sacerdotibus*. They branded the initials on their bodies as a signifying mark. They were known to the mediaeval world as the Swordbrothers."

Dobson hesitated, glancing uncertainly towards his senior officer. "I can go further, Singleton, explain how these Orders all fell into disuse, how the Knights Templar were destroyed as an organisation in the fourteenth century, how Freemasonry emerged in the seventeenth century and laid claim to many of the practices and mythology of the Templars to develop and expand their own organisation, but – "

"But that won't be necessary," Singleton cut in. "We can jump several hundred years, to get to the point. The first thing to note is that the Swordbrothers were a formal military organisation based in Riga in the thirteenth century. They faded from public consciousness, but the mythology was certainly kept alive in esoteric practices and rituals, albeit within a narrow circle of individuals." His cold glance switched to Charlie. "You mentioned the Nazi *Schutzstaffel*. Oddly enough, it was the activity of the Nazi SS that was partly responsible for the re-emergence of the Swordbrothers in the 1940s. For the Nazis in the early years of the war the occupation of Poland opened up new vistas. The planners and organisers of power in the *Schutzstaffel*, under Hitler's encouragement, saw Poland as an experimental playground. They were given a *tabula rasa*, a clean slate, to undertake more or less what they wanted. Military occupation, Germanisation of the territory, subjugation of the Slavic races, murder of the intelligentsia, and rape, confiscation of land and valuables, enslavement of the population, the unfolding of the euthanasia action to eliminate the incurably sick, these were all the consequence of the free hand given to the *Schutzstaffel*. And the ideological rationalisation which took place there after the German invasion was a precursor to the plans of 1941, which were designed to bring about Hitler's ultimate objective: the subjugation of Bolshevik Russia."

"I'm sorry," Charlie interrupted heavily, "but I don't see – "

"The fact was that the *Schutzstaffel*, as we know, did not have it all their own way. Various resistance groups were formed to oppose them. One of them emerged from a base in Riga. It had a political and patriotic objective. Its members were committed to resist the licensed barbarism of the Nazis. And this group of resistance fighters cast back to their own history to draw around them a cloak of patriotic respectability: they saw themselves as fulfilling the role that had been designated to their forebears in 1202: defence against paganism. Like their forebears over seven hundred years earlier, they called themselves the Swordbrothers."

Elaine Start leaned forward. "And they used the SS symbol? Are you telling us that this dead man, this Michael Podro, had been a Resistance fighter in the Second World War? Surely, that can't be."

"He would have been too young," Singleton agreed, nodding. "But that is not the point."

"In other words, the Swordbrother organisation continued to operate after the war was over," Charlie suggested.

"Exactly."

Charlie frowned. "A Polish resistance group formed in the 1940s...it's a far cry from finding a dead man up here."

"Victim of what seems to have been a deliberate assassination," Singleton added. "The work of a professional hit man, in your words in the report."

"So what is the connection?" Elaine Start asked.

Singleton hesitated. "We don't know yet." He glanced at his fellow civil servant. "Perhaps you should continue."

Dobson nodded seriously. "Just as the Freemasonry movement relied upon the mythology of the Knights Templar, partly to give their own existence some historical authenticity, the Resistance movement that emerged in 1940 leaned upon the Order of the Brothers of the Sword, the *Fratres Milicie Christi de Livonia,* to give themselves legitimacy and a sense of conjoined purpose. But in the same way that Freemasonry really has very little in common with the Knights Templar, so the Swordbrothers of the twentieth century also had basically different objectives from the earlier *Fratres.* They used the symbolism, they identified each other by way of the SS tattoo, but they were an evolving organisation dominated by thoughts of violence in a time of violence, without really having the spiritual objectives held by the earlier *Fratres.* Consequently, it was not long before their motivation became corrupted, in the aftermath of the Nazi setbacks, and final defeat."

"*Gotterdammerung,*" Singleton murmured.

"There is a body of evidence," Dobson continued, "to show that the process began quite early. To begin with, the Swordbrothers were devoted to the repelling of the Nazi barbarians, but as this necessarily meant a programme of destruction and murder it was not long before certain elements emerged in the group that began to see a way forward that had little in common with the original objectives of the order."

"In a word, the Swordbrothers evolved into a criminal organisation," Singleton averred. "The less altruistic elements took over. Wealth and power became the desired objectives. Murder, blackmail, the acquisition of wealth, dealings in the black market, political assassination... It is interesting, is it not, how the basic inhumanity of man will surface in spite of original patriotic intentions?"

"There were strong links forged later," Dobson continued, "with the Communist bosses in Poland and elsewhere, of course, as the organisation spread its tentacles throughout Eastern Europe. The group provided a useful, undercover terrorist organisation that could be used to good effect, if properly controlled. But control is not always possible with an esoteric group indulging in its own laws and rituals, and even the Communists found them uneasy bedfellows in the end. Consequently, by agreement among the Communist bosses at a meeting in East Berlin, there was a bloodbath and as an organisation, the Swordbrothers were suppressed in the mid-1950s."

"Suppressed," Singleton murmured, "but not, it seems, destroyed. Never actually *extirpated*, as they say."

There was a short silence as all in the room seemed to consider the implications, the consequences that had arisen from the bloody barbarism of life and death in the Eastern territories half a century earlier. ACC Jim Charteris cleared his throat. "So when did they emerge again?"

Singleton shrugged. "We cannot be absolutely certain. There have been various occurrences over the years which have been, shall we say, not entirely explicable. There have been rumours, suggestions of an underground organisation of some size, wealth and power, but with the collapse of the Berlin Wall, the general upheavals in Eastern Europe towards the end of the century, the disappearance of Communist regimes and the closing down of organisations such as the *Stasi*, it has been difficult to apportion blame, identify responsibilities. The world of terrorism is cluttered with swiftly changing factions, cults, movements... However, intelligence organisations have been monitoring events, identifying electronic chatter, until fairly recently it became clear that the Swordbrothers are indeed an active group. And a group of some consequence."

"What was the trigger point?" Charteris asked. "When did you become certain?"

Singleton wrinkled his nose in vague distaste. "You may recall the attempt at a political assassination in France last year. That rather foolish Minister, unable to stay away from his mistress, he was almost assassinated in the Midi-Pyr n es, at Argel s-Gazost. The attempt was foiled by the intervention of a multi-national group: the *Groupe Speciale Contre Terrorisme*. They were acting on information received from Interpol. They managed to prevent the murder, intercept and kill the assassins. But they wouldn't have been able thereby to strike off the head of the snake itself."

"The Swordbrothers?"

"The assassins were identified as members of the Swordbrothers organisation. They carried the *SS* identification marks: the shoulder tattoos." Singleton spread his hands wide. "It explained several things to the intelligence organisations in the West. So Interpol circulated details, called for co-operation from Western Governments, and in our case it meant trawling through old files. One of those files related to a man who had defected, in rather curious circumstances, in 1968."

"Michael Podro?" Charlie asked.

"We could not be sure. And the man was dead. So we asked your Chief Constable to reopen the file. The *SS* tattoo was missed the first time the crime was investigated, its significance not recognised. That was understandable. Now...well, it would seem that suspicions have been confirmed. This man Michael Podro had been a member of the Swordbrothers, and he had died a violent death here in the north of England. So much we can feed through to

Interpol. The question remains, however: *why* did he die, and who was responsible for his murder?"

Singleton looked around at the group, as though seeking an answer from each in turn. When none came, he sighed theatrically. "I have already said the man defected in curious circumstances. The reason I phrased it that way...well, you must understand that defections of that kind from Eastern Europe at that time caused a considerable brouhaha in the international Press. Consequently, they were always carefully arranged, carefully monitored. The arrangements were always made through unofficial channels, of course, but they were controlled. They were known to Ministers and to senior civil servants. But that was not the case with this man."

"How do you mean?" Charlie asked, mystified.

"Michael Podro seems to have made his own arrangements. He was not under any Government control officer. Not formally, at least."

"Are you suggesting he was smuggled in?" Elaine Start asked.

"You are perspicacious, young lady," Singleton patronised. "Yes, he was smuggled in, but the question was, by whom? And why? Our own Cold War systems were available if he wanted to defect. And we knew he could not have entered Britain without assistance from someone in the system." He paused, reflectively. "From the old files, it would seem that there were certain suspicions, but they were never proved in spite of interrogation of the individual civil servant. However, the man concerned was...persuaded that it was in his best interests to resign the Service. And, of course, it was not possible for him to receive the usual recognition that is customarily awarded to such long-serving officers – "

There was a tap on the door. The Chief Constable entered. He came straight to the point. "You'll excuse me Mr Singleton, but I need to interrupt your meeting briefly.

Charteris, and you, DCI Spate. A quick word outside, if you please."

In the corridor the Chief Constable turned on them both. "There's been another killing on our patch." His eyes glared at Charlie Spate. "And I hope to God it's not because of your bloody antics!"

Chapter Twelve

"So, just where do we stand with things right now?" Aline Pearce asked, as she sat facing Eric in the lounge of the Malmaison Hotel on the quayside.

Eric shrugged despondently. "I don't know. We seem to have come to a dead end."

The last few days had been frustrating. He had attempted to telephone Peter Olinger at his work but had been told the man was not available; it seemed he was away on business and could not be contacted. He had tried Olinger's home, suspicious that Olinger's secretary had been instructed to blandly turn away calls, but the electronic gates to the house were firmly closed and there seemed to be no sign of life in the house itself.

"We have discovered so much," Aline insisted, "there must be a way forward for us, something in what we know which will lead us to our objective. Maybe we need to go back to the beginning, identify each step in our progress in the search for this man Jason Sullivan."

Eric nodded in agreement. It seemed the only way forward at the moment. He had not told Aline about his suspicions regarding the man known as Frank Dennis, the fact that someone seemed to have been keeping a watch on their movements. But his failure to contact Olinger, to find out how the jigsaw fitted together, meant that they were cast adrift. He took a sip at his coffee and picked up his mobile phone.

The phone in the offices of Bradshaw and Savage was picked up almost immediately, the caller identifying herself at reception.

"Can you put me through to Ben Shaw's office, please?" He was aware of Aline frowning slightly, as she listened.

"At once, sir. Who is calling?"

The connection was made swiftly. The cool tones of Ben Shaw's secretary came on the line. "Ah, Mr Ward. We've been trying to contact you for some time."

"Sorry, I've been out of the country. Can I speak to Mr Shaw, please?"

The secretary's tone was even cooler. "I'm sorry to say that Mr Shaw is not available at the moment. He had been trying to get in touch with you on an important matter, but I'm afraid that he has been forced to leave the country for a few days on business."

"Can you give me a number I can contact?" Eric asked.

"I'm afraid I cannot. But he will be ringing in soon, I've no doubt. I can tell him you wish to speak to him. I'm sure he'll get back to you – he has after all been trying to get hold of you."

Eric recognised the implied rebuke in her voice: Mr Ben Shaw's time was far too important to allow his schedules to be disturbed by insignificant persons he had taken into contract.

"No luck?" Aline asked, casually, but unable to cover the curiosity in her eyes.

Eric shook his head. At this stage, there was no point in not revealing Shaw's name to her. "It's the man who retained me to find Jason Sullivan. There's a financial problem – "

"Surprise me," Aline said with a wry smile.

" – and it seems he's been after me for some time, to find out how far I've got." Eric grimaced. "I've been sort of avoiding him, and now I try his line, it seems he's out of the country. So we can't start there."

"So where do we start?"

"Mike Fremantle," Eric suggested. He explained briefly to Aline how Fremantle had been involved with Sullivan in the setting up of offshore accounts and the movement of funds destined for the Hollander Project. "That's why I've been trying to find Sullivan: my client, Ben Shaw's company, who hold a watching brief over the funding arrangements for Hollander want an explanation why the funds aren't forthcoming. I'll get in touch with him again, find out if he has any further information. Meanwhile, I think you'd better contact your friend Leclerc again. See if he's got anything more on Grabowski, or can suggest any other leads we might follow." And then, he thought to himself, it would be time for another talk with his ex-wife, Anne.

Aline was on the phone when he left.

He had decided to confront Mike Fremantle at his office, rather than ring ahead. It was only a short walk from the Quayside, and he was feeling frustrated by their lack of progress. As he headed up Grey Street Eric thought back over his earlier meeting with Fremantle. The man had been clearly nervous, aware that he had been unwise in his dealings with Jason Sullivan, foolish in his agreement to undertake the setting up of the bank accounts, scared now that he might be brought to account for the failure of funding for the Hollander Project. Eric wondered whether Ben Shaw had been bringing pressure on Fremantle, but thought it unlikely: when Eric had mentioned Fremantle to Shaw the banker had hastily insisted he didn't want to get bogged down in any of the details. And Eric considered vaguely the possibility that Fremantle might even know something more about Sullivan's disappearance than he was so far letting on.

When he arrived at Fremantle's premises there was a distraught air about the office and its inhabitant. She was perhaps thirty-five years of age, pretty in a rather faded way, unhappy and frustrated. She seemed less than pleased to see Eric, flustered and surrounded as she was by papers scattered on the two desks in the room. She looked up when Eric entered, brushed some errant locks of hair away from her vaguely panicked eyes, and said, "I'm afraid Mr Fremantle isn't here. You'll have to make an appointment."

Eric surveyed the room slowly. Everything seemed to be in a state of disorder: cabinet drawers half-opened, files piled on the floor under the window, ring binders lying open on the shelves. "Is everything all right here?" he asked.

"No, it bloody well isn't!" the woman snapped, losing control suddenly and close to tears. "How am I supposed to know where things are, what's been going on? I suppose you've come in to see him about the Hollander thing as well, but there's nothing I can tell you. I've not been involved; the other staff are in the same boat, and I just can't be expected to come up with the answers they all seem to want."

"They?"

She rubbed the back of her hand against her eyes in frustration. "Oh, all of them! The bank, the trustees of the Hollander Project, the contractors, they all seem to home in on this office with questions I can't answer." Her voice rose to a wail. "I'm just Mike Fremantle's personal secretary! I can't be expected to know what's been going on!"

"Where is he at the moment?" Eric asked.

"That's the point! I don't know! Everyone keeps asking the same thing, they want to talk to him, but I'm at my wit's end. He hasn't been into the office for over a week, I've tried his mobile but it seems to be switched off, I've tried his home, even driven around there a couple of nights, but I've no idea where he is. He's left me with no instructions, I don't know what's going on, and I haven't a clue where he might be right now." She gestured around the room with a look close to panic on her face. "I'm doing my best, trying to find files relating to Hollander, but it's all such a mess, and I don't have keys to his private file cabinet..."

Mike Fremantle had disappeared, made himself scarce. Eric doubted that there would be anything of interest in that private file cabinet. It looked to him as though the accountant had decided things were too hot for him with the search for Jason Sullivan being progressed, and pressure coming on from everyone involved with the Hollander

Project. Eric guessed the man had cut and run. Whether he had been involved more deeply with Sullivan than he had admitted, or whether he had simply decided to remove himself from the centre of things with all the difficult questions yet to be answered, Eric was uncertain.

But the secretary clearly was unable to help him. Eric would be getting no further information for the time being from Jason Sullivan's accountant and personal assistant. He made his way slowly back to his office, uncertain what the next step should be. He guessed that he would have to go out to Sedleigh Hall again, for another confrontation with Anne: he still held the suspicion that she had not told him all she knew about the disappearance of her lover Jason Sullivan. She had always been strong on loyalty, he considered grimly: that loyalty to her husband had wavered when Sullivan had come along, but maybe Eric himself was partly responsible for that state of affairs. Now, she would have transferred her loyalty to her lover, but she was playing a dangerous game if that was the case.

As he entered his office on the Quayside Susie Cartwright rolled her eyes, and jerked her head towards his room. "Someone to see you, Mr Ward. I told him it would be OK to wait in your office."

For a moment, Eric thought it might be Mike Fremantle. He opened the door and saw the man sitting at ease in the chair beside the window, gazing out at the people strolling in the sunshine of the quayside. Eric's heart sank: the visitor was not a welcome one.

Detective Chief Inspector Charlie Spate.

Chapter Thirteen

Peter Olinger's bedroom had showed few signs of disorder. There was little evidence to suggest the dead man had put up much of a struggle. The bedclothes had been thrown back, a bedside table overturned, a book lay on the floor beside the smashed reading light.

"How did they get in?" Charlie Spate had asked.

"Over the roof, it seems," the detective constable had replied. "The electronic warning at the gates had been bypassed – professional job, if you ask me – and the CCTV cameras made inoperative. There are no signs of forced entry on the ground floor. They walked out that way, cool as you like, after they'd done what they came to do, but the initial entrance was made through the window above the flat roof of the garage. Simple enough, really. Cut the glass neatly, shoved a hand in to slip the catch, and there you are. Inside the house."

"You say *they*," Charlie queried.

"Figure of speech, boss. Could have been one bloke, no signs Olinger put up much of a struggle."

"When did he die?"

The Detective Constable shrugged. "Forensic have been in and made preliminary calculations, can't yet put a time to it, like always, want to do their own checking on room temperatures, that sort of thing, but it was the cleaners who raised the alarm. Couldn't get in, tried phoning, checked with his office, and then contacted his security service."

"He employed local guards?"

"Down at the building works, not at the house. Anyway, they got suspicious and called us in."

Charlie surveyed the bedroom with a slightly bored air. Nothing kinky, he decided, and not at all expensive. The house itself, he had already considered, bore few signs of opulence, few of the trappings of the wealthy. The furniture, carpets, the things rich people accumulated about them seemed absent: the dead building contractor should have had plenty of money but had clearly not been a devotee of ostentatious spending. But then, with his gambling habit, maybe he had never been wealthy... And no signs of a feminine presence. Just the one man, living in a big, electronically-gated house. Dead now, with a bullet hole in the back of his skull, and a gaping exit wound at the front, that had removed most of his face. Blood, skin and bone had been splashed against the wall.

"Just the one bullet," the detective constable offered.

"You'll go far," Charlie scowled, "noticing things like that." He prowled around the house for a little while, but then left the minions to get on with details of the search. He had already made up his mind what to do.

He found Mark Vasagar at home. There was little resistance to his entry: the big-muscled character who designated himself as a butler stepped aside when Vasagar called from the sitting room. Charlie marched in, familiar now with the territory, to see Vasagar sprawled on the settee with a document in his hands, and a glass of whisky on the table beside him.

"I'd heard the news," he said immediately, laying down the document and rising politely to his feet.

"What news?" Charlie demanded harshly.

"Poor Peter Olinger." Vasagar's dark eyes were hooded, but calm. "I presume that's why you're here."

Charlie was too irritated to prevaricate, annoyed by the man's coolness, the richness of the room, his belief that Vasagar was undoubtedly involved in some way with the death of Peter Olinger, and tingling still from the Chief Constable's recriminatory comments. "You'll be in mourning, of course."

Vasagar frowned theatrically, raised a slim-fingered hand. "Saddened, naturally. And shocked. I liked Mr Olinger. But I did not know him well."

"Well enough to have him here in the house with that

crook Speakman; well enough maybe to have got angry with him and torch his premises; well enough to end a story by putting a bullet in his head when he failed to do what you wanted him to do."

Vasagar's white teeth glittered; his smile was wry. "I can't imagine what you're talking about, Mr Spate. But your tone is unnecessarily offensive. I shall be only too happy to co-operate in any way I can with your investigation into the murder of the unfortunate Mr Olinger, but I would prefer if you did not make the insinuations that you are indulging in." He gestured towards the document lying on the settee. "I am a respectable businessman; I sit here reading the company returns of one of my ventures, an import business set up in Sri Lanka, and I am quite prepared to allow you entry to my home – "

"Better here than down at the nick," Charlie snarled.

Vasagar observed him for a moment, then turned, calmly resumed his place on the settee, reached for his drink and sipped at it. He nodded thoughtfully. "All right, Mr Spate, let's talk for a few moments...without prejudice, as the lawyers say. Why do you drag me into this? Because you are aware that I knew Olinger, that you saw him here at my house, that I have had certain business dealings with him – "

"The race track, is my guess," Charlie interrupted.

Vasagar ignored the comment. "These things apart, what do you have? A connection that is only intermittent, joint involvement in a few building contracts, a few casual meetings of a social kind. Rather than me, maybe you should be talking with Mr Speakman for a more intimate view of Peter Olinger and his world: he knew him far better than I did."

"Speakman doesn't have his fingers in most of the dirty pies along the river."

Vasagar was silent for a little while, contemplating his whisky glass. Then he smiled slowly, a man still in control. "You exaggerate the extent of my business interests, Mr Spate. And perhaps tarnish them unnecessarily, but we may set that aside. I am a reasonable man. I can provide you with answers to all your questions regarding my movements over these last weeks, if you require; I can open my books to your investigators as far as they are relevant to dealings with Mr Olinger. But unless you have anything specific to raise with me, I don't think we have anything further to discuss in general terms."

"How much did Olinger owe you?" Charlie asked bluntly.

Vasagar raised his dark head; he regarded Charlie with cold eyes, weighing up the situation. "You came here alone, Mr Spate. No witnesses to our conversation."

"This is only the beginning of our conversations."

"But what is said here – such as your insinuations about my business interests – can be denied later."

"So?"

Vasagar smiled slightly, confident in spite of the aggression in Charlie's tone. "So perhaps we can talk, as reasonable men. You don't like me, of that I am aware."

"And I don't trust you. How much did Olinger owe you?"

"You don't like me," Vasagar replied, still evading the question. "You have a view about my position on Tyneside, suspicions about my earlier relationship with Mr Tenby – "

"Mad Jack Tenby used to be king of the river, or thought he was. My guess is he's handed over to you."

"I have been convicted of no offences nor charged with any since my arrival in Newcastle," Vasagar observed smoothly. "But as I already implied, this is an unrecorded conversation and in the present state of affairs, perhaps we might talk as reasonable men."

"Just what are you offering me, Vasagar?" Charlie asked contemptuously.

Vasagar took a sip of his whisky, then lolled back on the settee, staring up at the detective chief inspector. "A little co-operation, in return for a less belligerent attitude towards me. I will be frank with you, Mr Spate. This is not a time when I would wish to be involved with...shall I say...high-profile investigations. I am presently involved in certain delicate business negotiations which could suffer if our conversations were to become too protracted, and...sensitive. Off the record, here in my home, I would like to think I could offer you a few suggestions, a few pieces of information that otherwise I would be disinclined to proffer."

"In return," Charlie sneered, "I'd get off your back."

Vasagar sighed, lifted a deprecating shoulder. "Your tone is still offensive, but I take no offence. I can understand the strain you are under; the need you feel to try to place Olinger's death at someone's door, at my door perhaps, quickly. But I give you an assurance: I had nothing to do with the killing of Peter Olinger. Why would I kill him? He owed me money."

Charlie felt a small glow of satisfaction at the admission. "Maybe you wanted to make an example of him, for others."

Vasagar shook his head slowly. "You are melodramatic. I am a businessman. There are other ways..."

"Like setting fire to his premises?"

Vasagar took a deep breath, clucked his tongue sharply. "Well, yes, all right, that is one of the ways that a man can be shown the errors of his ways. An accident like that can give rise to an insurance claim; the money raised can be used to pay off debts, although there would be little left to rebuild the premises thereafter."

"He owed you that much?"

Vasagar raised a hand. "Ah, wait, Mr Spate, I did not say that the fire on the Gateshead bank was occasioned by anyone connected with me. I merely agree that it is a way in which...pressure can be applied. But what I am prepared to tell you is this. Peter Olinger established a construction business years ago which should have done well. But for various reasons it never achieved what it should have done. Contracts came his way, but the business itself had a rotten core to it: Peter Olinger himself. He had an addiction."

"Gambling," Charlie suggested.

"Quite so. We are talking about days long before I ever arrived on the scene. He borrowed everywhere; even when his business was prospering he was spending more than was coming in, and projects lagged, contracts were broken. His business was a shell, in the end. Hollow, empty, and he was a desperate man. Yes, he owed me considerable sums of money, but I was not alone. His paper was all over Tyneside. So, you see, anyone *could* have ordered the torching of the Gateshead premises. And I doubt you'll ever find out just what happened behind the scenes there. But let me give you this assurance: I had no hand in the killing of Peter Olinger. I can let you have the documentation for his debts to me; I can give you the names of some other people; I can testify to the weakness of the man, but I warn you that pursuing me over this matter can lead only to grief. And not for me."

Charlie did not care for threats. But, he considered later, as he left Vasagar's house with names and contacts to follow up, the man was probably right. Vasagar had already complained about Charlie's persistence and harassment; the brass at headquarters knew Charlie's history regarding Mad Jack Tenby, the man who had handed over his underworld business to Vasagar; and unless Charlie had hard facts to pin on Vasagar, all he would achieve would be a dressing down from the ACC.

That didn't mean he believed Mark Vasagar. The man was as slippery as a fish: Charlie was aware that the information he had been given was partly to put a squeeze on some of Vasagar's rivals, letting them share some of the pressure over Olinger's death. In his book, Vasagar still wasn't in the clear. It would be the man's style, to pressurise Olinger over his debts, fire the Gateshead premises, push for payment of bad debts. All the signs were that Olinger had been close to desperation, and if he couldn't pay his gambling debts, Charlie felt Vasagar could still have had the nerve to put the finger of death on him, if only to send a warning and a shiver around Tyneside.

No, Charlie wasn't convinced Vasagar was clean over the Olinger killing, but there was something else niggling at the back of his mind. Vasagar had collapsed too easily, given information without too much argument. He would have done that for a purpose. As to what the purpose might be, Charlie had no answer as yet.

When he returned to headquarters the paperwork awaited him. There was an initial forensic report to go through; he called a scene-of-crime consultation; he had a meeting with the ACC to report on progress. But he felt vaguely unsettled. The killing of Peter Olinger had been clinical: a single shot to the head. There were no signs of torture, yet there was an echo of the situation he had seen in the old Michael Podro file. And what the Home Office people had had to say about the mysterious existence of a centuries-old organisation still smouldered in his mind.

The Swordbrothers...

When DS Elaine Start entered the room he was still musing, hardly aware of the papers in front of him. He looked up at her: there was a sober expression on her face.

"So?"

"I've been helping out with the CCTV footage at Olinger's house," she remarked.

"Didn't have a system that was of much use," Charlie growled.

"He was keen on security. Electronic gates; security alarms – "

"Which were bypassed. None of that means he was *expecting* to get killed. What's your point?"

"The point is," she snapped, bridling at his tone, "I've been looking at the tapes during the days before his body was found. There was one of his entering – "

"He lived there, for God's sake, and that's where we found his corpse!"

"But there are tapes of the other people who visited the house as well. None of them gained entry. He was in there, was Olinger, but he wasn't answering the door. It looks as though he was lying low."

"His killers?"

Elaine Start shook her head slowly. "There's a few shots of a car doing the rounds, maybe it was them, but too hazy to make out in the dark. And we think they found a blind spot from the CCTV, climbed the wall under the trees at the back, went in over the garage roof, cut the security systems – "

"Yes, yes, we know that. Are you giving me something new?"

She shrugged, and passed a slip of paper across his desk. "There's this."

"A car number."

She nodded. "The car approached the house twice; the owner attempted to gain entry at the front gate. He failed. The car was a Toyota Celica."

"So?" Charlie frowned.

"The car sat there in front of the gate for a while. I ran a computer check on the registration. It belongs to someone we know."

Now, as Charlie Spate sat at ease in the chair beside the window in Eric Ward's office, he asked the question he and Elaine Start had wondered about. "So what dealings did you have with the deceased Peter Olinger?"

Charlie watched as the solicitor hesitated, then walked across the room to take a seat behind his desk, clearly playing for time to get his thoughts in order. At last he met Charlie's glance, frowning slightly. "Why do you ask? I've had no dealings with him."

"Is that so?" Charlie asked, shaking his head doubtfully.

"So he wasn't a client of yours?"

"No. And you say he's dead?"

"You didn't know?"

"I've been busy." Ward replied shortly, then took a deep breath, leaned back in his chair. "What's this about, Mr Spate?"

"It's about you being caught on camera, paying two visits to Peter Olinger's house, shortly, we assume, before he died. It's about you telling me what you were doing there, ringing his bell."

The solicitor was ill at ease. He linked his fingers together, frowned. "I...I was seeking an interview with him."

"With what objective?"

Eric Ward shifted in his chair. "I wished to obtain certain information from him. Look, Mr Spate, you must be aware I'm in some difficulty here. I am bound to protect the interests of my client – "

"Who is?"

"I can't name him, you know that," Eric Ward snapped.

"Can't, or won't, all the same to me, my friend," Charlie said menacingly. "What you got to know is that this is a murder investigation, and like it or not, you got to tell me what the hell you were doing at the scene of the crime. Otherwise, things could get rather difficult for you. We have a history, you and I; you know I'm a man of my word, and I know all the dirty tricks in the book. You also know I'll use them if I have to."

Eric Ward stiffened. "I don't react kindly to threats."

Charlie leaned back in his chair, relaxing. "All right, Ward, let's take this slowly. Why don't we start by your telling me what you can tell me, without damaging your precious client-lawyer relationship."

There was a long silence, as the solicitor thought things over. At last he nodded slowly. "All right, Mr Spate, I'll give you what I can. I can't tell you the name of my client, or the reasons why he employed me, but I've been trying to trace Jason Sullivan."

Charlie's eyes widened. He knew something of the relationship between Ward and Sullivan. An ex-wife, her lover, and the solicitor looking for him. "Why are you looking for him? You out to give him a thumping?"

Ward refused to rise to the bait; his tone was cool. "I told you, I can't divulge the reason. But Sullivan has disappeared, and for reasons I can't disclose I've been retained to search for him."

"What's this got to do with Olinger?" Spate challenged.

Eric Ward scratched at his cheek nervously, treading a careful trail. "My search for Sullivan took me to France. There things got complicated. Another reason for discovering the whereabouts of Sullivan emerged..."

"What the hell's that supposed to mean?"

Ward wriggled uncomfortably. "All I can say is that...I felt it advisable to pursue this other enquiry also, in an attempt to discover Sullivan's whereabouts. It brought us back – "

"*Us?*"

Ward hesitated, taken aback by Charlie's sharpness. "It brought *me* back to England. In the course of my enquiries I discovered a tenuous link with Olinger. So I went to see him. There was no answer at the house." Eric Ward held Charlie's glance steadily. "That's all there was to it."

"I don't think so," Charlie muttered. "Olinger's dead, and you were wanting to talk to him about something. It may have a bearing on our investigation. What was it? This tenuous link as you describe it – what was it?"

Eric Ward was clearly weighing things up in his mind in the silence that followed. "I find myself in some difficulty," he said at last. "But I take your point. I have to stress that my main objective is to find Jason Sullivan, but the trail has led me to believe there's also been a possible art theft. That in turn brought to our attention...brought to *my* attention a defection from behind the Iron Curtain forty years ago – "

"You're losing me, Ward," Charlie warned.

"I can't help that. And I can't say more than what I'm giving you. In a nutshell, the defection of this man called Grabowski was linked to Peter Olinger: it seems Olinger's father had assisted Grabowski in the early years of his living here in England. That's the lead I was following. That's why I wanted to talk to Olinger. I thought he would provide me with information that would lead to Jason Sullivan. That's all. There's nothing more I can tell you."

Charlie shook his head. "You got me running around in circles, Ward. You're going to have to give me more than this."

"There isn't any more, really. Just details which add nothing, as far as I'm aware."

"This Grabowski – "

"Michael Podro Grabowski," Eric Ward offered, then was silent as he caught the surprise in Charlie Spate's eyes.

"What did you say?"

"The man's full name. The defector, who came to live in England. He was called Michael Podro Grabowski."

It was too much of a coincidence. Charlie rose from his chair, walked towards the door. He had to get back to headquarters, get in touch with the Home Office people. "We're going to have to talk again, more formally, Ward," he warned. "I'll be in touch, so don't start running off anywhere."

"I don't understand," Eric Ward replied.

Charlie Spate smiled wolfishly. "This Grabowski character. He was known to us just as Michael Podro. You say there's a link between him and Peter Olinger. Well, Podro was murdered some time back, before I arrived up here in the north. Single shot to the head, professional job. And now Peter Olinger has also been murdered. And guess what? Another professional execution." Charlie Spate paused at the door. "I'll be in touch with you soon, Mr

Ward. Don't go away…"

Eric Ward was aware of a brief, murmured conversation between Charlie Spate and his secretary. The outer office door slammed. A few minutes later Susie Cartwright entered the room. She had a hard look in her eye. "What trouble have you got yourself into again, Mr Ward?" she accused.

Eric raised a weary hand. "Don't let's even talk about it."

"That Mr Spate, he wants me to keep close track of your movements, let him know what you're up to. The nerve of it! Does he think I've nothing to do but act as his lackey?"

Her indignation almost amused Eric. He waved his hand, calming her down. "Don't worry about it, Susie. I've got it all under control," he lied. He paused, thinking. It was even more imperative now that he put more pressure on his ex-wife: he had to find out where the hell Sullivan was. Everything was becoming too complicated.

"Have Bradgate and Savage been in touch?" he asked.

"There's been no call from them," she replied, dissent still grumbling in her tone. "But there's been a – "

"I need to speak to Anne," he interrupted. "Can you get her on the phone, please?"

Susie Cartwright's lips were pressed thinly in disapproval. "That's what I was just about to say to you. She's already been on the phone, while Mr Spate was in here. She wants you to call her back. If you'd only not interrupted me – "

"Thank you Susie. I'll call her myself, immediately."

His secretary marched out of the room, stiff-backed. Eric reached for the phone. He rang Sedleigh Hall, and got through to her immediately.

"Anne?"

"Eric! I've wanted to talk to you."

"I'm here now."

"It's Jason – he's been in touch with me!"

The feeling that surged in Eric's chest was part relief, part bitterness. "Where the hell is he?"

"I've got an address. I'll give it to you." Her tone was panicked. "Eric, he wants to meet you, urgently. He wants you to go to France; he needs to talk to you."

Eric nodded, his tone grim. "He's got a lot of explaining to do."

There was a short silence at the other end of the line. Then, in a more subdued tone Anne said : "He needs to talk to you urgently. Eric, he's scared…" The words faded as her voice dropped in concern. "Eric, he's really scared!"

# Chapter Fourteen

When Eric took Aline to the Greek restaurant that evening, there was an immediate disagreement. They walked down through the Bigg Market to the restaurant and settled upon a table under the awning, for the evening was pleasant, a late sun throwing long shadows across the roadway. While they took an aperitif, Eric explained what had happened.

"So where has Sullivan been hiding?" she asked quickly, in an excited tone.

"It seems he's kept on the move. But he's ended up at a place called Cordes-sur-Ciel."

She frowned thoughtfully. "Not a very big place. I know it. It's situated on top of a rocky outcrop, the Puech de Mordagne, overlooking the Cerou Valley. Cathar country." She shook her head. "But why there? There is a tourist industry, the town has winding, steeply sloping stone streets and some beautiful old houses, but why go there?"

Eric shrugged. "My guess is that he'd feel more in control there. He could stay a while, anonymous, blend in with tourists. If he's covered his tracks well, and he seems to have done that, he could be virtually untraceable for a while at least."

"So when are we going to meet him?"

"We are not. I am."

She flared at him. "You can't do that! I must come with you."

They were still arguing about it when their meal arrived. He pointed out to her that Sullivan was still on the run, and according to Anne, a frightened man. It could be dangerous meeting him: Eric had no idea what had prompted Sullivan to get in touch, but they surely had good reason to suspect that the death of Peter Olinger had some link to Sullivan's fears, and that meant it would be safer if he went alone to the rendezvous.

Aline's arguments were urgent, simple and direct: she

had helped him in the search for Sullivan; she could be close to recovering the looted artwork; he could not now deny her the opportunity to face the man she believed held the object she had been seeking with an almost obsessive urgency. It had become a driving force for her, and one she could not resist. Eric held out all evening, and they had reached no agreement: he insisted it was safer if he went alone. When they parted she seemed disgruntled and defiant. He regretted that, but was convinced he was right. He did not want to lead her into danger. Two men had already died in their search for Sullivan.

The following morning he flew from Newcastle to Stansted. It was a ticketless flight to Albi and he checked in early at the desk. When he turned to head towards the departure lounge he groaned. Aline was standing near the gate, a boarding pass gripped in her hand. "I drove down early this morning," she announced defiantly. "I've got a ticket. I'm coming with you."

For a moment he thought of denying her but realised it would not work. She stood in front of him, chin raised, eyes challenging his. He was headed for a meeting with Jason Sullivan at Cordes-sur-Ciel and it would be impossible to prevent her trailing him. It could cause more problems than it was worth. With ill-disguised annoyance he nodded. "All right. You seem determined; there's nothing I can really do to prevent you. So we'd better go together."

She relaxed somewhat, grinned, squeezed his arm and led the way through to the departure lounge.

The flight south took little over an hour. They picked up a hire car at the airport and headed north-east along the D600. The afternoon sun was bright, and on the hilltops the wind buffeted the car as they headed for the fortified town built by the Count of Toulouse during the thirteenth-century Albigensian Crusade. Cordes, Aline explained as they drove along, had in the thirteenth century become a favourite haunt for heretics and the Inquisition had found rich pickings there. But the end of the Cathar disturbances had ushered in a period of prosperity for leather and cloth trades in the town, and the beautiful houses built in that period bore witness to the wealth of the inhabitants.

Eric was barely listening. He was marshalling in his mind his strategy for his confrontation with Sullivan. He was unaware of what Sullivan actually knew about the death of Peter Olinger or the links that Eric and Aline had made with the defector Grabowski. Charlie Spate had reacted to the name in a surprising manner, but had offered no explanation after their brief discussion. But more important than this – in spite of Aline's own preoccupations – was the question how Eric was going to handle the issue that was uppermost in his mind. What had Sullivan done with the money for the Hollander Project, why was he on the run, and what specifically was he scared of? Anne's reaction had been clear: she told Eric that Sullivan was terrified, aware that Eric was searching for him, but now seemed to think his lover's ex-husband could provide him with some sort of lifeline.

They reached Cordes-sur-Ciel in the early evening.

"What are the arrangements?" Aline asked, somewhat subdued, edgy, clearly troubled by something. Eric guessed it would be the thought that she might be nearing the end of her quest.

"We're booked in at the Hotel de l'Horloge. Sullivan will contact us there, and arrange a rendezvous."

"He is a careful man," she said irritably.

"He's a frightened man."

The town, laid out in a diamond shape, was perched on the rocky outcrop and their hotel was located near the Terrasse de la Bride. They found a parking place near the portcullis gateway of the Porte de la Jane, took out the small hand luggage they had each brought with them and began the ascent into the upper town. They climbed through the narrow mediaeval streets past old houses, their fa ades constructed of warm pink Salles sandstone with hints of grey, through great mediaeval arches at street level, below the iron rings used to hang banners during festivals. From the Terrasse de la Bride, under the shady trees, they obtained a sweeping view of the peaceful Cerou Valley to the north-east, beyond the slender silhouette of the Bornazel belfry. The hotel was small, tucked away in a small alleyway, and the proprietor was quizzical.

"*Vous avez reserv une chamber a deux?*"

"*Non,*" Eric replied quickly. "*Deux chambres, s'il vous plait.*"

Aline was smiling as they entered the narrow lift. "He will be telling his wife he will never understand the English."

"Sullivan booked one room in my name. He wouldn't have expected me to be accompanied."

"One room would have been sufficient," she said carelessly. "It would not have been a problem for me."

Eric looked at her. In other circumstances the suggestion would have been a provocation that might have caused a reaction in him, but the studied carelessness in her tone seemed forced. She was an attractive woman, but there had been a nervousness about her during the last twenty-four hours, a dissonance that puzzled him. It was probably the tension of nearing her goal: it might have led her to think she could dissolve some of that tension by starting an affair with him. At some other time he would have had no problem with that, but right now he was too edgy himself, too uncertain of what lay ahead. They checked into their separate rooms without saying more. Eric took a shower, leaving the bathroom door open in case the phone rang, then half an hour later joined Aline in the bar, after instructing the proprietor to arrange for any calls for him to be passed through.

They took some pastis together. An hour later, they decided they had better get something to eat in the small hotel restaurant. They were half way through an indifferent meal when the waitress approached the table. Her English was precise. "There is a phone call for you, Mr Ward."

Eric rose immediately and went to the phone at reception. He could hear the quick, nervous breathing at the end of the line.

"Sullivan?"

"You're not alone. You've got a woman with you."

"That doesn't matter. Where and when do we meet?"

"Who is she?" the reply came back, almost hissing in its intensity.

"She's been helping me look for you."

"I asked *who is she*?"

Eric hesitated. He considered the matter for a moment, then decided it was best to tell the truth. "She's an employee of the Rijksmuseum. She was the negotiator for the artwork. She's still wanting to do a deal over it. We've been working together in a common cause. To find you. Now where do we meet, damn you!"

The anger in Eric's tone got through to the man at the other end of the line. There was a short silence, then a reluctant agreement. "All right. I need to talk to you, Ward, to find out what the hell is going on. But I need to be certain... Two hours' time. The house at the end of the flight of steps called the Escalier Pater Noster. Meet me there."

The connection was abruptly cut. Eric returned slowly to the dining room. Aline looked up at him expectantly. "Well?"

"In two hours. A house at the Escalier Pater Noster."

"It's called that because it has as many steps as the prayer has words," she muttered almost inconsequentially, her eyes fixed on the table in front of her. Her hands were trembling.

"Are you all right, Aline?" Eric asked sharply.

Her glance flicked up to him as he sat down opposite her. She took a deep breath. "We seem to be coming to the end of a line. I'm nervous…edgy. I'm sorry. Two hours, you say?"

"He'll be checking out the territory," Eric said grimly. "He's leaving nothing to chance."

The two hours slid past slowly.

The light had died by the time they emerged from the hotel and made their way to the steps designated by Sullivan. As suburbs had sprung up around the ancient town and citadel a fifth curtain wall had been added in the fourteenth century: the only remnant now remaining was the picturesque ruin of the Porte de l'Horloge. Eric and Aline made their way from the Terrasse de la Bride past the Barbicane and down towards the steps and the ancient gateway.

The street was dimly lit; the sky was cloudy and overcast; there was a hint of rain in the air and the atmosphere was heavy with the threat of thunderstorms. The house where they were to meet Sullivan had Gothic pretensions but they were half-hearted reconstructions of a much older building. The faade was distinctive enough, decorated at the second level with a high relief frieze depicting a hunting scene, but the lower level was blank-faced. The door was a modern desecration, sporting an electric bell. Eric pressed the button, then stood back, staring upwards. There was no gleam of light from the wooden-shuttered windows above. He rang again, impatiently, and then heard movement inside. The door opened slowly, still held with a security bar; a few moments of careful inspection and the man inside slipped the bar. Eric stepped inside, followed by Aline.

Jason Sullivan stood there in the dim hallway, staring at them. As Eric opened his mouth to speak Sullivan raised a hand, pushed past Eric and stood half-screened in the doorway, glaring down the steps to the lower town. His breathing was harsh and irregular. After a few moments he stepped back inside and closed the door, replaced the security bar, and motioned them towards the door at the end of the gloomy hallway. Eric walked forward, opened the door: it led into a small sitting room, plainly furnished, lit by a chandelier on which only two of the six possible bulbs glared. He turned to face the man he had been searching for.

Sullivan had changed. He seemed somehow wilted in appearance. Eric had known him as a tall, confident, handsome man; now his good looks seemed pinched, his manner uncertain, and he had clearly lost weight. There was an edginess about the way he moved, and his hand was trembling slightly as he headed for a chair beside the single table in the room. He lowered himself into the chair, then glared at Aline, before addressing Eric in an accusing tone. "You should have come alone."

"You're in no position to dictate terms," Eric replied harshly. "Aline has an interest here, even though it differs from mine."

A slight sneer appeared on Sullivan's lean features. "Ah, yes. The bloody artefact. Well, it's in a safe place, and I'm certainly still open to negotiations after all I've been through. But the price will have gone up, believe me, and I will want assurance – "

"That can wait," Eric interrupted harshly. "I'm not interested in all that. I'm here on other business."

A frown crossed Sullivan's brow, He grimaced. "Anne said something stupid on the phone when we spoke. She said – "

"What have you done with the money designated for the Hollander Project? That's why I'm here. To seek an explanation, and to bring you back to England to face the music."

Sullivan grinned mirthlessly. "Face the music? What the hell are you talking about? I've nothing to fear on that account. Haven't you talked to Mike Fremantle?"

Eric nodded angrily. "I've talked to him. He told me about the arrangement you made with him, to salt the money away in offshore accounts for your own purposes."

"It was a sensible arrangement," Sullivan flashed with a brief show of spirit. "Of course we would have got a decent commission out of it, but the money's still there, and it's available for Hollander any time I choose to put a signature to a few documents."

Eric stared at him in contempt, and slowly shook his head. "You're lying through your teeth, Sullivan. The money's gone. The accounts have been emptied."

Sullivan began to say something but the words died. He stared at Eric uncomprehendingly for several seconds. "You're talking rubbish. Only I have access to those accounts. Talk again to Fremantle. He'll be able to tell you – "

"Fremantle suddenly seems to be unavailable," Eric interrupted scornfully. "I think he's run for cover, knowing what you've done. He's out to save his own skin. You'd better save yours by returning the money – or whatever's left of it – and coming back with me to England to sort out the whole bloody mess." He gazed around the gloomy room. "It's certainly going to be better than this accommodation."

A shiver went through Sullivan's body. His hands were shaking with a subdued rage, and his eyes glittered. Eric was taken with the sudden thought that the man had been taking drugs, maybe to boost his confidence. And a cold feeling began to settle in his stomach as Sullivan leaned forward and spat out the words.

"Fremantle! That little bastard. He's set this up. I tell you there's no way he could have had access to the accounts. My system is foolproof. The accounts can't have been emptied. He's been lying through his teeth. I tell you he's up to some little scam of his own, but it certainly doesn't involve me! The bloody money is still there in Labuan and elsewhere, and I can bring it back whenever it becomes necessary!" He glared wildly at Aline. "All that's of no consequence. I can sort all that out as soon as I get back. It's this other thing that's got me trapped here."

"What do you mean?" Eric demanded.

"The Vasari. I wish I'd never heard of the bloody thing. Olinger had it; he'd acquired it from his father years ago, when the old man died, and the idiot tried to put it on the market. All right, I know Olinger was desperate, the weak bastard, and he'd got into such debt with his stupid gambling – and he was dealing with some of the hardest men on Tyneside. He offered me a considerable slice of the action if I'd get it into the market, find a private buyer. I had contacts in Europe, through my work in the European Community. I got in touch with Duclos, and he agreed to handle it as a front man. There was no way I wanted to be seen up front, any more than Olinger was keen to put his head above the parapet. But the trouble was, as soon as the word got out, people like this woman here got interested. The bloody Rijksmuseum! They'd have just jerked me around for months, and Olinger wanted the money desperately. But we were prepared to negotiate, until some funny things started to happen. We were being watched; we took the yacht out to St Martin de R  so we could talk in peace. But Duclos was edgy as hell; he told me there was a lot of interest in the Vasari, but it was the wrong kind of interest. Muscled stuff. I told him we'd better settle for a straight deal with the Rijksmuseum people. He was going to set it up." His eyes were cold as he stared at Aline. "That's when the poor bugger got suicided."

His breathing was heavy in the silence. Aline's eyes were wide. Eric leaned forward. "Are you saying Duclos was murdered?"

Sullivan's tone was scornful. "You never really believed he hanged himself, did you?"

"But why would – "

"When I got the news, that's when I decided upon a policy of discretion. I got out of there, went underground, to think things through. From what Duclos had hinted, there were some powerful players out there, looking for the

Vasari, and now he was dead. I wasn't keen to follow his example. So I've been lying low. But I can't see a way out. In the end I rang Anne, and she told me that you were among the people hunting for me. I've never liked you, Ward, but I know you're straight. You've been looking for me. Here I am. Now you got to find a way of getting me back safely to England."

"For God's sake," Eric snapped, "it's just a matter of getting on a plane! We can leave first thing in the morning if – "

There was a sudden buzzing sound. Eric looked at Aline, standing beside him. She was pale, her eyes shadowed, her body stiff with tension. "My mobile...maybe it's Leclerc," she muttered. She slipped a hand into the small bag she carried and took out the phone. She glanced at Eric apologetically, and moved away, back into the hallway.

Eric turned back to Sullivan. In the background he could hear the muttering of Aline's voice. He ignored it. "She's talking to the contact she has at the museum. Don't worry about it. All she's interested in is recovery of the Vasari, which I presume you've got in some secure place, so if you can get your hands on it by morning, we can all three be on our way. What you sort out with her is your own business. But you've got another problem now. Peter Olinger is dead."

"*What?*"

"He's been murdered. The sooner we get back to England, and get in touch with the police, the better. I'm in trouble myself if we don't return quickly: I've been warned to stay in touch with the Olinger investigation. So get the bloody thing you've been hiding and let's get back."

Sullivan swallowed hard. His eyes were wild; his fear was palpable. "Olinger's dead?" he asked in a stunned tone. "But that must mean they got to him – "

"We can sort all that out when we return," Eric assured him. "My main concern is to clear matters up in regard to the Hollander Project. You're on a hook there, Sullivan.

There's a hell of a lot of money involved, and the sooner you cough it back up the better. So, in the morning – "

He stopped suddenly as Jason Sullivan shot to his feet. The door behind Eric opened: he turned his head and saw Aline coming back into the room. She was ashen-faced. As she stepped into the room Eric realised she was not alone. Two men came in behind her: one of them was short, heavily built, clad in a black leather jacket. His hair was short-cropped; his eyes narrowed with caution. The second man was vaguely familiar to Eric. He stared at him and after a few seconds he remembered where he had seen him previously. Staring in through the window of the restaurant in Newcastle, where he and Aline had taken a meal. The man Jackie Parton had warned him about. The man in the photograph: the mysterious Frank Dennis.

They entered the room in a heavy silence. But there was someone else with them, coming in behind him. A big man, moving softly and easily. It was another man whom Eric recognised, this time immediately.

The banker, Ben Shaw. The man who had retained Eric to find Jason Sullivan.

He met Eric's shocked gaze with a confident smile. His glance slipped to the man standing beside Eric. "Ah, Mr Sullivan. You've been somewhat elusive. But we find you at last. Good…" He smiled again at Eric, then turned to the silent woman at his side. "All right, Miss Pearce. That'll be all for the moment. Go back to the hotel. I'll join you there in a little while. By then we should be able to give you what you want."

Aline's gaze was fixed on Eric. Her lips were pale. And he saw the betrayal in her eyes.

Chapter Fifteen

The silence in the room was electric. Shaw was looking at Aline, one eyebrow raised quizzically, a slightly amused lift to his mouth. He spoke soothingly, as though addressing a child. "Go on, off you go. You can leave the rest to me...and to my colleagues here."

It was several seconds before she recovered her voice. Her glance slipped to Jason Sullivan. "He says...he said he has the Vasari in a safe place."

"It will be locked away somewhere. A safety deposit box, perhaps. He'll tell us. Don't worry. We'll find it for you." There was a calm assurance in Ben Shaw's tone.

"I'll wait here with you. I'll – "

"No, there's no need for that," Shaw interrupted gently. "Go back to the hotel."

She seemed rooted to the spot. Eric was staring at her, bemused. Her eyes now avoided his, and he began to realise the truth. "You've been working for Shaw all along," he said accusingly, still puzzled.

She started guiltily, then shook her head, shamefaced. "No, that's not so. I told you the truth – I was acting for the museum; it was only after Duclos committed suicide and I thought the Vasari would be lost for ever... I've spent so much time searching for it, I couldn't just give up, so when I was recalled by the museum, and we seemed to be getting nowhere... It was when we were in Newcastle, I was approached..." Her glance flicked to Ben Shaw. "It was suggested that it would be useful if I continued to attach myself to you, worked with you, found the way to Sullivan..."

Her voice died away.

Coldly, feeling betrayed, Eric said, "You've kept in touch, all the while since. And tonight, the phone call, it wasn't Leclerc...You stepped out into the hallway under instructions, you let them in here..." A cold fist knotted in Eric's stomach as he began to piece things together. He glanced sideways at Jason Sullivan, trembling, hyperactive, his eyes glittering crazily, then turned back to Ben Shaw. "You retained me to find Sullivan because of missing money." His glance slipped to Frank Dennis. "But you clearly also employed this man...and then Aline...You didn't trust me?"

Shaw fingered the cleft in his chin in his characteristic gesture, and smiled. "I retained you because it was the best way, in my opinion, to get to Sullivan – through your ex-wife. I thought she might talk to you, where she would disclose nothing to anyone else... But, we have always had others working on it also. People here in France, at Poitiers and elsewhere. Dennis in the north-east. It would have been foolish merely to use you: we have had many searching. And, as you're now aware, even this young lady, ultimately." He smiled, glanced at her cynically. "We have learned that an obsession can drive people into dark waters."

Eric frowned. "And all this to find Sullivan and recover the missing funds for the Hollander Project? But he says there never was an emptying of the bank accounts."

Ben Shaw shrugged indifferently. "I'm afraid that's actually true."

"But Fremantle confirmed..."

"A little man, open to bribery," Shaw replied blandly. "You're quite correct in your assumptions. Fremantle received a substantial sum of money from us to persuade you that there was a large sum of money missing, and due to the Hollander Project. I had to find a reason for sending you after Sullivan. It was spurious, of course. As for Fremantle..." Shaw glanced at his companions, and smiled. "He suddenly seems to have got cold feet and run for cover. He always was a weak link in our chain. But we'll find him, never fear."

"So the search for Sullivan was never about the recovery of Hollander money," Eric said slowly.

"You're perceptive, at last."

"You wanted Sullivan because he had the Vasari."

Shaw shrugged carelessly. "That's not exactly true. We wanted to discover who was putting the Vasari into the market place. We were, shall we say, keen to tie up some loose ends, perhaps make a declaration of a kind. It's like closing the chapter in a book – one of long standing. There was a debt to be paid. The Vasari was incidental to those objectives. But that need not concern you." Shaw gave a suddenly irritated gesture. "But enough of this. We need to know where Sullivan keeps the Vasari, in order to tie all ends up cleanly. Miss Pearce, you don't need to be present. Please return to your hotel. I will call there in a little while. And you will obtain what you seek."

She half-turned towards the door, but her eyes were on Eric. There was an odd, pleading look in her glance, as though she sought forgiveness.

"Georges Duclos is dead," Eric said, grinding out the words. "And now Peter Olinger has been murdered. There's another thing too...when the police questioned me about Olinger, mention was made of another man. Michael Podro Grabowski. You'll surely remember, Aline, that he also was murdered?"

Shaw raised an eyebrow, mockingly. "That's old news now, Mr Ward. Miss Pearce, I insist you leave. *Now.*"

Eric fixed her with a warning glance. "Do you really think this man will keep whatever bargain he's made with you?"

She stared at him, shaking slightly. The obsession that had gripped her, that had led her to betray Eric was still with her, but he could tell that a new uncertainty had entered her mind. She had entered into an alliance that had always troubled her: Eric knew that now. Shaw had approached her, personally or through Frank Dennis, promised to help her in the search for the Vasari, stressed the resources at his disposal, in return for her assistance in keeping track of Eric's movements. All the information she had given Eric about Grabowski, she would have given Shaw. She had told him they were to meet Sullivan in Cordes-sur-Ciel. He would have assured her his objective was the recovery of Hollander money from Sullivan, but she had heard now from his own mouth that he had lied – to Eric and to her. There was a desperation in her eyes, as she flicked panicked glances between Eric and Ben Shaw.

At a final irritated nod from Shaw the man in the black leather jacket took her by the elbow, and began to push her towards the door. She looked back over her shoulder, shaking her head, asking for understanding from Eric and it was in that moment that the man called Dennis calmly took a handgun out of his deep jacket pocket. With a casual air he began to screw what Eric knew to be a silencer onto the muzzle of the weapon. Ben Shaw grimaced, raised a warning hand, but Aline saw the man's actions. The sight of the gun galvanised her into a sudden realisation of what was about to happen. Her voice rose in a scream, and she dragged herself away from the restraining leather-jacketed arm. "No!"

In the next second everything changed. Aline's leather-jacketed guard grabbed at her arm, swung her towards him and back towards the door. She fought against him, raised her hand and tore at his face, reaching for his eyes. Eric saw the red weals spring up on the man's face and heard his roar of pain. The man thrust Aline against the wall and next moment was pulling something out of his belt as she reached out for his eyes again. Eric caught the flash of a knife blade and it was enough to shock him into action. In a violent lunging movement he shouldered his way past Ben Shaw, sending the big man reeling, and threw himself at the man in the black leather jacket.

From the corner of his eyes he caught another swift movement, Jason Sullivan, also reacting to the moment, hurling himself at Dennis, still screwing the silencer onto the gun muzzle. But it was a momentary impression only because Eric was dragging at the arm of Aline's assailant. He heard her cry out as she fell, sliding down against the wall but her attacker was turning to Eric now, the knife blade slipping away from her and glinting as it came up towards Eric in a wild thrust. He felt the blade slice through the cloth of his jacket, was aware of its drag, a sharp burning sensation in his upper arm and then his hands were on the man's wrist, forcing the knife away. The two men grappled, staggered, then lost balance and fell crashing to the floor.

A fist thudded into the side of his head, and his senses began to reel, but fiercely he maintained his grip on the knife wrist. A knee came up into his stomach but he rolled, twisting away from the wall. As the man's face rose above him Eric lifted his own head, butted the knifeman full in the face, and he heard the crunch of bone and cartilage as the man's nose was smashed, and blood poured in a hot gush over Eric's head. He was vaguely aware of a gunshot booming across the room, of a thrashing sound as the others still grappled with each other and he heard a door slam, but he was still fighting for his life and he rolled again, forcing his way upwards until he was on top of the man in the black leather jacket. A fist still beat at the side of his skull, but he concentrated on the wrist still gripped between his fingers and he twisted slowly, inexorably, forcing the knife blade away from his own body. Through the mass of smashed flesh and bone he could now see the man's staring eyes, became aware of the panic that glittered in them through the mask of blood that still gushed redly from his nose and Eric pushed and pushed, twisting the wrist until the knife moved slowly towards the man's throat.

The black leather jacket was slick with blood; Eric's senses were reeling; he could hear a steady, rhythmic thudding that seemed to come from inside his skull but could have been from across the room, and then he became aware of a thick, gurgling sound. It was Aline, her lungs clogging with blood, coughing... The sound seemed to give him a surge of adrenalin, a mounting fury in his veins. Below him the man's eyes widened in despair as Eric made one last enraged effort: in that last moment the grip on the knife loosened in surrender but Eric's head was suffused with a red anger, and he drove hard, thrusting the knife down, mad with fury until the body below his slumped, the man's head lolled sideways, and the sliced carotid artery pumped blood in a steady, pulsating stream.

After a few seconds, Eric rolled away. He ran a hand over his face, clearing his eyes. He was exhausted. A sudden silence seemed to have descended about him. He looked across towards the door, then around the room. There was no sign of Ben Shaw: the banker had clearly decided not to get involved in the battle and had made good his escape. For another day, perhaps. Across the room Jason Sullivan was half sitting, one hand gripping the chair beside him for support. His head was lowered, and there was a spreading red stain across his chest, where he had taken the bullet from the handgun. The man Eric knew as Frank Dennis was sprawled on his back, motionless. His head was a shapeless mass of blood. He had been beaten to death in Jason Sullivan's drug-fuelled rage.

Eric turned, rolled towards Aline. Her eyes were wide, staring, glazed. Her breathing was laboured and there was a line of red froth along her mouth. He reached for her, and felt the slickness of her breast as the life pumped away from her.

"Aline," he whispered, half dazed, broken.

She heard his voice. Her lids flickered, and her eyes turned towards him. All he could read in them was pain, and regret. He fancied he heard her say something; her lips moved, and through the froth of blood he finally heard the whisper, light as dead leaves blown in the winter breeze. "I...I'm sorry..."

He leaned forward so that his face touched hers. Her skin was cold. "So am I," he said, shattered emotionally. "Aline, so am I..."

Moments later the red darkness engulfed him.

The darkness eventually became filled with half-seen dreams and images, unformed, drifting. All was confusion: he saw the dark alleys of his youth, down near the river, and dangerous men in shadowed places, cornered rats unwilling to be taken. There was the shadow of a man hanging by the neck, slowly twisting in a dusty room; there was Aline, reaching for him, pleading; there was the terror in the man's eyes when the knife slipped into his throat. And there was the old, familiar prickling at the back of his eyes, presaging the agonising pain that would blur his vision and render him helpless in the darkness. He had no idea how long he lay there in that middle, lost world between life and death and reality. It was only gradually that he became aware of sounds of movement, shouted commands, a hollow thudding, feet in the hallway, dragging sounds. He opened his eyes. Through a grey-red mist he could make out figures tramping around the room, white coats, a figure bending over him. Slowly his blurred vision cleared. He was lying on his back; kneeling at his side was a familiar figure. He blinked, not understanding.

"How...?"

DCI Charlie Spate grunted. "It was your ex-missus. After she'd sent you to your meeting with Sullivan, she had second thoughts, came to her senses, and decided there was too much going on, too much panic around. She decided she'd better call us in, tell us about it, come clean with us. She rang us, told us where you'd gone. I contacted the local police, came after you..." He glared around the room to where the paramedics were lifting Jason Sullivan onto a stretcher. "He'll be lucky to pull through this." There was disgust in his tone. "Hell's flames, it's like a bloody charnel house in here." His angry eyes flickered back towards Eric. "You should have listened to me in the first place."

He stood up, scowling. "I bloody well told you not to leave the country..."

Chapter Sixteen

The debriefing meeting was chaired by the Chief Constable. Singleton, the man from the Home Office, sat on his right. To his left was ACC Jim Charteris, slightly miffed that his senior officer had decided that he would take the chair. Charteris had made it clear that he had seen this as his operation from the beginning. But rank had its privileges.

"It would seem," the Chief Constable began, sweeping his glance over the assembled officers in the room, "that operations have been successfully concluded, by and large, to the credit I may say of our force..."

Charlie Spate glanced sideways to Elaine Start. She gave him a slight smile. She had no doubt, like him, that credit would not be given to individuals. For the Chief Constable, it was always a team effort – his team, of course.

"Before I go further, however, I should introduce Inspector Raoul Garcia, who is attached to Interpol, and who has been of considerable assistance to us in our investigations. I will ask him to speak, in a moment, but first perhaps we should clear up some of the particularly local issues."

"Yes, indeed," Singleton broke in smoothly as the Chief Constable was about to continue. "The immigration issues, and the on-going investigation on Tyneside. I believe the lady...?"

Elaine Start raised her head. She disliked Singleton's patronising tone. "Thank you, sir," she grated insincerely. "We have achieved a certain success in closing down some of the activities of the more obvious gangmasters. And it seems we have managed to crowd out the intruders who were seeking to establish new territories on Tyneside. Interestingly enough, Mr Mark Vasagar has shown himself to be most co-operative. He has been able to give us the names of several people who have been implicated, and our investigations continue. But we do have something to show for our efforts."

Charlie could not contain himself. "Let's not go overboard with our thanks to Vasagar. He'll have simply given us names of his rivals – so that he can take over their activities."

ACC Charteris leaned forward, a slight smile on his features. "Better the devil we know, hey?"

Grudgingly, Charlie had to agree with the sentiment.

Singleton pressed his fingertips together and glanced at the Chief Constable. "If I may be so bold, sir, as to suggest that it would be useful for all officers present to be briefed as to the origins of this whole business? Inspector Garcia has been involved in the Europe-wide investigation, and is perhaps best placed to explain what has been happening..."

The Chief Constable nodded ponderously. "I think that would be appropriate," he agreed.

Raoul Garcia rose to his feet. There were some thirty officers in the conference room: he allowed his glance to drift along the rows of faces. It lingered, Charlie thought sourly, just a little too long on Elaine Start. "One could say," Garcia remarked in his precise English, "that it all began some centuries ago, with the establishment of an organisation called the Swordbrothers. Their modern counterparts naturally have few objectives in common with the originals: it is a criminal network of some vicious extent. Their re-emergence during the Second World War was as a resistance movement in Poland against the Nazis, but they soon showed their true colours. As far as we are concerned, we can concentrate upon one of their interventions..."

Charlie leaned back in his seat, relaxing, and glanced at Elaine Start. He had already heard this part of the story. He admired her profile, the way her breasts moved slightly under her shirt as she listened, breathing softly...

"It appears that various artworks were looted by Russian soldiers in 1944, from a collection held by Count von

Sternberg, on behalf of Field Marshal Goering, and taken back to Russia. At that stage and later the Swordbrothers were working hand in glove with the Communist regimes, and they were given the task of dealing with recalcitrants, people who were seeking to profit personally from illegal activities. The organisation carried out reprisals against such people, but in so doing managed to grow as an organisation, feed off the support of the State, and become powerful in its own right. Some of the artworks were conveniently retained by the Order, and membership of the Swordbrothers grew, at least until the Communist bosses became uneasy with the monster they had encouraged, and tried to shut the Order down. The Swordbrothers went underground, but increased in numbers, power and strength."

Garcia paused, nodded slowly as he surveyed his silent audience.

"I need not go into detail, but some of this was known to Western Intelligence. However, by the seventies, it was understood the organisation had been extirpated. It proved to be false intelligence. It continued to grow, developing criminally into blackmail, murder, political assassinations for money. But for our immediate purposes, let me return to the late sixties. The organisation was still active, but there had been a certain disenchantment, a drifting away of members. This is something no secret organisation can accept. They have a habit of exacting revenge. Even if it takes decades." Garcia glanced sideways at the man from the Home Office. "And at about this time, a certain Mr Jarvis was acting as a cultural attach    in European embassies."

Singleton nodded reflectively.

"Jarvis was nearing the end of his civil service career," Garcia continued, "when he made contact with a man called Michael Podro Grabowski. This man was an athlete – a weightlifter – in the team working towards the Olympics.

But he was also a Swordbrother, and he wanted to leave both the organisation, and the Eastern bloc. He approached Jarvis, and a deal was struck. Jarvis made the arrangements to smuggle Grabowski out of Europe. It was done without the knowledge of Jarvis's superiors, and no formal channels were used. This suited Grabowski: he wanted a degree of anonymity, removal to a country where the Swordbrother organisation was not active. But why did Jarvis do it? Why did Jarvis bypass ordinary channels, and even give secret support financially to Grabowski thereafter, in England?" Garcia smiled cynically. "It's the old story. Grabowski had something to trade. A piece of artwork that had fallen to the Swordbrothers. An immensely valuable work by Paolo Vasari. Grabowski stole it, gave it to Jarvis as the price for his escape to the West."

There was a short silence. Garcia glanced at Singleton. The Home Office man nodded, somewhat stiffly. "We were not aware of this at the time, naturally. But there were…suspicions. It led to questions being asked, answers given that were not satisfactory, and, finally, the suggestion that Jarvis should retire. No retirement honour was given to him." Singleton gave a cynical smile. "It was perhaps of no importance to Jarvis. He was a collector: he had his pension, and his secret treasure to himself. However it may be, the file on Jarvis was closed thereafter. Not to be reopened until recently, when Interpol gave us certain information about the Swordbrother organisation, and its re-emergence in Europe."

"The attempted assassination of a French Minister of State, in Argel s-Gazost," Garcia confirmed. "And what became obvious was the professional execution of a man called Michael Podro in England." Garcia smiled thinly. "The Swordbrothers had long memories and deep-rooted vindictiveness. It took them some years, but they finally traced Grabowski, after they began to operate in England. Grabowski was living as Michael Podro in Newcastle, and they murdered him as a traitor to their organisation. But before they killed him, they tortured him, to discover the whereabouts of the artwork that had been the price of his freedom. They were frustrated initially: either he refused to tell them before he died, or he told them it was held by Jarvis, who had since died. Whatever happened, they did not make the link immediately to Jarvis's son, born out of wedlock. Peter Olinger."

ACC Charteris broke in, unwilling to be left out of the debriefing. "To clarify matters, I might point out how the Swordbrothers had finally entered the English underworld. It was they who had established a front in Newcastle through the setting up of a firm called Bradgate and Savage. The company had legitimate business in the financial world, but its real purpose was to provide finance for the development of the lucrative trade in illegal immigrants: it was the Swordbrothers who were muscling in on people-smuggling operations we believe were up to then controlled by Mark Vasagar – "

"Not that we could lay a finger on the bastard," Charlie Spate growled *sotto voce*. He shook his head in disgust. Mark Vasagar would have had his nose put out of joint by the incursion of the Swordbrothers, but was almost powerless to stop it. The empire Vasagar had taken over from Mad Jack Tenby was being chipped away: Charlie and Elaine Start had warned there was new money coming into the area. Now they knew it had been Swordbrother money, channelled through Bradgate and Savage.

"The Swordbrothers had eliminated Grabowski in a vengeance killing," Garcia continued. "But they had not traced the Vasari. However, within a year or so, new intelligence reached them from their European network. The Vasari had come into the market. It was an article they saw as theirs. They wanted its return, not simply because of its intrinsic value, but to send out a message to the brethren and all who dealt with them. The long memory; the ultimate revenge."

Garcia paused, picked up the glass in front of him and sipped at the water it contained. "They knew the article was in the market place and they sought it, and the person who owned it. Ben Shaw was the man who was entrusted with the search. He set up a network, used a local solicitor to find the man they suspected was acting for the person who held the Vasari. The trail led to one Georges Duclos: they murdered him. Then they sought the middleman – Jason Sullivan – if only to find out who he was acting for. They finally discovered it was Jarvis's illegitimate son, Peter Olinger."

Charlie closed his eyes, thinking. Eric Ward and the Rijksmuseum woman had been running along a parallel path with the police investigation: if Ward had only come clean, given Charlie all he knew, so that they could have combined their efforts, some of the later mess might have been avoided.

"Once the Order learned it was Olinger who owned the Vasari, they killed him too: it was all part of the chain they wanted to eradicate." Garcia smiled humourlessly. "*Pour encourager les autres,* as it has once been said. And then, finally, they managed to reach Jason Sullivan. It ended in a bloodbath."

Charlie caught Elaine Start's glance: he read sympathy in her eyes. Maybe she was recalling what he had told her of the scene he had entered upon in Cordes-sur-Ciel. He was used to scenes of violent death, but that had been carnage, blood everywhere. Jason Sullivan had survived, but the bullet he had taken had damaged a lung. He was still in hospital. Eric Ward had been lucky: a flesh wound to the arm. He was already back at work, hopefully a wiser man, and no charges would be brought against him for the killing of the Swordbrother assailant he had fought with. It would be treated as self-defence, though Charlie had his own views about that. But two of the Swordbrother organisation had died in that room, as well as the girl from the Rijksmuseum.

Garcia was still speaking. "I understand that we are now all co-operating in the on-going investigation into the Swordbrothers here in the north of England. Bradgate and Savage executives have been arrested. Their activities in relation to the Hollander Project would seem to have been legitimate, but their use of the accountant Michael Fremantle is questionable, and Fremantle himself has been located, in hiding in Scotland and has been arrested. The man Ben Shaw was taken into custody three days ago, at Limoges, as he was about to board a plane to the United States, well away from the spheres of influence of this secretive organisation." Garcia paused and smiled cynically. "In the final, rather bloody outcome at Cordes-sur-Ciel, Shaw took no part in the violence: he simply fled the scene. Clearly, he was one of those people recruited by the Swordbrothers not for the muscle he might provide, but for the intellectual and financial abilities he could supply. Not a man of courage, it would seem…"

Charlie Spate snorted. In his view, Shaw had been the only guy showing sense, getting the hell out of that carnage.

"We have to admit," Garcia was saying, "that while we can bring charges against these people which will lead to significant terms of imprisonment, it is unlikely that they will disclose much if anything of the activities of the parent organisation. The man Shaw, who has already shown a degree of prudence, might be the one to crack under interrogation, but it is unlikely. He will be aware of the possible repercussions. The arm of the Swordbrothers is long and deadly, and time is of no consequence to them. They can wait, in order to wreak their revenge, as has been demonstrated by what happened to Michael Podro Grabowski, and Olinger. So let us be quite clear."

Garcia paused, eyeing his silent audience dramatically. "The Swordbrothers are like rats. They have nests throughout Europe: their burrows extend deep into the East from whence they first emerged centuries ago. This particular battle is one that we seem to have won. But make no mistake." He paused again, his eyes hard and uncompromising.

"We have cut off merely one of the heads of the Hydra. There will be others. Believe me. This is not the last we will hear of the *Fratres Milicia Christi de Livonia*..."

The room was silent.

"This is not the last we will hear of the Swordbrothers..."